DE

This book is for anyone who has ever had a broken heart.
Sometimes people do things for reasons we never get the answers to,
or for reasons we can't possibly fathom. Sometimes those broken
hearts lead to happily-ever-afters.

I hope you find yours.

Because you deserve it.

You're pretty.

Boys are dumb.

You're smart.

Boys are stupid.

You're kind.

Boys are idiots.

You're a fucking mermaid.

—Abby O'Shea, poet, friend,
and Sterling All-Star :)

PROLOGUE

Jules

I DIDN'T PLAN on him. Or *for* him.

Or anything that had to do with Cal Donovan from Boston.

Meeting him was a surprise, taking me completely off-guard. I met new people every day in my line of work, and none of them affected me. Wasn't that the way of things, though? You could meet a thousand people and none of them would mean anything to you, but then you'd meet *one*, and suddenly they meant everything.

I was a self-professed workaholic, so everyone in my life knew I didn't date. It wasn't entirely intentional on my part; I just didn't make men a priority at this point in my life. But that wasn't to say that if I met someone who intrigued me, I wouldn't give it a shot. Because I absolutely would. But therein lay the rub—very few guys sparked my interest and managed to hold it.

And that was perfectly fine with me. Work came first, and I wasn't about to apologize for that or feel bad about it. Not even to my ex-boyfriend Brandon, when he broke up with me over two years ago because I spent too much time at the office, and he felt I should have been focusing at least a smidgeon of my time and attention on him.

He had played the role of the supportive boyfriend at first, telling me how proud he was of my ambition and accomplishments. But all the while, his resentment secretly brewed until it exploded from him one night as we sat in his living room. To say I'd been taken off-guard and shocked by his anger would be an understatement. I had no idea he'd grown so spiteful.

Brandon hadn't been entirely wrong in his frustrations, but even his leaving didn't make me want to change my priorities. All I'd felt when he was breaking up with me, delivering a speech he'd clearly practiced more than once, was a sense of relief. My heart leaped at the idea of focusing on my career without taking anyone else's desires or feelings into consideration. Oh, the freedom I looked forward to experiencing and the complete absence of guilt.

Yes, that might sound harsh, but I wanted to build a name for myself in the high-end real estate market, and I couldn't do that by dividing my time. Or maybe I could have. The point was that I didn't want to, and Brandon reminded me of that.

Besides, when did making yourself your number one priority become such a horrible thing? Men focused on their careers all the time, and that was completely acceptable. But not for a woman; not for me. I learned fairly quickly after the Brandon breakup that men didn't like being second on a woman's priority list. And they seemed to be intimidated by a motivated female, calling me things like *hard to handle*, *challenging*, and *difficult*.

The end result was that being single seemed to work best for me, and I had no plans to change my relationship status anytime soon.

Then I met Cal.

And he fucking ruined everything.

MR. PERFECT LIPS

Jules

I RAN INTO the hotel, my arms wrapped around my midsection to fight off the bitter cold outside. My long blond hair had whipped around my face in the bone-chilling wind, and I did my best to smooth it back into place as I stepped into the lobby.

Boston was freezing and I hadn't packed appropriately, tossing short-sleeved tops and sandals into my suitcase instead of cold-weather clothing that I didn't own anyway. How was I supposed to know an unexpected cold front could move through during early September? Back in Los Angeles, it was still at least eighty degrees every day, and with any luck, I wouldn't have to start wearing shoes with socks until almost January.

Fingers crossed.

So, yeah, I hadn't planned my East Coast wardrobe very well, and I hadn't heard the end of it since I met the three women I was currently hanging out with. They teased me relentlessly, but I enjoyed it. This was my first real estate conference out of state, and I was having more fun than I'd had in a long time.

The warm air from the hotel heaters hit me with welcome

relief, and I turned toward my new girlfriends.

"Bar?" I suggested, not ready to call it a night yet.

"Definitely," Robin from Boston said as the other two women nodded.

Robin was in her forties, had been married forever—her words, not mine—and owned her own real estate company. She was also hilarious, constantly cracking me and the other ladies up when we should have been doing anything but laughing.

"Nowhere to sit," Robin said as she nodded toward the circular bar, each seat currently occupied.

Glancing around the crowded space, I spotted a single free table that seated four. I pointed at it and we headed for it before I realized that there were only three chairs.

"You guys sit; I'll find us an extra chair," I said, scanning the area.

A group of guys sat at a large table nearby, surrounded by at least three extra empty seats as they pored over some notebooks and chatted with each other, oblivious to the crowd around them.

I walked over to them and pasted on my most charming smile, the one I used to close multi-million-dollar deals. "Hey, do you guys mind if I steal a chair, or are you using all of these?"

When they all looked up at once, I automatically smiled at them each in turn before stopping cold on a pair of attractive hazel eyes. My focus dropped to the man's lips and I sucked in a breath, completely mesmerized as I struggled to remember why I'd walked over there in the first place.

Chairs. Right. Chairs.

Holy hell, guys should not have lips that full and inviting

if they weren't going to be kissing me all night with them.

The man grinned up at me, revealing even white teeth, and I wanted to hop into his lap and show him how much I appreciated what God had blessed him with. His thick dark hair was cut short and spiked up in all different directions, a casual style that probably took him a while to style, but seemed natural, and I wanted to run my fingers through every single strand.

Instead of admonishing myself for my crazy thoughts about a complete stranger—and boy, were they growing crazier by the second—I went with it, probably a little too eagerly for someone like me. Maybe it was because it had been so long since I'd felt anything at all for a guy.

What harm could a little flirting do? And maybe if I was lucky, I'd find out what those lips felt like on mine before the night was over. It wasn't like I'd ever see the guy again, so who cared if I spent a few hours seeing what those beauties could do? Heck, my fantasy bank could use the inspiration.

"Help yourself," Mr. Delicious Lips said, his perfect mouth still smirking at me as his eyes remained focused on mine.

Suddenly, I didn't want to leave.

Ever.

The idea of chaining myself to his body and throwing away the key crossed my mind. *Too soon?* Probably, but I was rarely, if ever, this physically attracted toward another human being. It wasn't like me to fall all over myself for some random guy I'd just locked eyes with.

Sure, I tended to make friends and meet people wherever I went, but not like this. I'd never met someone who made the very idea of walking away from him seem all sorts of wrong, so

I refused to do it. I didn't think my body would have let me even if I'd been able to convince my mind. Which I hadn't, by the way.

Get a grip, Jules!

My only saving grace would probably be his personality. I'd bet money that once he started talking, I'd find something I didn't like. That tended to happen more often than not back in LA. When a good-looking guy opened his mouth, it usually ruined everything. So many lacked ambition and had no real work ethic. They relied on their good looks and sculpted bodies to get them ahead, and I was interested in more than just a pretty face. Although you wouldn't know it by the way I was currently obsessing over this guy's.

"Maybe I'll just sit here with you instead," I joked, unable to break eye contact.

"Please," he said, pulling out the chair next to him for me. "Sit."

I promptly sat down and mentally accepted my award as world's shittiest friend as I ignored my new girlfriends sitting behind us and chatted up the group of guys. My complete focus was on the one sitting to my right, so close, I could almost feel him. If I leaned in a little closer, I could just . . .

"I'm Jules Abbott," I said, extending my hand.

"Cal Donovan."

When he took my hand with his in a firm handshake, squeezing way too hard, I jerked it from his grasp, my face pinched in pain.

"Jesus, Cal, I'm a girl. You don't have to impress me by breaking my hand." I frowned and shook out my hand as if he'd really hurt it.

"I'm sorry, was it really that hard?" He cocked his head to

the side as he frowned back at me.

"Yes!"

Reaching for his hand again, I squeezed it as hard as I could to prove my point. But he wasn't fazed in the slightest, his intriguing gaze still glued to mine.

"Is that supposed to hurt?" he teased, and I growled, narrowing my eyes as I tried to squeeze his hand even harder, but couldn't.

Damn it. How could I make my point if I couldn't even hurt him with my wimpy grip?

I moved on to the next guy at the table, who reached for my offered hand and shook it gently.

"Charles," he said, and I smiled.

"Nice to meet you, Charles. Now, that's how you shake a lady's hand." I glanced at Cal with a smirk.

The last one in their group introduced himself as Simeon, and when I repeated his name, hoping I pronounced it right, he nodded his head.

"Thanks for letting me crash your party."

"No, thank you," Cal said, brushing his knee against mine, and my entire body heated with the contact.

"Can I invite my girlfriends over?"

I glanced back at the girls, who were thankfully carrying on a conversation without me. It made me feel a little less like a jerk to see they were perfectly fine without me. Then again, this wasn't high school; grown women tended to usually be okay on their own.

"Of course," Simeon said with a smile.

Waving in their direction, I called out, "Girls, do you want to come over here with our new best friends?"

I laughed when they immediately pulled their chairs over

to the table without question, squeezing in and forcing me to inch even closer to Cal.

Cal's thigh pressed against mine as I scooted over, and I made no move to shift away. He didn't either, but maybe it was because he couldn't. The table was packed now, and I couldn't have been happier about that.

So we stayed that way, our legs touching. My body was fully aware of every move he made, every muscle twitch, each time his leg pressed against mine a little harder than it had been a second before. My heart raced at the contact, each movement he made stirring an excitement buried deep inside me.

I'd read plenty of romance novels that talked about this sort of thing happening—the immediate connection between two people, that indescribable pull. And for the last few years, I'd rolled my eyes whenever I'd read those words, half calling them bullshit and half wishing they could be true. But in this moment when my entire being was being shaken to life by the simple act of a male thigh pressing against mine, I finally understood.

I *got* it.

Those words weren't just something the author wrote to make the story sound pretty or give it more meaning—it actually happened to people. And it was currently happening to me. I felt like a live bomb, a firework, something on the verge of exploding. Nothing made you realize how much you'd been ignoring your heart, until someone came along and smacked it awake simply by existing.

Please let him feel it too. Because how much would it suck if I was the only one feeling this heart-altering stuff here? It would suck. A lot.

The seven of us chatted, introducing ourselves. My girls and I explained that we were in town for a conference, and the guys told us they lived here in Boston but were staying at the hotel for an office retreat. They worked in the finance industry and dropped terms about stocks, covalent bonds, and other things that honestly sounded like a foreign language to me.

When Cal spoke about his job, his face lit up. He was smart, and apparently good at what he did; I could tell that simply by the way he talked about it. His passion for his work only turned me on more. There was something so incredibly attractive about a smart, hard-working guy.

"I also help coach a kids' hockey team," he said. "And I'm a math and finance tutor at an afterschool program."

I stifled a shocked laugh. "You're telling me that kids actually want to talk about math and finance? Come on, Cal, don't bullshit me," I teased.

He smiled. "What? You wouldn't want to listen to me talk about that stuff?"

No, but I'd like to listen to him talk about other stuff. "I'm just shocked that kids are even interested in that at their age."

"You'd be surprised at the things that kids are interested in. It actually gives me hope for the future," he said.

"Yeah, Cal here is a real do-gooder."

A new guy walked up to our table, and Cal rose to his feet to give him a one-armed hug.

"Ladies, this is Lucas," Cal said before mussing up the guy's dark blond hair. "Lucas, this is everyone." He waved toward the table.

"Hi, everyone." Lucas's light blue eyes beamed as he grinned at all of us. "Can't stay. Date with a ridiculously hot cop. Don't wait up," he said to Cal.

"Make good choices," Cal warned before Lucas hurried off as quickly as he'd arrived.

Cal sat back down, his leg pressing against mine again as he leaned in, closing off our conversation from the rest of the group. "That was my best friend. We work together."

"He's adorable," I said with a grin.

"Too bad you're not his type."

"Why are all the good ones gay?" I teased, tucking my hair behind my ear.

"What am I, chopped liver?"

"I've never liked liver."

"It's an acquired taste."

Well, damn. So much for his personality sucking. The least he could have done was have a crappy one, be overly cocky or unintelligent, something that might shut my heart down. It would have only been fair to the rest of the male population.

"Where are you from?" Cal propped his elbow on the table and angled his body toward mine, giving me his complete attention.

"Los Angeles." Actually, I lived in Malibu, but it seemed easier to just say LA to people who weren't from there. "You?"

"New Jersey. But I came here for college and decided to stay."

Someone at our table laughed, but neither Cal nor I looked up from our conversation.

"Do you like living here?" I asked.

"I love it." He took a sip of his drink. "Have you seen much of the city yet?"

"A little. It's really pretty. Completely different from California."

He nodded. "Tell me about this conference. What are you learning, and do you think it will help your business?"

What am I learning? God, could this guy be any closer to my own business-minded heart?

"It's actually pretty interesting. They brought in a bunch of speakers who are experts in their territories to share their marketing techniques, personal stories, and what they feel works and doesn't work in terms of relationship building. There's a lot of information on advertising and social media. It's hard, though, because each market is completely different. What works for someone in Alabama most likely isn't going to work for someone like me."

"Why not?"

Cal's genuine interest in my thoughts and opinions fanned the fire in me. I could talk about what I did all day, every day, if he'd let me.

"I work in Malibu mostly. I can sell anywhere in the general LA area, but I'm focused on that particular stretch of beach. It's a lot bigger than people realize. I tend to have clients with a lot more money to burn, so the rules that might apply to, say, someone who only deals with young couples looking to buy their first homes, they don't apply to me. I have to take all this information that I'm learning and figure out what parts of it might work with my clientele."

"Are you self-employed?"

"I work for a broker. Haven't decided yet if going out on my own is the smartest thing for me. I'm still building my client roster and making a solid name for myself." I shrugged. "And to be honest, I'm not sure that in a state like California, it would make sense for me to be my own boss. The tax implications on small businesses are killer, and the very idea of hiring employees makes me nervous."

He nodded. "Makes sense. California is brutal. You should move." His lips curved up. "Probably to Boston. I've heard it's great here."

I laughed. "Yeah? I don't know. I'm sort of attached to where I live."

He glanced up at the ceiling and then back at me, his hazel eyes filled with mischief. "I want to argue, but I'm not sure I can. How the hell do you argue with Malibu?"

"You don't. You can't." I grinned back at him. "What about you? Do you work for a big firm?"

"It's not big by New York standards, but it's not a five-person shop either. We're considered a midsize company. But I want to make partner, so I pretty much spend all my time networking and trying to bring in new clients."

I leaned back slightly. "Is that what you're doing? Trying to bring me in as a client?"

He cocked an eyebrow. "Give me all your money, Jules. Let me triple it for you."

"Well, when you put it that way . . ." I reached for my purse before playfully shoving the entire thing at him. "Here. Take it."

He laughed. "You're smart."

"So are you."

"I don't meet a lot of smart women. No offense," he said as I pursed my lips, willing him to remove the foot he'd just placed in his beautiful mouth. "It's just that women tend to see themselves one way, but they're usually the opposite."

I bristled, needing more of an explanation than that for why he was putting down my entire gender. "Explain."

"Okay, but don't get pissed. Hear me out." He put his

hands up in surrender. "One of the first things women always say is how independent they are, how motivated. But in my experience, they're usually neither of those things. They're either searching for a rich guy to provide for them so they don't have to work, or they're still living on Mommy and Daddy's money. And neither of those things are signs of an independent or motivated woman, in my opinion. Unless you count trying to land a sugar daddy motivation," he said with a grin.

I wanted to disagree with him, but the truth was that a lot of my clients were women who didn't work at anything except spending their husband's money. Granted, the men in those situations also tended to want nothing more than eye candy on their arm, so it worked both ways.

Cal spoke again, interrupting my thoughts. "Most people don't know what they want to do with their life, and they aren't working toward a goal. I rarely meet anyone who is as together as you are. It's a compliment, Jules. Take it." He smiled at me, and I focused on those damn lips again as my irritation faded.

Listening to him speak was almost like having a conversation with myself. Hadn't I just thought virtually the same thing about the guys in LA, that they were all looks and no substance?

It had been a long time since I was around a guy whose thoughts seemed to mimic my own. It was almost more of a turn-on than the rest of him. I wanted to take him upstairs and make love to his mind. Was such a thing possible? *I volunteer as tribute!*

"Thank you."

"My turn," he said expectantly.

"Your turn what?"

"What do you like about me?" he asked before taking another sip of his drink.

I giggled. "Who says I like you at all?"

"Those green eyes do. They give you away," he said as he stared into them.

"I might like you a little." I pretended to glance over his shoulder for a second, anything to break the intense eye contact before meeting his gaze again. "But honestly, your motivation and passion for the things that you love—" I let out a little sigh, all but moaned out loud. "It's so damn hot."

He laughed. "You're adorable."

"Yeah? And you're sexy."

Cal's hand brushed against mine under the table. He squeezed my thigh and left his hand there, caressing me through my jeans with his thumb. His move was a bit forward, and I found myself enjoying it way too much for my own good.

That touch wasn't accidental and I wanted more of it—more of him. I wanted his hands all over me. Hell, I'd already imagined those full lips pressed against mine the second I'd first laid eyes on him.

"I'm so tired, you guys," my new friend Kristy from Connecticut said. "I don't want to, but I think I have to go to bed." She pushed up from her seat and stretched her arms above her head.

"Oh, thank God," Sue from Arizona said before standing. "I didn't want to be the first to leave, but I think I might fall asleep at this table if I don't head upstairs."

I told them both good night and watched as they headed toward the elevators. When I glanced at Robin, I was surprised to see her sipping a cocktail that I hadn't even noticed her order. Clearly, I'd been distracted.

"I'm not going anywhere, so don't look at me like that," she said with a smile, and I found myself only marginally thankful.

The entire hotel lobby could empty out for all I cared; I wasn't leaving Cal's side. No matter how tired I might have been from the day's seminars and team-building activities, I refused to be the one who walked away from whatever was simmering between the two of us. If we came apart instead of falling together, it would be his doing, not mine.

"Don't go yet."

I turned toward Cal's whisper as relief filled me, willing him to want the same thing I did. With our faces mere inches apart, I fought the pull I felt as my attention kept drifting between his hazel eyes and those damn lips.

"Didn't plan on it," I said softly.

Our bodies leaned closer, inexplicably drawn together, and I almost laughed at how we must have looked to everyone else. *Like a couple.* Definitely not like two people who had just met.

As his hand squeezed my thigh again and he smiled, my brain turned to mush. All I could think about was Cal and how much more I wanted of him.

So much more.

BREAKING RULES

Cal

I WAS CURRENTLY sitting at a table with my hand on Jules's thigh, breaking my number-one rule: No women.

Work was too damn important to me, and women were a distraction. Even the best ones seemed to turn into something else once we started dating, taking on personality traits that hadn't been there when we first met. They were good at hiding the parts of them they didn't want you to see until just the right time. And while I understood that most women needed things from a relationship that were seemingly normal, like my time and attention, I couldn't give it to them.

That was what led me to formulate my life plan in the first place—too many clingy, needy women, and my realization that I wasn't ready for any of that yet. My plan was solid and ladies didn't factor into it; at least, not for another three or so years. Yes, I even had a timeline.

Women had their own timelines. They wanted to be married by a certain age, have two point five kids and a house by another. The only problem was my timeline and theirs tended to be off by several years. I needed two more years to make partner within my firm, another six months or so to get settled into the role, and then—and only then—could women possibly come back into the equation, depending on what else I was involved in by that point.

To fill what little spare time I had after spending long hours at the office, I took on some volunteer projects. At first it was to impress my bosses and show them that I was well rounded, dependable, and thought outside the box when it came to positive publicity for the firm. But I soon realized that I really enjoyed the mentoring and coaching, and it had become less about impressing anyone else and more about making a difference where I could. I found a deep sense of satisfaction in my volunteer work that my job couldn't fill.

Coldly categorizing my life into a series of boxes I wanted to check off wasn't a romantic notion, but my career had nothing to do with romance and everything to do with reality. I wanted to be firmly rooted in it before allowing myself to be distracted by a relationship.

But right now, with my hand touching Jules's thigh, my brain wasn't the least bit involved, and I wasn't sure what was real at this point. She was real. Her long blond hair and fierce green eyes, those were real.

I wasn't lying when I'd told Jules that most women didn't have it together. It wasn't meant to be a slap at her gender; it was the truth from my experience. But Jules was motivated and determined the same way I was, and damn it if I didn't find everything about that sexy as hell. Not to mention the fact that when Jules spoke, she reminded me of myself; she had ambition in spades and the gusto to make her dreams a reality. I could relate to her on every level, and I couldn't even remember the last time that had happened.

Jules was funny too. She always smiled when she spoke, and her eyes closed with genuine amusement each time she laughed at something someone said.

And beautiful—God, she was so beautiful. She looked like she'd walked straight from the sands of some warm beach, wearing a sleeveless shirt and strappy sandals in the chilly Boston air. Jules was a vision, and I had a hard time keeping my hands off of her. Granted, I wasn't trying very hard, but I found myself not wanting to. What I did want was to get her alone and familiarize myself with every square inch of her body.

That was something I hadn't done in a very long time. My right hand and I had become the best of friends, and I'd convinced myself it was easier that way. My hand didn't talk back, didn't demand that I take it to dinner or buy it expensive gifts. I'd put sex on the back burner for my career, and before this moment, I'd been fine with that decision. It had always made the most sense.

But now, staring at Jules's honey-colored hair, something nagged at me, telling me that if I let her go, I'd regret it. And I hated regrets more than I hated nagging.

What was it about this woman that had me so twisted up already? It made no sense at all. The logical parts of me wanted to fight this nonsense and not give in to it, but my body betrayed me at every turn. My hands had a will of their own, acting without permission as they touched her at every opportunity.

It was official; I couldn't keep my hands off of her. She was like a siren, drawing me in so she could have her way with me. And I'd be damned if I wasn't going to let her.

HE CHANGED EVERYTHING

Jules

CAL'S HAND WARMED my leg, spreading heat wherever it landed. It was all I could focus on, that sizzling touch of his. His fingers splayed out across my leg, inching closer to my most private area.

As much as Cal turned me on, I refused to go that far in public, groping beneath a table like we were in middle school. So I placed my hand on top of his and gave it a light squeeze, stopping any further movement. I'd intended to pull my hand away, but he laced his fingers with mine and held them there.

"What are you drinking?" I looked into his glass, wondering if he was drinking straight liquor.

"Bourbon."

"Seriously? I thought so, but are you sure you're even old enough to drink?" I asked with a laugh.

"Twenty-nine, babe. So just barely."

He grinned at me then, a mischievous smile baring lots of perfect teeth, and my heart leaped at the sight. Or maybe it was the term of endearment. It was silly to get excited over something so small, but I'd been so focused on my career the last few years that I'd forgotten what my heart was even for, or how a simple nickname from the right guy's mouth could cause it to hammer against my chest. Now, it seemed to be trying to remind me of its role with every single beat.

Prior to walking into this lobby tonight, I would have bet money against my heart ten times out of ten when it came to love. I was convinced that it didn't care about anything other than work and my success. It especially didn't care about the opposite sex. My heart didn't need a man, didn't want a man; it was perfectly fulfilled, beating only for my career.

I would have lost that bet the minute I met Cal Donovan.

My heart was clearly meant to *want*. It was meant to *feel*. It was meant to do more than just keep me alive. Oh, how I had forgotten.

"How about you?" he asked, and I struggled to remember what the hell we were talking about.

I glanced down and lifted one shoulder in a little shrug. "I'm only nineteen, so no. Not old enough to drink. At least, not legally."

He froze for a second before he jerked his hand from my thigh as if it were scalding hot.

I burst out laughing, amused at the look of surprise on his face, which was slightly paler than it had been a moment ago. "I'm just kidding."

"Oh, you're hilarious." He took a few deep breaths, clearly exaggerating his response and playing along.

"I'm twenty-seven," I said truthfully, hoping his hand would return. And it did.

"Just a young'un."

"Tell me about it, old man."

He grabbed at his heart like my words wounded him before asking, "Do you drink bourbon?"

"I have before. But I didn't enjoy it," I admitted, fully

expecting him to make fun of me about it. Everyone else always had.

"That's because you didn't drink it right," he said, poking my shoulder with his finger.

"There's a right way to drink that wretched alcohol?" I cocked my head to the side, not believing him.

A slight smile appeared as he leaned closer, bringing his lips a breath away from mine. "Of course there is. Let me teach you how."

Lost in his eyes, I sucked in a quick breath. "Okay."

I watched as he brought the glass to his mouth and pressed it against his bottom lip. Damn, I wanted to be that glass.

He inhaled but didn't drink a drop.

"Do that three times," he said. "Just breathe it in. You'll start to feel it in your mouth, in your throat."

As he repeated the movement twice more, my focus remained firmly trained on those damn lips. They had me under a spell. Seriously, that was one lucky glass.

His smirk reappeared when he caught me staring. I was probably drooling and had no clue.

"And now you sip it."

He tilted the glass further back as the smallest amount of the amber liquid poured into his mouth and he swallowed. I was surprised he had no visible reaction at all, as if it didn't burn like hell as it coursed down his throat. I wasn't sure about most people, but just the smell of bourbon evoked a physical reaction from me.

"Your turn." He set his glass on the table and pushed it in front of me.

I smiled as I reached for it, bringing it to my lips as he watched me with the same intensity as when I'd watched him.

But it was unnerving, the way he stared. His hazel eyes were almost *too* intense, filled with too much of something I couldn't entirely read, and it made me uncomfortable.

"You can't watch me," I said as my face heated.

"Okay, but do what I told you." Playing along, he closed his eyes.

"No peeking," I warned before bringing the glass to my mouth and breathing it in. The scent of the bourbon mixed with the air and traveled down my throat and into my belly. After a moment, I repeated the process twice more like he'd suggested, enjoying sensing the alcohol like this instead of drinking it.

"Can I watch yet?" he asked, squinting his eyes tighter, and I laughed.

"Yes."

Cal's eyes opened and met mine instantly, capturing me. It was as if no one else existed around us. I heard nothing else, saw no one else. My new friend Robin wasn't there at the table in this hotel lobby, and neither were his coworkers. Cal and I were the only two people in the entire hotel, as far as I was concerned.

Glancing at my mouth, he licked his lips. I willed my body not to react, but it heated anyway.

He reached out again and squeezed the top of my leg before resting his hand there as if that was where it belonged. On my body. Touching me. And I couldn't remember what I had been doing before that moment. One touch from him caused my thoughts to scatter.

"Take a drink."

That's right. I was supposed to be drinking this damn bourbon. I stopped focusing on his hand caressing the inside of my thigh and stared at the glass.

I tilted it back, sipping it like he had instructed, and I almost couldn't believe it when the liquid didn't burn me up from the inside out like it always had before. Everything about it tasted completely different. It was tolerable, good even, to drink it straight when you followed Cal's advice.

"And?"

"I guess there is a right way to drink bourbon," I said with a nod, pushing the glass back toward him.

"Was it good?"

"It actually was. I'm impressed."

"I'm pretty impressive," he said, and smiled at me with a mock smugness.

I stared at his smile, wanting to photograph that mouth for all the world to see. No, not the world. Just me. I wanted photographic proof of those lips. What if I never saw them again after tonight? I was pretty sure I'd die if I didn't get to kiss them.

Dramatic, yes, but this man woke up the sleeping beast that had lain dormant inside my chest for so long. It was all his fault that my heart decided to come back to life the moment it found him.

"Where did you learn about the right way to drink bourbon?" I asked.

"My best friend, Lucas, the one who said hi before running out of here earlier, he's from Kentucky."

I raised my eyebrows as I waited for him to explain. When he didn't, I simply said, "Kentucky?"

"Yes, Jules. Kentucky. The bourbon capital of the United States." He looked at me like I was crazy.

"I didn't know," I said with a shrug. "I think of horses

when I think of Kentucky."

"They have those too. Horses and bourbon." He nudged his shoulder against mine before his tone turned serious. "When do you leave?"

"Two days. You?"

"We check out tomorrow morning."

"Oh."

Well, that sucked. I wanted Cal to be here at the hotel for as long as I was. That might have been an unrealistic expectation, but it was how I felt. I enjoyed his company and didn't want this to end yet. Was it too forward to want to spend more time with him?

"Two days, huh?" He cocked his head to the side.

"Yep."

"Do you have any free time?"

"I do, actually. We have activities and presentations, but I don't have to go to every single one. And all of our evenings are free. Why, Cal, what are you thinking?"

I'd sensed the wheels turning in his head and kept it light, asking my question in a teasing tone. I hoped he wanted to spend more time with me too.

Cal's voice lowered a little, turning husky as he said, "I'd like to see you again."

Heart, meet floor. Floor, meet my heart.

"That can maybe be arranged," I said while I tried not to smile like an idiot.

"Maybe?" He leaned in close, his gaze pinned to mine. "Tell me what I have to do to convince you."

"Kiss me," I blurted before I could stop myself. I blamed my forwardness on his lips—they'd turned me stupid.

Without another word, he slipped his hand behind my

neck and held me tight as his mouth drifted closer to mine.

Shit, was he really going to do it here, in front of his coworkers and my new friend from the conference? The words had just slipped from my mouth before I'd thought it through, but I sure as hell wasn't going to stop him if he was going to give me a kiss, even if we were in public.

When Cal's lips touched mine, my brain stopped all rational thought. Those lips were so soft. And warm. Our mouths opened and his tongue brushed against my bottom lip, making me moan into him.

The sound of cheers and whoops broke through our haze, making us abruptly pull away from each other. If looks could kill, I would have murdered both Charles and Simeon on the spot for breaking up that epic first kiss.

"So I win, right?" Cal said to me with a satisfied smirk.

Oh no, buddy, my fuzzy brain insisted. *I think I'm the winner here.*

"Yeah," I said on a long breath. "You win."

"You owe me, Cal," Charles said from across the table.

Cal turned away to scowl at him. "Owe you for what? You're lucky I don't hit you for trying to ruin my kiss."

"Simeon wanted to record that and post it online."

"Do that and I really will hit you," Cal growled out.

Simeon's eyes grew wide as he shoved his phone back into his pocket. "I would never really do it."

"That was hot," Robin said, breaking the tension, and I laughed when I saw the look on her face. "Seriously. That was . . . whew." She rolled her eyes and fanned herself with one hand.

My cheeks heated as embarrassment rushed through me. I didn't normally put on a show with guys I'd just met, but Cal had me doing and feeling all sorts of things out of character for me tonight.

A chair squeaked across the floor as Cal pushed to his feet. With his hand extended toward me, he asked loud enough for everyone to hear, "Can I have your hand?"

"Yes?"

I gave him a confused look as I accepted his hand. Smiling, he tugged me to my feet.

It was the first time we'd stood since we met, and I realized that before now, I had no idea how tall Cal was. He stood more than a handful of inches above my five feet six inches; not over six feet tall, that I could tell, but he was close enough. Honestly, I wouldn't have cared if we were the same height at this point. My attraction for him had nothing to do with his ability to tower over me or not. Cal was all man, no matter his height.

"Dance with me?"

"Really?" I glanced back to see our tablemates all grinning at us, and then looked up at Cal. "Sure."

He spun me around once, his hand firmly gripping mine as he twirled me twice more. Then he led me away from the table and before I knew it, we rounded a corner and disappeared from their view.

I had no idea where we were going, but part of me didn't care. Cal had me all caught up in the adventure of it, and for once in my life, I went with it, enjoying the rush.

He smiled and led me toward the bank of elevators. "I just wanted to get you alone, and it was taking too long to get you away from your other friend. Why won't she go to bed?"

My pulse raced as he pressed the call button. I stood there, half stunned, half impressed, watching his mouth as he spoke.

My lust for his lips was becoming ridiculous.

Becoming? I was completely lusting after that mouth of his. No question.

"Where are you taking me?" I thought to ask.

"To my room, if that's okay." He shifted his weight, and his confidence disappeared for a second.

"But what about Lucas? Didn't he mention that you two were sharing a room?"

Cal laughed. "Yeah, but he said not to wait up, remember? Charles actually texted me at the table, telling me to grab you before you got away."

"He did not," I said, slightly taken aback.

"He did. He mentioned something about our highly combustible body language, and that we should move it upstairs before we set the bar on fire."

When my mouth dropped open, Cal chuckled again. I stared into his eyes, lost somewhere in the depths of them. I'd honestly forgotten how it felt to be *this* attracted to someone, the way my body came alive as it buzzed with desire. It really had been too long.

Cal was all consuming, and I was happily being consumed.

The elevator arrived and we stepped inside. The moment the doors closed, he pressed the button for his floor before stalking toward me like I was his prey. I stepped back until there was nowhere else for me to go. As he pressed me against the mirrored wall of the elevator, his eyes burned, as if he couldn't wait a single second longer to have his mouth on me.

An exhale later, his lips crushed against mine, claiming them, claiming me. They were everything. These were the lips people wrote books about. As our mouths moved in perfect sync, that kiss ignited me. A single spark and a fire was born.

DEAR HEART, I HATE YOU

His hands gripped my waist, pulling me flush against him. Pressed together from mouth to knees, our bodies merged, and the feel of his hard-on pressed against my body instantly aroused me even more, making my sex tingle, alive with want.

My hands were relentless, pulling, gripping, and grabbing every part of him as fast and hard as they could. I couldn't get enough. I wanted all of him, and if the elevator took much longer to arrive at his floor, I'd let him take me right there if he tried.

His hands were just as needy, his fingers digging into my lower back, cupping my cheek, tugging at my neck, feeling me everywhere. Our mouths never left each other, our kiss never breaking, no matter how frantic our touches became.

We breathed the same air, caught up in the passion as if our lives depended on it. If the doors had opened and someone had walked in on us, I wouldn't have noticed. I was too caught up in the moment, in the feel of his lips on mine. His touch had drugged me, the way one of his hands clutched at the small of my back, pulling me closer to him, and the other hand wrapped in my hair. Cal was singlehandedly bringing me to life, and he didn't even know it.

As the elevator dinged before coming to a shaky stop, Cal reluctantly pulled away from me, leaving my mouth tingling and a little numb. He reached for my hand again, twining his fingers with mine before he led us down the long hallway in the direction of his room. He pushed the key in the slot, and the light flashed green before he held the door open for me to walk through ahead of him.

"Your room is huge," I said as I glanced around at the giant space.

"Is yours not this big?"

"I don't think so." No, my room was nowhere near this size.

Walking toward the window in the darkened room, I took in his impressive view of the Boston skyline at night. All the buildings lit up from within, casting reflections on the water below.

"Is your view the same?" He stepped behind me, pressing his body against my back as he swept my hair over one shoulder and touched his lips to my neck.

"No. We face the other direction, I think. Who cares," I said on a breath before turning to face him.

His lips landed on mine without hesitation, our tongues again frantic and wild in their need for each other.

"You're beautiful. You know that?" he said as he placed kisses along my cheek, my neck, and then back to my lips, which had craved him since we left the elevator.

When I didn't respond, Cal gently moved me toward one of the two beds. He kicked off his shoes, and I found myself doing the same before moving on top of the comforter.

He pulled off his shirt and tossed it onto the moonlit floor. I sat there for a moment, staring at the beauty of his naked chest and the patch of dark hair there that I would have never expected. Then he reached for me and pulled me on top of him, making my long hair spill down between us. His fingers found the strands and tucked them behind my ear.

"Beautiful," he whispered before kissing me softly, the once frantic pace slowing to something more intimate and intense. His kiss took on a different rhythm, his tongue gentle in its quest for mine.

If the elevator had been a minefield, this room waved the white flag of surrender. The battle was over, and we'd both won.

Cal reached for my top and pulled it over my head. I helped him, knowing I had another layer underneath. The fitted tank top that was left molded to my body like a second skin, and I froze when he sucked in an audible breath.

"What's wrong?" I asked.

His gaze followed the curves of my body, looking me up and down before returning my mouth. "Nothing. You hid this from me earlier," he said, running his hands along the curves of my hips as if in total appreciation.

I smiled. "Yeah, I guess it was under my other top."

"Stand up," he said, and although I thought it was odd, I did as he asked. When I started to turn toward him, he said, "Don't move, Jules. Please."

Standing next to the bed wearing a skintight tank and jeans, I had no idea what was happening behind me. "What are you doing?"

"Looking at you. Memorizing the shape of your body. That ass—it's perfection. And I had no idea it was there this whole time."

My cheeks warmed at his brazen compliments. Before I could say anything, he stood up and pressed his body against my back without warning, every part of him molding against me. He touched my shoulders to turn me around to face him, his eyes locking onto mine the way they'd done all night, as if he saw right through me to the *real* me. It was as unnerving as it was intriguing.

Cal's fingers grazed across my stomach as he reached for the bottom of my tank and tugged it over my head and discarded it, leaving me in just my lacy bra and jeans. An appreciative sound escaped his lips, and it did something to me to know that I turned him on in this way.

"Sorry. I can't help the way I react to you," he said, and I found myself speechless again.

He crouched to his knees before pressing his lips against my bare belly. I stood there, finally allowing my hands to rake through his soft hair as I'd wanted to do all night, while he alternated between planting kisses on my bare stomach and licking a trail along my ribs. I sucked in a quick breath and shuddered slightly as chills raced through me.

"I need to lie down," I said, his attention throwing me off-balance.

My legs couldn't be trusted to hold me up any longer, and I moved toward the bed. I stretched out on it again, my excitement warring with a touch of fear of taking things too far, too fast.

Cal lowered himself on top of me, peppering me with kisses as his warm hands explored my body. I welcomed his touch, reveled in it.

"I want you, Jules."

I closed my eyes, knowing that this was the moment in which everything would change. If I crossed this line, there would be no going back; I could never uncross it once it was behind me.

The reality of the situation was that Cal and I had just met; we were perfect strangers. Granted, I'd willingly come upstairs with him and had practically mauled him in the elevator, but actually having sex with him when we'd just met hours before wasn't something I typically did.

One-night stands weren't for me. I was far too emotional, feeling things way too deeply to just give my body away to any guy who wanted it. I learned that the hard way back in college after I'd given myself to a guy who had halfheartedly pursued me for months. I thought he really liked me, but when I slept with him after a party one night, he never spoke to me again. I was traumatized by his actions and quickly realized that I wasn't the type who could sleep with someone and have it not mean anything to me. Tami, my best friend back home, could do that—the friends-with-benefits, no-strings-attached, fuck-buddy thing—but not me. I honestly wasn't cut out for it emotionally.

"I want you too," I admitted. "But . . ."

When I hesitated, he pushed up on his elbows. "But?"

"We just met. And if I have sex with you, it will mess me up." I shook my head, not liking the way my words tumbled out. They were too raw, too honest.

"Mess you up how?"

"I can't sleep with someone and not feel anything for them. I know you probably think that's stupid because we're both adults and we should be able to—"

Cal's finger pressed against my lips, stopping my words. "I don't think it's stupid. I understand what you're saying."

"Really?"

"Of course. I'm not a complete dick, Jules."

I huffed out a quick breath. "Obviously I didn't think you were, or I wouldn't be here with you now. It's just that I'm sure you thought you'd get lucky, and it's not like I didn't give you that impression. I know that I did. But if we have sex tonight, I'll only end up getting hurt."

"I don't want to hurt you." He leaned over and pressed a kiss against my forehead before rolling off of me and lying on his side, propping himself on one elbow to give me his full attention.

"It wouldn't even be your fault. It would be mine," I said, trying to explain.

"What do you mean?"

I turned to face him, mirroring his position, hoping my words would make sense and wouldn't make him run like hell out of his own room.

"It's just that I'd want to see you again if we did something like that. And I wouldn't be able to not feel that way about it, you know? Sex isn't just something I do. I consider it really intimate and personal."

Why did I feel the need to explain myself to Cal? Maybe it was my hope that he would understand my heart better, even though we'd just met. Or maybe it was because I believed people tended to give themselves to each other too easily these days, without thought or hesitation, and I couldn't bring myself to be so cavalier about it.

When a woman has sex, we allow a man inside us, allow them to take a piece of us with them forever. Having sex means that a guy *enters* us, pushes their way into our bodies and becomes a part of us, an extension of us. We don't enter men; we don't invade them. Instead, we welcome them inside us and cover them, hold them, surround them with our softest, most private parts. There was something extremely personal about letting someone inside you that way, being vulnerable to them like that.

And it scared me to do that with someone I'd just met.

"So you're saying you want me to book a flight to LA right now? If I plan on seeing you again, we can have sex tonight?" Cal sat up and pulled his phone from his back pocket and opened a travel app.

"Oh my gosh, stop it," I said, swatting him on the shoulder.

"I'm not joking, Jules. Hell, I'll book two separate trips. Say the word."

"Stop," I said again with a giggle, but I didn't really want him to stop. If he wanted to book a hundred trips to see me after tonight, I'd encourage it.

"Okay," he said with a grin, "but remember that I tried to see you again." His mouth moved to mine, kissing me long and hard before pulling away. "And you wouldn't let me."

"Cal, if you want to come out and visit after I leave here, I won't be the one to stop you. And I'll definitely have sex with you then."

And I meant it. Not having sex when we'd just met was one thing, but if I saw Cal again after tonight, I'd totally give myself to him. Because that would mean that we'd kept in touch after this night. And hell yeah, that earned him a little hot sex. Which meant it earned me sex too.

"I can't wait to see you again," he said, making me smile. "I love everything about you, Jules. There isn't a single thing I don't like."

I wondered how much of that was the bourbon talking, considering I'd watched him down a few glasses.

"We just met, Cal; of course you love everything about me. Get back to me in a few months."

"Deal," he said before his lips met mine.

JUST HAVING FUN

Cal

HELL, IF JULES had called my bluff, asked me to actually book a flight out to see her so we could have sex tonight, I would have done it. I was *that* caught up in the moment. Or maybe it was just her that I was that caught up in.

Ridding myself of that fantasy, I crash-landed back into reality. It was a hard fall, but I needed it. I had two more days to spend time with Jules, and I planned on doing exactly that. Two more days and then we'd never see each other again. Which sort of sucked, but it was what it was. She lived in Los Angeles and I lived in Boston; there was no future for us. But that didn't mean that I couldn't enjoy her while she was here.

Jules stopping us tonight from having sex had been pretty respectable. I wouldn't have thought any less of her if we had done it, but had to admire the fact that she knew herself well enough to know what she could and couldn't handle emotionally. Most people generally didn't have that level of self-awareness, myself included at times.

Plus, the last thing I needed was to sleep with someone and have her go all crazy psycho on me. Been there; done that. And it wasn't fun. Hence, my timeline. It saved me from all sorts of potential drama.

I lay back down and reached for Jules. "Come here." Wrapping my hand around her waist, I pulled her against me, and she lay her head on my chest as I ran my fingers through her hair. "Wanna just talk a bit?"

Her head lifted slightly. "Seriously?"

"Seriously."

"Only if said talking has kissing involved." She looked up at me and ran her thumb along my bottom lip. "These things right here, they do something to me." She pressed her lips to mine before her tongue swept across them, teasing me.

"You don't play fair."

She smiled before moving her head back to my chest. "I know. I can't help it. Those lips. They'll be my ruin."

I laughed, my ego loving her compliments, but I needed to change the subject or I'd end up being the type of asshole who didn't stop trying to have sex with her until she finally gave in. I wanted to be better than that.

"No more talk about my lips. Or your lips. Or any kind of lips," I said sternly.

She giggled, her shoulders shaking against my chest. "Now all I want to do is talk about them."

I cleared my throat, trying to calm myself down from the thought of her mouth and what it could do to my body, and came up with a safe question that wouldn't turn me on. At least, I hoped it wouldn't. With my luck, Jules would tell me she had an identical twin sister, and then my willpower and my plan to behave would be shot to hell.

Going for a conversational tone, I said, "Do you have any brothers or sisters?"

She giggled against my chest again. "Nice subject change, but I'll play along. One older sister. I think I was an *oops*, although my parents will never admit it. But who has two kids seventeen years apart? No one does, that's who. At least, not on purpose."

"Your sister is seventeen years older than you?" I couldn't believe it. That seemed crazy to me.

"Yes!" She looked up at me again, then moved her hand on top of my chest before propping her chin on it. "And my parents are like, 'We planned for you, Jules.' Bullshit. Liars!" she said with a laugh.

"Do they all live near you?"

"My sister took a job in London about a year ago. I don't think she's ever coming back. And my parents keep taking 'extended vacations' there," she said, using air quotes around the words. "One day they're going to send me an e-mail saying they're staying forever."

"Could you blame them?" I asked with a smile.

"Not really. I'm sort of in love with London."

I nodded in agreement. "I understand that feeling."

"You've been?"

"Once, after college. But I've never gotten over it and I've always wanted to go back."

She smiled like she could once again completely relate to my words. "What about you?"

"What about me, what?" I asked, not sure what she was inquiring about exactly.

"Siblings?" she reminded me with a smirk. "Do you have any?"

"I have one older brother, and a younger brother and sister," I said as thoughts of my siblings made me smile to myself. We had grown up close, but now we only saw one another during the holidays.

"So many," she said, her tone almost awestruck.

"We're Irish," I said as if that was reason enough. Which to be fair, it was.

"No wonder you love this city so much. It's like Irish Central."

I'd never thought about that before, but Jules might have been on to something. I loved Boston in general because it was a really great city, proud and filled with hardworking people, but she was right. The Irish ruled this town.

"I do love it. Is this your first time to the East Coast?"

She shook her head. "It's my first time in Boston, but not the East Coast. I've been to New York a handful of times. I wanted to go to school there so bad when I was younger."

"Why didn't you?" Strange; Jules didn't seem the type to let anything stand in her way.

"I didn't get in," she said, her expression revealing her regret and sadness.

"That sucks. I'm sorry. New York's a great city."

"I know. I love it there; I always wanted to live there. Not forever, but for a few years, you know? Just to experience something different from what I was used to."

I nodded. I did know. It was why I'd moved out of Jersey. Granted, I didn't go very far, in the grand scheme of things, but Boston was completely different from my hometown. The people weren't the same, the city wasn't the same, nothing was the same except that they existed in the same general area of the map.

"That's why I wanted to get out of Jersey too. I was afraid that if I didn't leave for college, I never would."

She sighed, seemingly lost in memories. "It's hard when you plant that seed in your mind. You convince yourself that moving across the country is the only thing you want, and then it's all you can think about. When I didn't get in, I was crushed. I hadn't even applied to any other out-of-state schools. I just assumed I'd get in." She shook her head. "God, I was so clueless."

"So you stayed in LA for college?" I asked, feeling disappointed for her.

"Yep. Which was fine, don't get me wrong. I had a great experience. It's just that that lust for adventure, that want for a location change never really goes away when you don't get the chance to fulfill it." Her gaze drifted away, going a little unfocused as she said, "Sure, I stuff it deep down and try to tell myself I don't want it anymore, but that's a lie. It's still there. It rears up its head every now and then, begging me to toss all my things in a suitcase and just leave." She bit her lip and stopped talking, as if she only now realized she had an audience.

"Don't stop," I said, wanting Jules to keep going. Her honesty was beyond refreshing. Most people didn't share their heart very easily, and she did it so willingly.

She shrugged and laid her head back on my chest. "That's basically it. For the most part, I'm really happy where I am. But sometimes I feel so pulled away, like I'm supposed to be somewhere else. Do you ever feel like that? I'm crazy, right? Totally not normal?" she asked with a slight smile.

"I think that if I hadn't ever left New Jersey, I'd feel that way too. A hundred percent. You're not crazy." I put my hand on hers and gave it a squeeze. "You actually sound a lot like my little brother's fiancée. Must be a California thing."

"How so?"

"She basically said the same thing as you did about moving

away for college. That she wanted to get out of LA and experience something new."

Jules's head snapped up. "Wait—she's from LA? What part?"

I racked my brain. "Shit. I know this." I snapped my fingers and squeezed my eyes shut as I concentrated. "Bur-something?"

"Burbank?"

"Yes! That's it. Katherine's from Burbank."

"That's not too far from where I live. Where is she now?"

Her voice took on an excitement that made me smile. Jules might have wanted to move somewhere else for the experience, but she loved where she was from. It was written all over her face, reflected in her eyes and in the tone of her voice.

"She and Cooper, that's my brother, live in Chicago. He plays professional hockey. You know, he has a game in town tomorrow night, if you're interested."

"Really?" She stared up at me, her green eyes big and trusting as I leaned over to kiss her forehead again, loving the way it made me feel protective of her. "You want me to go to his game with you?"

"Yeah. Unless you don't like hockey." A lot of girls weren't into sports, so I offered her the opportunity to say no. But I hoped like hell she wouldn't.

She huffed out a breath. "I don't know anything about it, to be honest. Obviously, I know what hockey is, but I've never watched it on purpose. And I've never been to a game."

"Stop." I moved to sit up, lifting her with me. "What is it with you California girls and hating hockey?"

"I don't hate hockey," she said with a laugh. "My dad didn't watch sports when I was growing up, and I didn't play any. He used to be a big baseball fan, but after they went on strike one year, he stopped supporting it. Quit baseball cold turkey."

That made sense. My dad had stopped watching baseball too after the strike.

Hugging Jules close, I said, "We're a huge hockey family, especially now that Cooper's gone pro. My dad's been obsessed with all things Rangers since we were kids. He had all of us on the ice as soon as we came out of the womb, even my sister. But Cooper was the best of us by far."

"That sounds nice, though. Having so many brothers and sisters," she said almost dreamily.

"It is," I wholeheartedly agreed.

"Will Katherine be at the game tomorrow?"

"Yeah. She usually travels with Cooper, especially when he comes to a town where one of us lives."

Her smile widened. "That's cool."

"So you'll come with me?"

"I'd love to."

"It'll be fun. I promise."

"I know it will," she said with a smile.

Glancing at the clock on the nightstand, I noted how late it was. Or early, depending on how you looked at it. While I had no qualms about staying up with Jules until dawn, I knew that she had to attend a bunch of meetings tomorrow—or later today, technically.

When her gaze followed mine, her shoulders slumped. "I should probably go."

I knew it was coming, but that didn't make it suck any less. "You could stay," I offered, knowing she'd never say yes. But you couldn't blame a man for trying. *You can't win the game if you don't play.*

"Tempting," she said with a grin before giving me a sweet kiss. "But I should probably sleep in my own room. That way, I'll actually sleep."

I knew that answer was coming too. Still sucked, because wasn't ready to let her go.

"Give me your phone," I said as she pushed off the bed and stood up, stretching her arms above her head before she tossed her phone at me without question.

So trusting, I thought. Like she had nothing to hide. And maybe she didn't.

"Where did you throw my shirts?" she asked.

"In the trash." I smirked as I turned her phone on, noting the lack of a password, and programmed my number in before sending myself a text so I'd have her number too.

"Ha-ha," she said sarcastically. "Found them! And not in the trash."

My phone vibrated with my own text message as Jules pulled her tank top over her body and covered herself up. It was a damn shame to hide those curves. Pushing myself from the bed, I found my own shirt on the floor and pulled it on.

As she slipped on her blouse, she asked, "What are you doing?"

"Walking you to your room."

"You don't have to do that," she said, giving me an out I had no intention of taking.

"I know I don't have to. I want to."

The smile that brightened her face reassured me that even though she'd said I didn't have to, she wanted me to. I wasn't a total dick when it came to women. Hell, maybe I was when I wasn't interested in them, but I genuinely enjoyed Jules. She brought out the gentleman in me, and I was fairly certain men like that were sorely lacking back in Los Angeles, which only made me want to be more of one.

If Jules and I were never going to see each other again, I'd send her home with memories of that really hot, sweet guy she met in Boston. The one she compared all others to.

Wait—was that my ego talking or my pride? It might have been a combination of both, but I couldn't be sure. My head was a little messed up, alternating between the reality of our situation and some fantasyland where no one existed except for the two of us.

I held her close as we walked to the elevator, and once the door shut behind us, I attacked her mouth with mine. I wasn't sure what it was about Jules and elevators, but the second those doors slammed together, I wanted her pressed against the mirrored wall, giving herself to me. All my self-control was lost when I had her in a confined space like this.

We exited the elevator and when we arrived at her room, I kissed her softly as I wrapped my hand in her long blond hair.

"I had a really nice time tonight," she whispered, almost as if she was embarrassed to admit it.

Hell, I wasn't sure at all what she was thinking. Maybe she thought I didn't have a nice time because we didn't have sex?

"I'm sorry we didn't . . . you know," she said, stumbling over her words. "I mean, I'm not sorry. I'm just sorry if you were disappointed."

There it was. I loved how she seemed to say what she felt when most people, myself included, kept those things locked inside.

"I'm not disappointed. I had a great time with you to-night. I mean that," I said, her tenseness ease with my words.

"I did too."

"I'll see you tomorrow."

"I can't wait," she said with a small smile.

"Me either." Leaning in to give her one last kiss, I waited for her to open her door and walk all the way inside before I headed back to the elevator.

WHEN I WALKED back through my room's door a few minutes later, I was nearly knocked over by a rapid-fire barrage of pillows.

"What the hell? Those had better be yours!"

"Where were you?" Lucas said from his now pillowless bed.

Frowning as I stepped over all the pillows on the floor, I said, "Just walking Jules to her room."

"Jules, that hot blonde I saw you with downstairs?" He waggled his eyebrows.

"Yeah. How was your date? Why are you back already?"

"Exactly," he said with a groan. "Why am I back already?"

"Because your date sucked? No pun intended," I said with a grin as I walked into the bathroom to brush my teeth and get ready for bed.

"You're hilarious. Tell me about Jules." Lucas stepped into the doorway before moving to the edge of the bathtub and making himself comfortable.

I stopped brushing my teeth and talked around the toothpaste in my mouth. "There's nothing to tell. Except, oh yeah, you're not coming with me to Coop's game tomorrow. Sorry." I delivered the news quickly, hoping he wouldn't throw a complete fit.

J. STERLING

"Seriously? You meet this girl, what, four hours ago, and I'm already getting pushed aside for her? Not cool, man. Not fucking cool at all. You're a dick." He scowled at me, and I almost felt bad.

"I know," I said before rinsing out my mouth.

It was sort of a dick move, but Lucas had seen Cooper play a hundred times. And Lucas didn't even like hockey. He only went to the games so he could meet the other players and see if any played for *his* team.

A small smile appeared. "I'm just messing with you. It's cool. But I can't believe you're bringing some chick you just met to a game. Are you feeling all right?"

I tried not to read too much into his words. Jules was going back to California soon enough, and that would be that.

When he stood up and placed a hand on my forehead, I gave him a little shove.

After wiping my face with a towel, I said, "She's fun. And she leaves in two days, so I figured, what the hell?"

I actually hadn't figured *what the hell*. I hadn't thought this through at all. When I asked Jules to come with me to Cooper's game, it was because I genuinely wanted her there. All the potential reasons why hadn't even crossed my mind. Until now.

"She leaves in two days?"

"Yeah, she's just here for a conference."

"Where's she from?"

"California."

"So you plan on hanging out with her until she goes back home?" He sat back down on the edge of the tub and cocked his head to the side, his brow creased.

I shrugged. "Yeah. Why? What's wrong with that?"

46

His smirk reappeared. "Nothing. That sounds like a great idea."

"Then why are you acting like I'm crazy? Just spit it out already," I demanded as my patience with this stupid conversation faded.

He glared at me. "You know I don't spit!"

"I didn't, but now I do." I rubbed my temples, wishing Lucas would just say what was on his damn mind. He might come across as macho as any other guy, but damn, sometimes he was such a girl.

"I'm just saying this isn't like you. What about your rule?"

I opened my mouth to defend myself, but then closed it again. Why was I getting defensive when Lucas was right?

"What about it?" I finally said. "She'll be gone and then everything will go back to normal. My rule's still in place. The world continues spinning."

But Lucas's concern bugged me; after all, he had been my best friend since college. When we graduated, we were hired on at the same large investment firm in Boston. I hated it. Not the job—I absolutely loved the job—but I hated the company. It was too big, and it seemed like their sole focus was only on getting bigger. I always had this feeling that no matter what anyone did there, it would never be enough.

Within a year, I found myself longing for something smaller, where I didn't feel like a replaceable cog on the proverbial wheel. Before then, I would have bet money that it was exactly what I'd always wanted. But it wasn't.

Lucas had been just as frustrated as I was, which helped me feel a little less crazy. So when he got an offer at a smaller firm and accepted it, he put in a good word for me and I was brought on. That was where we still worked, the company I was busting my ass to make partner for, but Lucas didn't have the same drive that I did. He enjoyed being an employee without the extra pressure. He always claimed to enjoy his free time too much, something he said I didn't know the meaning of.

He stood up and clapped me on the shoulder. "I think it's cute that you're going to spend time with some smoking-hot girl from California for the next two days," he said with a laugh.

"Cute? What are you getting at?"

"Look, Cal, I saw your body language downstairs. I should have taken a damn picture so you could see what everyone else around you saw. I'm afraid of what two more days with her might do to you."

"It's two days, Lucas. And she lives across the damn country. What could possibly happen in two days?"

"I guess we'll see," he said, grinning at me as he brushed past me to leave the bathroom. And it only pissed me off more.

"I guess we will," I called after him.

I shrugged off his concerns, fully convinced that spending two days with Jules would do me absolutely no harm. Hell, I didn't get what Lucas was even worried about in the first place. I'd get to enjoy the company of a smart, beautiful woman, and then we'd both go on with our lives.

It would be easy.

DREAM LIPS

Jules

'D TOSSED AND turned during the few hours of sleep I got, my mind constantly replaying snippets of the night I'd just had with Cal. I felt him touching my body, heard him tell me I was beautiful, and saw the way he looked at me with those beautiful hazel eyes. My brain was on a loop of memories with Cal that I couldn't stop. Not that I wanted to.

When my alarm buzzed and I opened my eyes, my first thoughts were of him, and my body hummed with the knowledge that I'd get to see him again later today. If I was being honest with myself, which I always tried to be, getting through this day was going to be pure torture. I couldn't wait to see him again and spend more time with him. It was all I could think about.

As I walked into the last presentation of the day, I noticed Robin flagging me down, so I sat next to her.

"What happened with you and Mr. Hot Stuff last night?" She leaned over to elbow me in the ribs, making her coppery ponytail sway.

"Nothing." I bit back a smile.

"Nothing, my ass. Where'd you guys disappear to?"

"His room," I whispered as my cheeks burned, and added

quickly, "But nothing happened." The last thing I wanted was for her to get the wrong impression.

"Why the hell not?" she said, and I almost laughed.

"Because I just met him, that's why."

Oh my God. Why was I always the only one who seemed to think that having sex with strangers wasn't a good idea?

She narrowed her eyes at me. "Please tell me you're seeing him again to remedy that."

"He's taking me to a hockey game tonight," I confessed as a thrill of excitement shot through me.

Robin's eyes lit up. "Please jump his bones, and then I want all the details. Give me something to vicariously live through. I've been married for twelve years, you know," she said, giving me a knowing look.

I patted her hand in mock sympathy, as if being married for so long was the worst thing that could happen to a person.

The speaker took to the lectern and began a presentation on interest rates and how to navigate around potential bank-client issues. As she droned on, my mind continued to replay the scenes from last night.

It was troubling that it had been one night, and I was already this consumed by Cal. My only excuse was that it had been so long since I'd wanted to spend any time with a guy, my emotions were heightened to the point of overload.

Forty minutes later, my phone vibrated. I pulled it from my pocket, just to make sure it wasn't my office calling. It was a text message notification, and when I opened it, I laughed out loud in the middle of the presentation that I had only been half listening to anyway.

The people sitting in front of me turned around to stare. Robin glanced at me, then leaned over to try to peek at my phone as I turned it away from her view.

DREAM LIPS: Can you be ready in an hour?

Apparently Cal had added himself to my contacts list as "Dream Lips," which was what had made me burst out laughing.

Tapping quickly, I adjusted my text notifications for him, assigning the dark blue smiley face that I used for any guys who sent me texts. Organized person that I was, I'd assigned green to my dad and other family members, and red to my boss and coworkers.

Since Cal was the only guy in my life texting me at the moment, anytime I saw the blue smiley appear, I'd know it was from him. I briefly considered changing his name or adding "Cal" to the end of it, but couldn't bring myself to do it. "Dream Lips" made me laugh, and I couldn't argue with the nickname. His lips really were dreamy.

As I typed out a response, I smiled.

JULES: Dream Lips?! Nice. LOL Yes, I can.
DREAM LIPS: Good. Dress warm. The rink gets cold.

Shit. Shit. Shit. I really wasn't prepared for this arctic city. I responded to his text, which set off a flurry of messages.

JULES: Can you do me a solid and bring me a sweatshirt? I didn't pack well for this trip.
DREAM LIPS: So California of you. I'll take care of you, babe.
JULES: Thanks. Meet you downstairs in an hour?
DREAM LIPS: Perfect. See you soon.

Each time my phone vibrated just now with a message from him and that blue smiley face appeared, my heart did a little flip inside my chest and a dumb smile spread across my face. I knew it was a dumb smile because it felt foreign and awkward as I bit down on my bottom lip. I was almost giddy with anticipation of what he might say.

It was ridiculous. I was being ridiculous.

What was even more ridiculous was the fact that I enjoyed it. Every single second of this craziness made me . . . *happy*. All the feelings I'd been avoiding for years came rushing back with a vengeance, and I welcomed them as if I had any choice in the matter.

"I'm gonna go get ready. Let me know what I miss?" I whispered to Robin, who told me to *get some* before I crept out of the presentation twenty minutes early.

Back in my room, I changed into a pair of jeans and a fitted blue sweater. I used the term sweater loosely because it was made of the thinnest material, practically transparent. It was made for looks, not warmth, and I had to wear a tank top underneath it so no one could see my girls.

Twisting my hair around my curling iron, I added a few loose waves to my typically straight hair. The curls added volume and texture that I'd missed while being away from the climate in LA.

DREAM LIPS: Here.

That stupid smile appeared on my face again, and I tried to shake it off as I replied that I was on my way down. After mussing up my hair and giving it a spritz of hairspray, I headed out.

In the elevator, I started to get nervous. What if being with him wasn't as fun and nice as it had been last night? What if our connection was only because he'd been drinking, or because I had been tired? What if I'd imagined everything, and when I walked out of this elevator and saw him again, I felt nothing?

Oh God, I was suddenly sick with trepidation.

The elevator dinged and I stepped out into the lobby, stuttering mid-step as I saw Cal standing there, holding a single pink rose.

Relief flooded through me. I hadn't made up anything last night. It had all been real.

He looked delicious in his dark jeans, black button-down shirt, and leather jacket. His brown hair was much like it was last night, spiked up in the front, albeit a little messy in places that seemed to work only on someone like him. And his lips were as incredible as they'd been in my imagination all day today.

"Hi," I said with a smile.

"Hi, yourself." He bent down to give me a kiss.

If that was how this night was going to go, I was all in.

"This is for you." He handed me the rose, which I immediately brought to my nose to appreciate.

"Thank you." I clutched the flower, a little overwhelmed by the sweetness of the gesture. It had been a long time since I'd received a rose from someone other than my parents.

"You look beautiful," he said, his tone so sincere that I felt myself blush with the compliment.

"And you look hot." I gave him a once-over before settling my gaze on his mouth and licking my lips.

"Jules," he said, practically growling a warning, and I quickly returned my gaze to his eyes. If I didn't behave, we'd end up back in my hotel room, and we both knew it.

"Sorry," I lied.

"I don't think you are. Come on." He placed a hand on my lower back and steered me toward the side exit. "I have a sweatshirt and a jacket in the car for you."

"Thank you so much. I didn't bring anything warm with me at all. See?" I pointed at my manicured toes peeking through the straps of my sandals.

He shook his head. "What am I going to do with you?"

I said nothing, the response running through my head way too crazy to say out loud, let alone think. *Love me? Kiss me? Marry me? Give me babies?*

Cal held the hotel door open as I walked outside and pointed toward the charcoal-gray Mercedes parked at the curb. The car beeped to life as the locks clicked open and the lights all turned on. He opened the passenger door for me, and I slipped into the cool leather seat and placed the rose carefully on the backseat next to the jackets. When Cal slid into the driver's seat, it automatically adjusted to his body.

I breathed in deeply. "Is this new?"

"About a year," he said as the engine purred to life and the music turned on. His hand immediately came to rest on my thigh like it had last night, and I placed my hand on top of his, longing for the connection to him.

"It still smells new," I said, sniffing the air.

He gave the dashboard an affectionate pat. "I take care of her."

"Her?"

Cal shot me a glance. "Of course she's a her. Isn't your car a girl?"

I laughed, because no, my car was most definitely not a girl. I'd considered all of my cars boys and had even given them boy names. I'd never thought about that until now; it was just something I did.

"My car's a boy."

"See?"

"We're weird." I smiled as I watched him drive.

"You might be, but I'm normal." His fingers moved on my leg, his thumb drawing circles as he drove.

Silence quickly filled the space between us. It wasn't awkward or weird, and neither one of us seemed eager to fill the quiet with anything other than our breathing. It was just one more thing to add to my mental list of how natural it felt being around Cal.

The fact that I didn't feel the need to rack my brain to think of something to talk about was refreshing. I'd driven with clients I'd known for years to look at properties, and there was always a level of awkwardness when the conversation lulled. Someone would eventually fill the empty air to avoid the silence.

The sound of the radio playing softly in the background caught my attention, and when I realized what was playing, I said, "Country? Really?"

To be honest, I hadn't even thought about what kind of music Cal might enjoy, but hearing him hum along to the song now playing on the radio made me giggle.

He stopped humming and glanced my way. "I like all kinds of music, but I'm on a country kick right now. I can put on something else if you don't like it. What's your favorite?"

Grinning at him, I said, "I'm sure you'd love to listen to some Top 40 pop music. I can see you now, singing along to Bieber and One Direction." I liked a lot of music too, but I loved pop the best. Always had.

He stifled a smile as he yanked his hand from my leg. "You

like Justin Bieber and One Direction? Out of my car." He pointed at the door as the city whizzed past.

"Oh, please," I said with a huff. "You probably love all their music and you don't even know it."

He laughed before returning his hand to its rightful place. "I might. Do you want me to turn it on?"

"No, it's fine. I like country. I like everything except hard rock and old metal. Ick." I stuck my tongue out and made a face.

Nodding, he said, "I can tolerate pretty much anything except techno. It all sounds the same, and it makes me want to punch someone in the face. Repeatedly." To make his point, he scowled as he mimicked the *nst-nst* sound of a synthesizer.

"I think that's the exact opposite reaction you're supposed to have when listening to techno, Cal. Something's wrong with you."

A moment later, we came to a stop behind a long line of cars. He released my leg and opened the glove compartment, removing a pass of some sort as the stadium came into view.

When we pulled into the parking lot, Cal rolled down the window and stopped next to a young guy walking toward us wearing a bright yellow vest and carrying a handheld machine. Cal showed him the pass.

"You know where you're going?" the attendant asked.

"Yep. Thanks."

"Don't forget to put that on your dashboard so it's visible."

"Will do."

Cal pulled forward and navigated his way through the massive parking lot. I had no idea where we were going but I was already in awe, and we hadn't even entered the stadium yet.

THE DONOVAN BROTHERS

Cal

AFTER PARKING THE car, I grabbed both the sweatshirt and the jacket for Jules, not knowing how cold she might get during the game, and reached for her hand.

She looked even prettier than she had last night, that blue sweater doing a number against her tanned skin. I had to admit I'd been a little worried that things might be uncomfortable between us, not for any particular reason other than a little time had passed and things from last night had been able to settle.

But the second I saw Jules step out of the elevator, all those concerns disappeared. There was no weirdness at all. Yes, there were lots of other feelings and thoughts—desire, want, lust, *holy hell, she looks good enough to eat*—but no awkwardness, which both intrigued and scared me. So I pushed them away, shoved them deep inside as if they didn't exist.

I picked up our tickets from the will-call booth and led Jules into the arena, knowing exactly where our seats were located. The visiting team's seats were always in the same section each year.

"Do you need anything?" I asked Jules as she walked at my side.

"I'm good."

"You sure you're not hungry?"

She smiled and leaned against me. "Not yet."

"All right."

Suddenly, she blurted, "Katherine will like me, right?"

I stopped and grabbed her by the shoulders, bringing us face-to-face. "She'll love you. She's really nice, and so are you. You have nothing to worry about." I gave Jules a quick kiss and waited for her reaction, but she just stared at me. "Okay?"

"Okay," she said as she wrapped her arms around her midsection.

"Cold?"

She nodded. "It is pretty cold in here."

"That's why I brought you these."

When I held up the sweatshirt, she snatched it and quickly pulled it on. It hung loose on her, all but completely covering her up. She looked adorable.

Grinning, she pulled the neck to her nose and breathed in. "It smells like you," she said before snuggling into it even more.

As we walked down the stairs and toward our seats, I spotted Katherine's long brown hair. I pointed at her, and Jules nodded as we made our way to her.

"Katherine," I called out and she turned, a big smile on her face.

"Cal! It's so good to see you." She launched into my arms and squeezed me tight before noticing my hand was still clasped with Jules's. "No Lucas?" she asked with a pout.

"Not tonight. I want you to meet someone," I said as I moved to the side.

"Hi. I'm Katherine." She extended her hand toward Jules,

unable to hide her surprise.

I hadn't warned Katherine that I was bringing a girl. Not that she needed the warning, but I could have at least given her a heads-up since it wasn't something I normally did.

"Jules. It's nice to meet you."

The two girls shook hands politely, but when Jules commented on Katherine's engagement ring, that apparently broke the ice. They both broke into a fit of giggles and started hugging.

Chicks were weird. Half the time they couldn't stand each other and the other half they'd kill for one another. You never knew which half you were going to get.

Heading for my seat, I said, "I was going to sit between you two, but seeing as how you're both from LA, I figured I'd better let you ladies chat."

And that was all it took from me to get the two of them practically squealing with delight again and talking about all sorts of shit I knew nothing about. They mentioned specific restaurants and hotels and beaches they both knew, all while talking a million miles a minute. How women did that and still understood what the other was saying, I had no idea. But I did manage to pick up on the fact that they had a few mutual friends, which was surprising, but sort of cool.

When the game started, the two of them didn't slow down for a second. Their voices lowered to whispers, but I could still hear them chatting away like long-lost friends.

I focused my attention on my brother, who was currently tearing up the ice, as usual. Cooper Donovan was a badass. Each time he scored a goal or got an assist, I wanted to announce to the entire arena that he was my brother. I was totally that relative.

Jules leaned over and whispered in my ear, "Hey, she's really great."

"I'm glad you like her."

Since my hand was already on her thigh, of course, I gave it a quick squeeze in agreement and leaned in to kiss her. Instead of pulling away after a quick kiss like I should have, I deepened it, unable to resist her lips the way she seemed unable to resist mine. Our tongues touched briefly and I realized I had to stop. Otherwise, I'd have a woody the size of Canada.

When I pulled away, I noticed Katherine watching us, her attention more focused on Jules and me than on my brother skating around the ice. And I knew why. She'd seen me with other women in the past, but I'd never brought anyone to one of Cooper's games before. It just never seemed to work out—I was either single whenever he was in town, or wasn't serious enough about the girl to introduce her to my family.

I refused to read into exactly what it meant that I'd brought Jules here tonight, because it meant nothing. She was leaving tomorrow, and then life could go back to the way it was before I ever knew she existed, and everything would be fine.

I just wished I believed that.

WHEN THE GAME ended, I asked Katherine where we should meet for food, and she suggested we go to the hotel first so Cooper could decide what he was hungry for. They won the game, so at least he'd be in a good mood. He was a pain in the ass when they lost and typically sulked in his hotel room afterward, so I was thankful we wouldn't have to deal with that.

Instead of waiting at the locker room for Coop to shower and deal with the press, I wrapped an arm around Jules and headed toward the car. I had offered Katherine a ride back to the hotel but she declined, saying she already had one with one of the other hockey wives.

"That was fun," Jules said once we were inside the privacy of my car.

"Did you even watch the game?" I asked with a grin.

"I watched it! Sort of." Her face crinkled as she looked at me with a worried expression. "I'm sorry. That was rude of me, wasn't it? To spend more time talking to Katherine than watching your brother play? Shit. You'll never take me again, will you? I'm a bad hockey date. You probably hate me now. I understand if you never want to see me again."

Her unfiltered thoughts kept spilling from her mouth, each sentence more paranoid than the last, but instead of scaring me, her words actually excited me. "You're nuts. I don't hate you."

"Promise?"

"Promise." I leaned over the center console and kissed her soft cheek. "You can come meet my brother, right?" I hadn't even asked her if she had other commitments.

She frowned at me. "Why wouldn't I?"

"Sorry, I just wanted to be sure that it's okay that we do that. You don't need to get back early and go to bed, or have an early meeting in the morning for your conference? I just realized that I hadn't even asked you." After starting the engine, I turned on the seat heaters for both our seats.

Her expression relaxed. "I'm good. I'd love to meet him. But thank you for asking."

I placed my hand back on her leg where it belonged. "Ready?"

"Yep. Ooh, have I ever told you how much I love whoever invented seat heaters? Because I do. I love that guy."

"What if it was a girl?"

"Then I love her."

She was absolutely adorable.

I drove us to Cooper's hotel and let the valet park the car. Based on the number of scantily clad girls hanging around in the hotel bar, we had obviously arrived before the team. Not wanting Jules to see that shit, I walked us toward the lounge area near the elevators.

I spotted Katherine before I noticed Cooper walking behind her. He was taller than me, which should be against the rules. Older brothers should always be taller, smarter, and stronger. *Damn it.*

When I said, "Here he comes," Jules sucked in a breath.

"Shit, Cal, he's a giant. And he looks just like you. Only bigger."

Cooper and I did look a lot alike. He had green eyes instead of hazel and his hair was a little darker than mine. But with our features and the shape of our faces, you could definitely tell we were brothers.

"I'm aware," I said, trying not to roll my eyes.

"Bro!"

Cooper's booming voice filled the small area as I rose to my feet and gave him a manly hug. We clapped each other's backs before he tossed an arm around my shoulder and looked curiously at Jules.

"Who's this beautiful lady?"

"This is Jules. Jules, this is my little brother, Cooper."

Cooper scoffed at me, obviously bristling at the word *little*, and stepped over to give Jules a giant bear hug, lifting her off the ground so her legs swung in the air, and Katherine laughed.

"You're much prettier than Lucas. Don't you dare tell him I said that," he directed toward me before returning his attention to Jules, "It's really nice to meet you."

"It's nice to meet you too." When he plunked her on the ground and she added, "Great game tonight," I bit back a grin, knowing that she had no clue how Cooper had done.

"Thanks. What are you doing with this knucklehead?" He grinned, nodding his head in my direction.

"Slumming it," she deadpanned without skipping a beat, and Cooper burst out laughing.

"I like her," he said, and I had to bite my tongue to keep from saying that I did too. Obviously I did but I wasn't ready to declare it—to him, to her, or to anyone else.

He reached for Katherine's hand and pulled her in for a tight hug. I loved Katherine like a sister, and couldn't have been happier that my little brother found someone like her to spend his life with. They went through some crazy shit back when they were in college together, and after a freak accident, both of them had almost died. I wasn't sure what that kind of thing did to two people who cared about each other, but I was pretty certain it created a bond that wasn't easily broken. Trying to remember a time I'd ever seen them argue or fight, I searched my mind, but I couldn't think of one.

"You guys hungry?" Cooper asked, and I blinked twice before nodding.

"I'm starving. You hungry, babe?" I asked Jules, the term of endearment rolling off my tongue so naturally that I didn't even realize I'd said it until I saw the surprised looks on Katherine and Cooper's faces.

"Yes! Food please."

Jules batted her eyelashes at me, and I realized that I'd never gotten her anything to eat during the game. Like an idiot, I'd asked her once and then never asked her again. It was getting late, so she had to be as hungry as I was.

"Should we go out, or do you want to just order room service?" Cooper asked.

Ordering room service meant awkward eating positions on the beds in the hotel room, and while I liked the idea of complete privacy, I wasn't sure I liked the idea of that. The hotel had a restaurant, but some of the players would probably be there, cheating on their wives or hooking up with their latest puck bunny, and I didn't want to expose Jules to that shit.

"We should go out," I suggested. "There's that sports bar nearby."

Cooper frowned. "Should we really go to a sports bar after we just beat the home team? They'll probably throw beer at me."

"I'll protect you, little brother," I joked before pulling out my phone and looking at the time. "It's late enough that everyone who watched the game is probably already gone for the night, but I'll scope out the crowd before we go in. If it's too crazy, we'll go somewhere else, but our options will be limited because it's so late."

He sighed. "You sure you don't wanna just stay here?"

"Come on." Considering it a done deal, I reached for Jules's hand and pulled her toward the lobby exit. She looked so damn cute all bundled up in my sweatshirt.

When we reached the sports bar around the corner, it was all but dead, the hard-core hockey fans already gone.

"Cal?"

A couple of my college buddies waved to me from the bar. I steered our group toward them and gave them each a firm handshake before introducing everyone.

"This is my brother, Cooper; his fiancé, Katherine; and this is Jules," I said, showcasing the girl currently wearing my sweatshirt and curled within my arm.

Pride filled me at the idea of showing Jules off. It was a foreign feeling, having someone I wanted people to know was with me, and not simply because she was pretty. Jules was so much more than that.

We chatted briefly before I excused us, saying that we had to eat before we killed someone. The waiter seated us at a booth toward the back, as far from anyone else as possible at our request. He dropped off four waters, menus, and a giant basket filled with an assortment of breads and rolls before Jules stopped him from leaving.

"Can you take a picture for us, please?" she asked sweetly as she handed him her phone. "I hope that's okay?" She glanced at Cooper and Katherine, who both nodded.

We huddled together and yelled *Cheese!* as the waiter took a few pictures, looking annoyed as he handed back her phone.

Jules grinned as she scrolled through. "These are really cute," she said and then handed over her phone to me.

She was right. The pics were pretty cute.

"Text them to me please," Katherine insisted, and Jules tapped away on her phone. When the hell had they exchanged numbers?

I leaned toward Jules. "Tell me you eat carbs," I said as she put her phone away.

Reaching toward the basket, she grinned. "I eat everything. Especially carbs." She tore off a big piece of the bread and shoved it in her mouth while I laughed, returning my hand to its rightful place on her thigh.

"Hungry?"

She nodded, her mouth too full to respond before she swallowed. "I'm starving. Sorry." She looked at Katherine and Cooper, who both waved her off. He couldn't even speak, his mouth was so full.

"Don't be sorry," Katherine said as she buttered her own roll.

Cooper swallowed hard before taking a drink of his water. "So, Jules, when did you meet my dashing older brother?"

"We just met yesterday, actually."

Cooper practically choked before punching at his chest. "Yesterday?" he squeaked out.

I knew what he was thinking—that not only had I brought a girl I'd just met to his game, but also to hang out with him. This was so out of character for me, I'd never hear the end of it; that much I knew for sure.

"Yeah," I said, cutting in. "She's just here for a conference. I had a retreat, and we were staying at the same hotel. She stalked me relentlessly, followed me everywhere I went." Taking a bite of the sourdough bread, I relished the fact that it was still warm.

Cooper gave me the eye. "I'm sure she did."

"Oh yeah, she definitely looks like the stalking type," Katherine added with a smile.

"I don't even know why I'm here. You're all horrible people," Jules said with a laugh before taking another bite of her roll.

"When do you leave?" Cooper asked.

"Tomorrow evening."

When Jules said that, I felt something inside me sink. I didn't want to talk about her leaving while I still had her here. My hand squeezed her thigh, and she rested her hand on top of it before weaving her fingers through mine.

"That sucks," Katherine said with a frown as Cooper tossed his arm over her shoulder and carefully moved her long brown hair out of the way so he wouldn't pull it. He was so thoughtful when it came to her.

"It does suck," Jules agreed before looking at me.

The sadness written all over her face gutted me. In that moment, I realized that I didn't want her to go. I was tempted to ask her to change her flight, to beg her to stay, but I couldn't do that.

"It's not like you guys can't see each other after she leaves," Katherine said, always the optimist. "Right?"

I glanced back at Jules. It wasn't as if the thought hadn't occurred to me since she'd left my bed last night, but I hadn't voiced it to anyone before now, not even myself. When our eyes met, hers were filled with hope.

"That's true," I said, shrugging in a noncommittal way. "It's not like you're flying back to Sydney, or somewhere a thousand hours away."

"Nope. Not Sydney. Just LA."

Jules might have agreed, but her tone was off and I couldn't read it. I didn't like not knowing what she was thinking, and right now I had no clue.

Maybe Jules didn't want to see me after she left. She was as busy with work as I was, and had no more time for a relationship than I did. Was she fighting her feelings the same way I was? I had no idea.

The waiter came back to take our drink order and told us that the kitchen closed soon, so we needed to get our orders in. We focused on our menus and quickly placed our orders before the conversation started up again.

Katherine turned toward Cooper. "If I had moved home after freshman year in college, do you think we still would have ended up together?"

My brother didn't miss a beat. "Yes." He kissed her cheek and looked at her the way a man truly in love looked at his woman. Their over-the-top mushy shit usually made me a little sick, but tonight I found it sort of sweet.

What the hell is happening to me?

"You two met in college, right?" Jules asked, and Katherine nodded. "Why would you have moved home?"

When Katherine and Cooper exchanged glances, I knew what they were thinking. They had a unique history between them, and the accident that had landed them both in the hospital fighting for their lives was only part of it. There was more to the story that they didn't share with anyone, some big secret only the two of them knew.

As much as my curiosity had been piqued by that fact, I'd never pushed them for details. They wouldn't have told me anyway. When pressed on the subject, they always said that some things were just too personal to share.

Katherine gave Cooper an adoring look before turning her attention back to Jules. "It's hard to explain, but I basically had a really difficult freshman year. I went through a lot of stuff and almost failed out."

"Really?" I'd never known that before and was shocked,

unable to believe it. Katherine wasn't the type to fail at anything.

She nodded, her eyes sad. "Yeah. It was pretty bad."

"What would you have done if she had?" Jules asked my brother.

"Gone to LA and gotten her," he said matter-of-factly. When I laughed, he glared at me. "What are you laughing at?"

"You say that like it's so easy. You were just a kid. How the hell were you going to *go to LA and get her?*" I used my fingers to make air quotes around his words.

Cooper shifted in the booth, getting a little heated. "I would have flown there, would have brought her back to school, or moved there, or demanded we date long-distance. I wouldn't have just done nothing."

Jules sucked in a long breath, her voice dreamy as she said, "That's the sweetest thing I've ever heard."

"Thanks, bro." I tossed a piece of bread at my brother's head and he dodged it effortlessly. Cooper was always making me look bad.

Giving me a smug grin, he said, "It's not my fault that I'm the romantic in the family. Sorry, Jules, but Cal doesn't have a romantic bone in his body."

Jules looked at me and shrugged, a small smile playing on her lips. "I don't know, Cooper. He's done all right so far."

Take that, little brother.

Cooper raised an eyebrow. "Really? I'm impressed."

I glared at him. "Contrary to popular belief, you're not the only one who knows how to be sweet to women, okay?"

He narrowed his gaze at me before looking at Jules, his gaze shifting between us. "Okay. If you say so."

Katherine rolled her eyes. "Oh my gosh, stop it. You're

both amazing, romantic, and hot, okay? No one can beat a Donovan brother."

"You hear that, Coop? Your fiancée thinks I'm hot." I leaned back and tossed my arm around Jules, who was biting back a laugh.

Katherine threw her hands up in the air with a laugh. "Why do I even try?"

"Because you love me," I said, looking right at her.

Cooper looked at my date. "Jules, why'd you bring this knucklehead again?"

"He looked lonely," she answered quickly, and he nodded.

"I could see that."

Jules smiled. "Can we go back to the subject of the two of you in college again?" She wagged a finger between my brother and his fiancée. "I'm sorry; I'm just intrigued by you guys. I don't know anyone who found the person they wanted to spend the rest of their life with so young. Well, I guess I have known a few people, but they're all miserable or divorced by now, and you both still seem happy and suited for each other. So, would you really have dated long-distance at that age? I don't mean to pry—I'm just impressed."

Cooper nodded. "I would have, for sure. I would've done anything for her."

"I probably would have said no and fought him on it," Katherine said with conviction.

I recoiled a little, shocked for the second time that evening. "Really?"

As Katherine nodded, Cooper added, "She definitely would have been the more difficult one to convince. But I refused to give up on her, even when she wanted me to."

Katherine's smile faded. "I'm sorry for wanting you to,"

she said, as if whatever they'd gone through still bothered her.

Damn! What exactly happened back then?

"That was a long time ago," Cooper said softly. "You know I understood." He kissed her temple and focused on her, caressing her cheek and playing with her hair.

A little uncomfortable, I cleared my throat, reminding them that we were still here. Those two tended to do that sometimes, get lost in their own world and forget anyone else existed.

Our waiter came back with another waitress in tow, interrupting us when they set our plates in front of us. As soon as they walked away, the four of us attacked our food as if we hadn't eaten in weeks. The sudden silence was almost laughable. It was the longest we'd gone without talking since we first sat down.

After dinner, Cooper and I fought over the bill, as usual. After he won, we all walked back to his hotel so I could get my car and drives Jules home. We said our good-byes at valet parking, the chilled air mimicking how my insides felt. As much as I loved seeing my brother, I hated telling him good-bye. We never had enough time together anymore.

"It was really nice to meet you," Katherine said to Jules.

"You too. Good luck with the wedding planning, and let me know the next time you're in town. I mean it."

Katherine nodded. "I will for sure."

The sight of the two girls exchanging a hug warmed me inside. I liked the fact that they had gotten along well. It made things so much more pleasant when the females didn't want to claw each other's eyes out.

I hugged my brother tight and released him with a pat on his shoulder. "Miss you. And great game tonight, by the way."

"Thanks. And thanks for coming. Maybe you can come out to LA to visit Jules and meet me at a game there?"

Cooper made it sound so innocent, but I knew what he was doing. He was trying to push me to commit to seeing her again after she left tomorrow.

"You never know," I said with a shrug. At this point, I had no idea what would happen after Jules left, and I couldn't think about it. Not right now.

"Just trying to help, brother," he said before giving me another quick hug.

"Don't need it, brother," I said, mimicking his tone.

"You might need it a little bit," he added with a smile that looked exactly like our father's before he reached for Jules. "It was really nice to meet you," he said, then whispered something in her ear that I couldn't hear.

I didn't like that. Not at all.

Pushing aside my annoyance, I pulled Katherine into a hug and pressed a quick kiss to her cheek. "It's always good to see you, sis."

"You too. I really, really like her, by the way," she said softly as we hugged, and I nodded in agreement.

I liked Jules too, but she was leaving tomorrow, and that would most likely be the end of our story.

It had to be. It was the only thing that made sense.

GOOD-BYE

Jules

"WHAT DID MY brother say to you?"

Cal kept badgering me in the car on the way back to our hotel, trying to get me to spill, but I refused. It was much more fun to torture him.

"He said it was nice to meet me," I said with a sly smile.

"No, what did he whisper to you?" he asked again, and I played dumb.

"He didn't whisper anything. You're imagining things."

He wasn't. Cooper had told me that he'd never seen Cal so happy, and he hoped that things worked out between us. I didn't know what that meant exactly, considering I was leaving tomorrow, but the last thing I wanted was to scare Cal off. If I told him what his brother had said, Cal would probably run for the hills. And I wasn't ready for him to run yet.

"All right, Jules, I'll let you keep it to yourself. For now," he teased before squeezing my leg.

I watched as the city flew by us, my sense of direction completely out of whack. I had no idea where we were, where the hotel was, or if I'd seen any of these landmarks before. Everything looked different at night.

"You okay?"

When Cal's voice broke through my thoughts, I turned away from the view outside my window and admired the other view—the one in the car.

"Yeah. I had a really nice time tonight," I said sincerely. Meeting Cooper and Katherine had been so much fun. They were an awesome couple.

"I did too. They love you, by the way," he said, and I couldn't stop myself from smiling.

"They're really great. And Katherine already friend-requested me on Facebook."

"Double trouble."

"The best kind," I teased. "They're a really sweet couple, though."

"Yeah, they are. So annoyingly in love, but we all have our faults."

As he chuckled, I stared at those lips. Realizing how much I'd miss them, I pulled out my cell phone and took a picture of him while he drove. *God, he's handsome.*

"Did you just take a picture of me?" He glanced at me before refocusing on the road.

"Yes. It's hot as shit too, so don't ask me to delete it, because I won't."

"I think you might be using me for my lips." He puckered, and when I moaned out loud, his hand gripped my leg tighter. "Don't make sounds like that if you expect me to keep driving, Jules."

"Sorry, but you can't just go around puckering those things whenever you feel like it. They're lethal."

He grinned as he slowed the car to a stop. Surprised, I looked out the passenger window and saw with disappointment that we were in front of the hotel already. Since Cal had already checked out this morning, he had no reason to come inside.

"You don't have to come in, okay? I promise I won't think any less of you," I said, glancing at the clock on his dashboard.

Not to mention how tired I was from my lack of sleep. If Cal walked me inside, I'd most likely ask him to come to my room and we'd have a repeat performance of last night. But this time, I probably wouldn't be able to tell him no. Then I'd be really screwed. *Pun intended.* No, I needed Cal to stay put in his car.

Unless this is the last time I'm seeing him before I leave . . .

That thought sent panic through me. I hadn't mentally prepared for tonight to be it for us. I'd assumed I'd at least see him again tomorrow, but what if he was busy or had plans?

"Are you sure?" He frowned at me. "I don't like not walking you inside, Jules."

"I know you don't, but I'm a big girl."

Cal sucked in a long breath. "What time is your flight tomorrow?"

A sliver of relief shot through me. "Six fifteen."

Concentrating on our joined hands, he said, "I won't walk you in on one condition."

"And what might that be?"

He looked up. "I get to drive you to the airport."

My heart stuttered a little at his words. "I'd like that a lot."

"Good."

He leaned across the console and cupped my cheek before pulling me in for a kiss. Our lips parted and we tasted each other, the thrill of it making my thighs clench together. Cal's kisses set my entire body on fire.

"God, I love kissing you," he said against my mouth before

he traced my bottom lip with the tip of his tongue.

"I was just thinking the same thing," I breathed into his mouth, then tugged at his bottom lip with my teeth. Biting lightly, I let it go as he ravaged me with his mouth, our kisses desperate. It seemed even our mouths knew our time together was short.

When we finally pulled apart, my lips tingled with the absence of his touch. Reaching in the backseat for my rose, I grabbed it before leaning in to give him one last kiss good night.

"I'll talk to you tomorrow," he said.

"Okay."

I felt like a giddy schoolgirl again as I opened the car door and stepped out into the bitter cold, my body still warm from his kisses and his sweatshirt. When I realized I was still wearing it, I almost turned around to give it back to him, but decided I'd sleep in it instead. If I wasn't going to really be sleeping with Cal, the scent of him would have to do.

THE LAST DAY'S schedule was light, mostly opportunities for us to ask questions, mingle, and network. Trying to focus on word, I did all three, hoping to bring something helpful back to my office in Malibu. If my boss, Jonathan, deemed this trip a total waste of time, he'd most likely never let me attend a conference like this again. And to be honest, it had been fun to get away and meet new people.

I spotted Robin mingling in the sparse crowd before she saw me, and prepared myself for her onslaught of questions. Our other two friends, Kristy and Sue, had left yesterday, so Robin and I were the only ones left from our group.

Her face lit up and she hurried over to me. "There you are."

"Here I am."

When I played nonchalant, she swatted my arm. "How was last night? Tell me something that will get me through the next month with my husband." She put her hands together as she pleaded. "I beg you—lie if you have to."

With an uncomfortable laugh, I said, "He's fantastic." It was a lame response, but wasn't sure how else to describe Cal, or what I should say.

"In bed?" she said hopefully. "Please follow that up with 'in bed.'"

"I'm sure he is." I grinned. "But I wouldn't know."

"Damn it, Jules. I counted on you," she said with a huff.

Lowering my eyelashes, I pretended to be upset. "I'm sorry I let you down."

"You should be," she scolded before laughing loudly. "Will you see him before you leave? Do you need a ride to the airport?"

I couldn't stop the smile that spread across my face, and Robin's eyes widened.

"Oh my gosh! He's taking you, isn't he?" When I nodded, she said, "Then I'll want another full report. Don't think just because you're going back to California that you don't have to keep me up-to-date. I expect e-mails."

"You got it," I promised.

Actually, I was excited at the idea of e-mailing Robin about Cal. I knew that she'd make me laugh and encourage me to be brave when it came to him, not that I would need it. Normally I wouldn't be all gung-ho about a guy like this, but my usual attitude had all but left the building when I sat down at Cal's table the other night.

My phone buzzed with several notifications in quick succession, and I pulled it from my pocket. When I saw the dark blue smiley face, I couldn't get the text app open fast enough.

> DREAM LIPS: *When can I come get you?*
> DREAM LIPS: *Now? How about now?*
> DREAM LIPS: *Are you done yet? Jules!*

My insides warmed as I smiled.

"Is that from him?" Robin asked. "You should see your face right now."

I didn't need to see my face; of course I looked crazy. There was no way I couldn't, considering how I felt.

My heart raced, beating in double-time as I composed a response to his message.

> JULES: *I'm ready anytime. Say the word.*
> DREAM LIPS: *Word.*

I stashed my phone in my pocket and pulled Robin into a hug. "I'm going to go hang with him until I leave. It was so nice meeting you, Robin. You're hilarious."

"It was nice meeting you too, sweetie. Don't forget that I need to live vicariously through you. If you don't send me e-mails, I'll harass the living shit out of you and call your boss," she threatened.

Laughing, I shook my head. Robin from Boston was crazy.

Moving a little quicker than usual, I headed to the front desk and handed the concierge my ticket. As she disappeared to get my things, I tapped on the counter, impatient to get going.

As I was rolling my luggage toward some empty chairs, Cal

appeared at my side and took my suitcase off my hands.

"You're already here?" I looked at him with surprise.

He cocked his head to the side, his hazel eyes filled with mischief. "Nope."

Smartass.

"I have your sweatshirt from last night," I said, hoping like hell he didn't want it back.

Yes, I had become *that* girl, the type who wanted to keep a piece of clothing because it smelled like him. If I was never going to see Cal again, the least he could do was give me a damn souvenir.

"Keep it." He didn't even hesitate. "You know you want to," he added, seemingly unable to resist being a smartass tonight.

I sent a sideways look in his direction. "You're sassy tonight."

"And you like it," he shot back.

Stopping short, I stared at him. When he realized he'd lost me, he turned and looked back at me with a smug smile.

I shrugged. "I do sorta like it."

"And you wanted to keep the sweatshirt. Admit it," he said as he reached for my hand.

Threading my fingers through his, I lied, "I wasn't going to give it back to you anyway," and Cal barked out a quick laugh.

"I might miss this a little," he said as he dropped a kiss on top of my hand. "Our banter."

A little? Hell, I was going to miss this a lot.

"Me too. But just a little." I lied again, holding back my real feelings. Protecting myself, I shoved them deep inside for the moment and refused to let them escape. Because if I let them out, I couldn't take them back.

"I know I'm a little early," he said, "but I thought I could take you to my favorite diner before you left."

"You have a favorite diner? They still have diners in Boston?"

What a charming notion. We didn't really have diners in LA, not in the traditional sense like the ones you saw on TV.

"We have a few diners here. Why is that so hard to believe?"

"I don't know. I guess I don't picture you as a diner sort of guy."

He frowned at me, actually scoffing. "I'm from New Jersey. Of course I'm a diner guy. And I'll have you know that this particular diner serves the best burgers in all of Boston. Not to mention that it has the best waitresses who remind you to eat when you've spent hours in a chair studying for exams."

I squeezed his hand. "All right, Cal Donovan, take me to your diner and feed me your favorite diner food."

"You got it, lady."

THE DINER WAS exactly how I'd pictured it, intimate and well-worn. Checkered cloths covered the tables, and swivel bar stools lined the front of a long counter.

Cal led us toward two empty seats, and when I started spinning on mine as soon as I sat down, he laughed.

"Jules."

"Cal?" I said, spinning around one more time. "Okay, I'll stop."

"Don't stop on my account. Or the guy sitting next to you." He pointed at the burly man sitting on my other side.

DEAR HEART, I HATE YOU

"Sorry," I said to my new neighbor, feeling silly.

The man leaned toward me and said in a confidential tone, "I used to spin in them too as a kid. I get it."

I was wearing a victory smile as Cal handed me a menu, but I pushed it away. "Huh-uh."

"You're not hungry?" He pouted at me in disappointment.

I grinned back at him. "Oh no, I'm hungry. But you said it's your favorite place, so I want you to order for me."

This was a new one for me; I'd never allowed a guy to order a meal for me before. Chalk this up to another first in my weekend of firsts.

"That I can do." He winked at me and then greeted our waitress when she approached.

Cal ended up ordering identical meals for us, their famous Boston burger with homemade pickles and fries. I had no idea why the burger was so mouthwateringly delicious, but it was. It might have been the seasoning or maybe it was the bun, but whatever it was, it was one of the best burgers I'd ever eaten. The homemade pickles and fries were top-notch too.

After pushing back my plate, I rubbed my stomach, feeling overly stuffed. "That was so good."

"I told you. But save some room," he warned.

I patted my belly. "There's no more room. It's full."

"But you can't leave without having a slice of their Boston cream pie."

Scrunching up my face in an attempt to pout, I said, "Cal, I'm stuffed. Like a turkey on Thanksgiving day."

"Then I'll only order one piece and we can share it. You have to try it. You won't be sorry." He raised his eyebrows, knowing that I would give in.

"Fine," I huffed. "What's in it?"

He gave me an incredulous look. "What? You've never had Boston cream pie before?"

"I haven't. I've seen it, of course, but I've never actually tried it."

Cal shook his head at me and clucked his tongue. "Jules, I don't know how you've lived such a sheltered life all these years. Let me introduce you to the best thing to ever hit your taste buds."

The waitress brought over a piece of what looked like cream-filled sponge cake covered with a layer of chocolate drizzle.

"Ladies first," Cal said, pushing the plate in front of me.

Eager to please, I grabbed my fork and took a bite. *Holy hell.* It was unbelievable, so moist and light with just the right amount of sweetness.

"Jules?"

I heard Cal say my name, but he sounded far away. When he spoke again, I threw my hand up between us to stop him.

"Don't talk to me. I'm busy." When he laughed and tried to stick his fork into the cake, I said, "I will hurt you," poising my fork over his hand.

"Hey! You didn't even want any, remember?"

"I was stupid then, but I'm much smarter now. Get your own piece."

I glared at him, half serious and half joking. But when he flagged down our waitress to order another piece for himself, I was relieved I didn't have to share.

Looking sadly at the crumbs left on the plate a few minutes later, I had to stop myself from scraping them up and set down my fork instead.

"Done?" he asked, grinning at me.

I nodded, too full to speak. Cal paid our check and we walked out of the diner and down the sidewalk, the fact of my leaving hanging in the air like a little cloud of sadness over our heads.

"Thank you for bringing me here," I told him. "It was everything you said it would be and more." I stood on tiptoe to press a kiss to his cheek.

He curved an arm around my shoulders and steered me toward his car. "Thanks for coming with me. Did you like the pie?"

"I had to stop myself from licking the plate, so yeah, it's safe to say I liked the pie."

CAL PULLED TO a stop in front of the airport terminal, clicking on his hazard lights before popping the trunk.

Neither of us moved to get out of the car. We both sat there, staring wistfully each other as if saying good-bye was the last thing either of us wanted. I had no idea how Cal felt, but it was definitely the last thing I wanted. I hated the thought of never seeing him again.

"One more picture?" I said as I pulled out my phone.

"Of course."

He pressed his head against mine in the middle of his car while I snapped a picture of us looking into my phone, both of us smiling big. Then he planted a kiss on my cheek and I took another. When his fingers turned my face to his and his lips met mine, I melted. And took another.

"Now a serious face," I said with a giggle.

"Why?" he said, pursing his lips as if he was annoyed, but I knew he wasn't.

"The lips. I need them in their full glory," I insisted.

Cal nodded before throwing up a gang sign, and I burst out laughing as I took the picture of us. I didn't even care that I was a blurry blond mess. His lips looked amazing, and I knew I'd be thankful for these pictures once I was back home and a million miles away from him. They'd get me through any withdrawals I might have.

And I might have a lot of them.

His expression turned serious. "I had a really great time with you."

"Me too. I had so much fun. The game was awesome," I admitted. I was fairly certain I'd never be able to hear about hockey now without thinking of Cal and his brother. "I should go."

"I know. I just don't want you to," he admitted, and I inhaled sharply.

Everything Cal said was so sweet and exactly what I wanted to hear. A few simple words strung together in a particular order, and I found myself turning into the sort of girl who had always believed in love—I hadn't. And the kind of woman who had always wanted to give her heart away—I didn't.

I moved first, opening the passenger door and stepping out into the chilly evening air. Cal stood next to the driver's side of his car, watching me, his eyes sad. We both walked toward the trunk of his car, where Cal pulled out my suitcase and lowered it to the ground.

"Thank you."

"Of course," he said as he pulled me into a hug. His arms wrapped me tightly as I breathed him in. "Call me when you land?" he whispered, and I had to stop myself from cheering as I read way too much into his simple request.

Cal hadn't asked me to text him, he'd asked me to call, which meant I got to talk to him once I was back home. In my own state. Twenty-six hundred miles away. Our communication wasn't ending the second I walked into the airport, and I couldn't have been more excited about that.

"I will," I said as I pulled away.

He leaned down and pressed his lips against mine again. I let him take the lead, letting him decide how deep and long this good-bye kiss would last. I was half-tempted to miss my flight if it meant I could keep kissing him.

In the story of us, was this it? Was this really our last kiss?

No sooner had the thought entered my mind when Cal slowly pulled away, disappointing clouding his features. "You'd better go."

"Okay."

Conflicting emotions welled up inside me. I was simultaneously thankful for meeting him, sad at having to leave, confused at what this all meant, and hopeful that I might possibly see him again. It was too much at once.

I will not cry.

I will not get emotional.

Because crying at this point would be bat-shit crazy, and I was not bat-shit crazy.

Steeling myself, I reached for my suitcase and pulled it next to me as I walked away from Cal, his Mercedes, and his dreamy lips.

I hadn't even gotten inside the terminal before I heard him call my name.

"Jules."

At the sound of his voice, I stopped and turned to find him striding toward me like a man on a mission. Was I that mission?

When he reached me, he wrapped a hand behind my neck and pulled me close, his mouth devouring mine as if it would be the last time. This was the good-bye kiss; I could feel it in my bones, and it both surprised and saddened me. Oh, how I didn't want this kiss to be our last.

Wiping any thoughts from my mind, I reveled in the feel of his tongue, the softness of his lips, and the taste of him. I wished the world would pause in this moment so I could simply enjoy it longer, with no care for the consequences.

"Sorry," he whispered as he leaned his forehead against mine. "I just couldn't let you go without giving you one last kiss."

One. Last. Kiss.

Cal released me, and my heart ached as I walked away. I didn't even look back at him—I couldn't. I knew I wouldn't be able to leave if I saw him watching me the way I knew he was.

Only once I was on my flight did I finally allow the feelings from the past few days to overwhelm me. I pulled out my phone and scrolled through the pictures I'd taken of us together, my heart thumping in approval. We looked good together, Cal and me. I continued scrolling until I reached the picture of us kissing in the car, and I pressed my fingertip against the screen, wishing I could jump in and experience that moment again.

That picture was taken little more than an hour ago, and it already felt so far away. *He* felt so far away.

It was heartbreaking when you recognized that moment when pieces of your reality turned into memories. Everything I'd just gone through with Cal, all the time we'd spent, it now only existed in my mind.

At least I had the pictures. And the sweatshirt.

Closing my eyes, the sleep that I'd been avoiding the past couple of nights quickly caught up with me, and I passed out before the stewardess finished her emergency spiel. Only once the wheels hit the tarmac in Los Angeles with a jolt did I finally wake up.

Holy shit, I'd slept through an entire cross-country flight. That had never happened before.

HOME IS WHERE THE HEART IS

Jules

T HE PLANE WAS taxiing to the terminal as I switched my phone from airplane to regular mode, and it started pinging with notifications almost immediately. A text message from Cal appeared first.

DREAM LIPS: I hate that you're not here.

My heart resumed the same pounding as earlier, and I couldn't stop smiling like a fool. Six words and I was over-freaking-joyed, filled with so many feelings that I thought I might burst all over the cabin of the airplane.

E-mail notifications popped up as well.

CAL DONOVAN HAS FRIEND REQUESTED YOU.
CAL DONOVAN IS NOW FOLLOWING YOU.

It was official; I had a stalker. Did it count as stalking if you were totally into the guy?

Calculating the time difference in my head, I typed out a text message to him, even though he'd asked me to call when I landed. Maybe he hadn't really meant it now that I was back on my side of the country? It was super late there, and I didn't want to wake him up if he was sleeping.

JULES: *Just landed. I miss your face. Among other things.*
DREAM LIPS: *I told you to call.*

His answer came through instantly, as if he had been waiting up. I typed out a quick response.

JULES: *Sorry. I'm still on the plane and my crazy best friend is picking me up. Talk tomorrow?*

Smiling, I pressed SEND and my phone instantly rang. My heart soared as I glanced at it, thinking it was Cal, but it was my best friend, Tami.

We met after college when I'd taken a temp job at a law firm to answer their phones. Unlike other recent college grads who knew exactly what they wanted to do out in the "real world," I had no idea. So I temped at various jobs for about a year, hopping from industry to industry until I found something that interested me—high-end real estate.

Tami was a paid intern at the firm when I worked there, and we'd bonded immediately over our distrust of people who preferred tea over coffee, and over the lack of good men in Los Angeles.

"Hey, I just landed. Still on the plane," I tried to whisper, but I was extremely bad at lowering my voice to an acceptable level whenever I was on the phone. I always thought I was being quiet, but had been told that I was anything but.

"Good. I'm almost there. Pick you up out front or in baggage claim?"

"No, out front's fine. I just need to grab my suitcase and then I'll be out."

"I can't wait to hear all about this super-hot guy you met!" she said loudly. "I've been dying. Jules! Hurry! Get off the plane, people! Move!" Then she hung up on me.

I looked over at the older gentleman sitting next to me and forced a smile. I knew he'd heard her. Hell, half the plane probably heard her.

I had sent Tami a text that first night after I'd met Cal, giving her only the CliffsNotes version of things. She was my best friend, and I'd felt like I might explode if I didn't talk about him with someone. Of course she had flipped out, in the best way possible, and demanded to know every single detail, but I'd been too busy to fill her in since then. Needless to say, she was dying to get the scoop, and I was dying to share it with her.

Luggage in hand, I made my way out the airport doors and braced myself for the cold air that never came. I'd gotten so used to being in Boston that I completely forgot I wouldn't be freezing to death now that I was back home.

A horn honked, and I saw an arm wave from the driver's side window of Tami's car. She was insane. Her antics reminded me of Robin from Boston, and I laughed as I imagined the two of them together. They would have loved each other. Apparently I was drawn to outgoing, ballsy women as friends.

Tami hopped out of her BMW and squealed like a seventh grader as she ran over to me. She stopped short before hugging me, her normally brown eyes a bright blue today thanks to the colored contacts she wore.

Scanning me from head to toe, she blurted, "You look different. Oh my God, you had sex, didn't you? You little minx!"

"Lower your voice! I did not have sex. Nice eyes, by the way," I said, knowing she'd appreciate the compliment on her blue eyes, and also to take the attention off of me long enough to get into the car.

Tami was Filipino, so she had this amazing jet-black hair, so straight and slick. No matter how many times we cut our hair at the same time, hers always grew back three times faster than mine. It was completely unfair.

She also had flawless skin and never wore foundation. She didn't need it and actually looked super weird the one time I forced her to wear some. It was as if her skin got angry, drinking in the foundation from her cheeks and spitting it out in other areas of her face. She looked blotchy and unnatural. I, however, needed the stuff to even out my skin tone in an attempt to appear flawless. For me, flawless took work. For Tami, it came naturally.

The crazy girl was obsessed with colored contacts and wore them in all sorts of bizarre colors every time we went out. It was hilarious to hear guys compliment her on her purple eyes after asking her if they were real . . . if her purple eyes were *real!* Yes, guys were that dumb. Or maybe it was Tami who rendered them that stupid. In my opinion, it was a toss-up.

The only thing I had over her was the fact that I could drink alcohol and you'd never know I was drunk just by looking at me. Tami, on the other hand, turned bright pink the second any alcohol passed her lips, no matter what kind of alcohol it was or how small the amount. One drop and her entire face exploded with color. I thought it was great but it royally pissed her off, which only made it better.

I buckled my seat belt as Tami pulled away from the curb and into the stopped traffic. She clicked the button on her steering wheel to turn down the radio and then gave me her complete attention.

Start talking. I'm dying to hear all about Mr. Calvin Not-Klein."

I laughed. "His name is not Calvin. It's just Cal. And thanks, now I'm picturing him all scantily clad on some underwear billboard on Sunset." At the thought, I swiped my hand across my lips just to be sure I wasn't drooling.

"How would you know what he looks like in underwear if you didn't have sex with him?" she shouted. "You liar!"

I groaned. "Why the hell would I lie to you, of all people, about sleeping with someone?" She knew that I confided in her about everything, not that there had been anything to talk about on the guy front in years.

"I don't know," she said with a frown. "I just got excited at the idea that you might be a little reckless. It's been a long time since you let your guard down, you know."

"Of course I know. But you know me. And you know that I don't do one-night stands."

"Such a shame. Letting all of that go to waste." She waved her hand at my body.

"You're ridiculous."

"Of course I am." She gave me a big grin. "It's what makes me awesome."

Traffic started moving, so she refocused on the road, yelling at someone for being a shitty driver. Once the cars ahead of us achieved a steady pace, she glanced my way.

"Tell me more about him. What's he like? Did you see him before you left?"

"He drove me to the airport."

My final kiss with Cal replayed in my head and I shivered, thankful the car was dark so Tami couldn't see. I pressed a finger to my lips, wishing I could still feel his.

Shaking my head, I dragged myself from that delicious memory long enough to fill her in on my weekend, and answered all her questions about Cal and his brother. It was nice to have someone to talk to, but it also made my brain start working overtime. When Tami commented how awesome it was that I'd finally met a guy who didn't make me want to run away from him, I almost cried.

"I don't know, Tam, it's just—" I stopped short, not knowing what to say. There was so much going on inside me, I wasn't sure how to organize my thoughts into something remotely coherent.

"It's just what?" she asked.

"It's just a bad idea. All of it."

Now that Cal and I were separated by distance and time, worry had begun to creep in. Not only did my heart long for him, but every part of me missed him, and it scared me. I'd always been such a take-charge kind of person, in control of my own destiny, and now I was being swept away by something I had no control over. Common sense told me I should probably forget about Cal instead of craving more of him.

Tami glanced at me, her brows scrunched in confusion. "What the hell are you talking about?"

"I'm going to get hurt at some point with this one." The realization hit me so hard, I felt the unwelcome truth of it settle into my bones.

"Why are you saying that?" Her voice softened with concern, sounding almost sad.

I took a minute, thinking about how to word it in a way that made any sense. "He lives in Boston and I live here. We're both workaholics who don't normally date. There's no way this doesn't end badly for me. Just remind me that I knew this would hurt and I still did it anyway. Remind me that I thought he was worth the impending pain."

Tami drew in a long breath and shook her head. "You're sick, you know that?"

"I think I'm just being realistic."

"I think you never know what can happen. He might prove you wrong."

"Who are you," I said in disbelief, trying to tamp down my irritation, "and what have you done with my best friend?"

Tami dated a lot, but she never seemed to settle down with one guy for too long. She was pragmatic rather than a hopeless romantic, and I liked that about her. She was the only one who understood when I decided to close off my heart to love, and didn't give me a hard time about it.

She shrugged as she signaled to exit the freeway. "I'm just saying that you never know. You obviously met him for a reason, right? And you had fun when you were with him?"

"Yeah, I really did. I had a great time." My voice went all dreamy as I indulged in my memories for a second.

"When's the last time you had fun with a guy?" she demanded. "I can't even remember, Jules. Honestly."

"I know, okay? I know all of this."

"Did you two talk about seeing each other again?"

A lump that was certainly filled with disappointment lodged in my throat. "No. We didn't talk about anything like that."

"That sucks."

"Yeah," I said softly. "It does sort of suck."

I looked out the window as we neared my apartment complex, my mind filled with so many thoughts I didn't know how they all stayed in. I was half-convinced that if I dipped my head a little lower to the right, some of them might spill out of my ear.

Tami sighed as she pulled into my gated complex and punched in the security code she knew all too well. The heavy gate swung open and she drove to my building and parked behind my car, blocking it in its assigned covered space. After putting the car in park, she turned to face me and studied me for a moment.

"I feel like it can't be over. I mean, why meet him if that was it?" Then her face lit up. "Unless his whole purpose was to wake up your dead black heart for the next guy," she said with a laugh.

Three days ago, I would have laughed too, but I didn't laugh tonight.

"I don't want a *next guy*. I'm not done with this one," I said without thinking, the words slipping out before I could stop them. But it was true.

She gave me a smug grin. "I knew it. I'll bet you money that you two see each other again."

I shook my head. "I can't see it happening. He's too focused on work. And I don't factor into that equation."

I wanted to be wrong, but in my heart, I knew that I wasn't. I couldn't begrudge Cal his ambition. After all, I had my own.

"Sounds like someone else I know." She poked my shoulder with her finger.

"I'm aware. I think that's part of why we were so attracted to each other. We thought about things the same way. We're very like-minded, you know?"

"That's hot. Seriously. Hey, speaking of, please tell me you have a picture of Cal Not-Klein."

My mouth dropped open. "I can't believe that wasn't the first thing I showed you!"

I pulled out my phone and opened the gallery, scrolling through the pictures to my favorite. It was the one of us in the car from earlier today when our heads were smooshed together. We were both wearing genuine smiles that were reflected in our eyes; we looked really happy.

When I handed Tami my phone, she gasped.

"Shit, Jules. Cal Not-Klein is stupid hot. You two look amazing together."

I tried to smile, but couldn't quite manage it. "We're cute, huh?"

"Yeah, that's not really the word I'd use, but okay. We'll go with cute." She moved to hand me back my phone, but scrolled through the other photos instead. "You were holding out on me," she said as she zoomed in on the picture of Cal kissing me. "Now this, this is hot! Damn, where can I find me a Cal?"

How could I help her find a hottie when mine was in another state? And he wasn't even technically mine in the first place?

Tami tossed the phone into my lap and said the first thing that had made the most sense all night. "You're in trouble."

I nodded. "Exactly. That's what I've been trying to tell you."

CAN'T TAKE IT

Cal

JULES HAD ONLY been gone for less than twenty-four hours, and I felt like I was losing my damn mind. The first thing I'd done this morning—after feeling disappointed that she was no longer in town—was to fire off a text to her so she'd get it when she woke up. It was sweet, a gesture that even my romantic brother would approve of. I pressed SEND on my phone before I could talk myself out of doing it.

It seemed like the only saving grace at all was the time difference between us. Knowing she was three hours behind me made it easier to resist calling her just so I could hear her voice.

Wait . . . just so I can hear her voice?

Looking at me now, you'd never know I wasn't always like this. Jules had me affected . . . infected . . . whatever, and it was making me crazy. I couldn't stop thinking about her. I could be in the middle of working on a trade or checking a client's portfolio, and her smile would break into my thoughts. Before I knew it, I'd be sitting at my desk just staring off into space, daydreaming about being with her.

It was horseshit.

To be honest, I hated that she was gone and that I wished

she were still here. No woman had ever gotten me so twisted up in her so quickly before. Three days with Jules and I'd already grown used to the idea of seeing her all the time, used to her being around.

Was that how quickly it took for a habit to form? Jules had become a habit that I didn't want to break, but I needed to.

My mind was relentless, constantly reminding me of the cute way she laughed, the way she felt in my arms, the way her green eyes sparkled when she looked at me. I struggled to push the thoughts away, but in the end, she always won out. I was a desperate man, missing someone I barely even knew. Somewhere between dropping her off at the airport yesterday and this moment, reality had slipped away, leaving me in dreamland.

I pulled up a florist website on my computer and looked at the arrangements, torn between wanting to send Jules flowers to let her know I was thinking about her, and thinking it was the stupidest idea I'd ever had.

"What are you doing, dipshit?"

Lucas's voice stopped me cold. I quickly switched to my screensaver before glancing up at him and waved a hand over the papers scattered across my desk.

"What's it look like, asshole?"

"Looks like you were about to send someone flowers."

"I wasn't," I lied.

Lucas leaned against my cubicle wall and crossed his arms over his chest. "I think you were."

"You're wrong."

"Not likely," he said with a huff.

"Did you want something?"

"I did, but now I can't remember. Your mental vacation to

la-la land with a certain blonde distracted me." He walked over to my desk, pushed a folder out of the way, and sat in the space he'd just cleared.

"I can't stop thinking about her, okay," I admitted, feeling defeated somehow, as if I'd lost some sort of important internal battle. I wanted him to tell me that I was crazy to be hung up on a girl I'd just met, but I knew he wouldn't.

"That's what happens when you actually like a girl," he said, as if this were news to me.

Leaning back in my chair, I scoffed at him. "I don't want to like the girl. She lives three thousand miles away. It's beyond unrealistic."

"Sorry to break it to you, bro, but your heart doesn't care about reality or miles. Cal," he said, speaking slowly in a tone one might use with a small child, "a heart is this thing that lives right here." He pointed to his chest. "That's where most people think they feel everything related to love. Now, love is—"

"Shut up," I growled out, and he laughed hard as he tried to talk through his laughter to continue teasing me. "Come closer so I can hit you." I swung at him but he was just out of reach, and I almost fell out of my chair.

Laughing, Lucas pointed at me. "That's a hate crime."

"You're a hate crime."

"That's probably also a hate crime."

Rolling my eyes, I groaned before I tilted my head back and rubbed my temples. "You're an idiot."

"I knew I should have bet you money that this would happen," he said, grinning like some all-knowing guru. "I could be a rich man right now."

"Please shut up."

"Cal, for once in your life, forget about your rules and your stupid timeline, and be flexible."

My fingers still pressed to my temples, I glared at him. "You're reading way too much into this."

"I don't think I am."

"We had fun together. We enjoyed each other's company. That's it." I wasn't sure who I was trying to convince, but Lucas's expression told me that he didn't believe a word I said.

He shrugged before saying something that surprised me. "Maybe you're right."

I leaned toward him, cupping my hand to my ear. "I'm sorry, what? Could you repeat that?"

"I *said* maybe you're right. Maybe it was so great with Jules because she doesn't live here. Maybe you were just caught up in the moment."

"That's it! I'm acting all crazy because I thought it was perfect, but it only seemed that way because Jules doesn't live here. You, my friend," I said as I pointed at him, "are a genius. I probably won't even miss her in a week."

As I was speaking, my cell phone vibrated on my desk, and I reached for it to find a text from Jules on the screen.

> JULES: Good morning, or good afternoon, in your case. Time differences are weird. Hope you have a great day. I'm showing a $3-million house today to some new clients. Wish me luck! :)

Hell. One text message from her and all my thoughts flew out the window.

Lucas gave me a big grin. "Is that her? Dude, your face."

"It's your mom," I said as I flipped him off.

"Gross."

Staring at my phone, I hesitated, wondering if I should

respond to Jules now or later, but found myself unable to resist.

> *DREAM LIPS: Three mil? Chump change. LOL Good luck, babe. You got this.*

I smiled as I pressed SEND. A response I wasn't expecting came within seconds.

> *JULES: I sorta miss you.*

Hell. My body instantly relaxed as I read her words. I hadn't realized until this moment how much I'd wanted Jules to feel that way. Knowing she missed me too made me feel a little less vulnerable. I might have tried to convince myself that I'd be over her in time, but that time was certainly not today.

> *DREAM LIPS: I sorta miss you too.*

"What's she saying?" Lucas said, straining to peer over my shoulder to see my texts. "What are you saying?"

"She misses me," I tried to tell him, but my voice came out funny. I sounded like a damn eighth-grader going through puberty.

"Who wouldn't?" he said, giving me a *duh* look, then nudged my shoulder. "You should do it, by the way."

"Do what?" Confused, I frowned at him, and Lucas nodded at my computer.

"The flowers. You should send her flowers. It's a nice gesture."

Sighing, I shook my head. "A nice gesture for what? What would be the point?"

Lucas crossed his arms over his chest and gave me a knowing look. "No girl would ever complain about getting flowers from a guy she just met. It's obvious you like her, even if you keep trying to convince yourself that you don't."

"But I don't want to give her the wrong idea . . ."

"And what's that? That you enjoyed meeting her?"

Scowling, I shoved his ass off my desk. "What would you think if I sent you flowers?"

He laughed and shot me a wink. "I'd think that you liked me."

"Exactly."

"But you do like me," he said, making his point.

"Of course I like you. I'm just not sure if I should advertise that fact."

Lucas paused. "Advertise it! Definitely advertise it. And I like calla lilies. In white," he said in a stage whisper before walking away.

Before I could talk myself out of it, I opened the floral website again and sent a giant bouquet of mixed flowers to Jules's office. Lucky for me, she'd mentioned the name of her agency, so I found the address within seconds of searching for it.

Should I be doing this kind of stuff? No, but I couldn't help it. I wanted to. Jules had me breaking every rule, going against my better judgment at every turn. The battle inside me was a struggle, and I didn't know what was right or wrong anymore.

THE REST OF the workday flew by in a blurry haze of numbers, research, and the memory of Jules's green eyes. There was something captivating about the way a woman looked at you when she wanted you. If you felt the same way about her, it was mesmerizing, sexy. If you weren't interested, it bordered on creepy.

After I left work, I'd stopped by and spent a couple hours with the kids at the afterschool program, worked out at the gym, and was now sitting in my one-bedroom condo, waiting for my dinner to finish cooking. It was nice that the time difference between Jules and me worked in my favor, leaving me plenty of time to take care of other things and then be free to talk to her.

I had sent her a text earlier asking her when I could call, and she told me she would call when she was done for the day. So I found myself glancing at the clock and waiting for my phone to ring. Like a girl.

The timer for my steak buzzed at the same time as my phone rang. It was Jules. My heart gave a little lurch at the sight of her name on my caller ID, but I ignored it as I answered.

"Hey."

"Hi," she said, sounding as if she was in her car.

Even with the traffic noise in the background, the sweetness of her voice came through. I hadn't realized how much I enjoyed the sound of it until I heard it again.

"Damn, I miss your voice."

She breathed into the line. "Me too. It's ridiculous," she said with a giggle.

"How was your day? How were the three-million-dollar clients?" I asked as I cut into my steak.

She groaned. "Ugh. They're becoming increasingly difficult. I love them to pieces, but it's hard to get people to be rational sometimes."

I wasn't sure what she meant exactly, but I wanted to learn more about what she did, day in and day out. "In what way?"

"When I first meet with clients, I ask them questions and make a list, like what are their must-haves as opposed to the things they want, but could live without. Basically, I find out what their deal-breakers are, like some people will insist on a three-car garage and an infinity pool. And if the property doesn't have both of those things, they don't even want to see it."

I nodded my head as she talked. "Right. Okay. That makes sense. Go on."

"Well, the property I showed them today had everything on their must-have list, but it wasn't grand enough for them. They never mentioned wanting something grand or showy before, but now it's a must-have. Which is fine, but they don't really want to pay more than their budget. And it's hard to explain to people that what you can get for three million in, say, Beverly Hills isn't what you'll get in Malibu. They're not the same."

"So now you have to find them other options in the same price range?"

"Yeah, but I'm also going to have to show them a couple that are beyond it, just so they can see the difference. Like, hey guys, if you spend half a million more, you can get all this and this. That usually pisses people off, but sometimes it's the only way to make them understand."

"I don't envy you, babe."

Dealing with people like that sounded like a pain in the ass. I worked with difficult clients too sometimes, but not very often. Since I was an expert in my field, most of them listened to my advice. But when push came to shove, the client was the boss, and I'd ultimately do whatever they wanted. It was their money, after all.

"How was your day?" she asked.

"Good. The market didn't tank, so that's always a plus."

"Tell me exactly what you do again. I know you work in finance and you handle people's money, but when you and the guys were discussing it that night, you were talking in Chinese, so I didn't understand."

I laughed. "Yeah, we were talking about investments. Technically, I'm a financial advisor, but I like to think that I do much more than that for my clients."

"How so? Say I was your client. What would you do for me?"

"We'd start off sort of the same way you start off with your clients, going over their list of wants and needs."

"Really?"

"Yeah. I'd probably start by asking you what your goals were for the future. Like, do you plan on purchasing any property in the next five years? Do you want to travel, and if so, where? Are you going to start a business? Will you want a new car? Are you going to be getting married or adopting a kid? Basically, I'd learn about your long- and short-term goals."

"Okay. Then what?"

"Then I plan for it. I invest your money in different ways and get you set up for things you may not have thought about, like life insurance or a will. It all depends on the needs of the client and what they want from me. But I talk to them all the time, and I'm invested in their success. I want them to succeed so that I succeed."

"That all sounds very fancy," she said, sounding impressed.

"And grown-up. And sort of awesome."

I laughed. "Thanks. I love it."

"It sounds like it."

"I have to build relationships with my clients the same way you do. The only thing that sucks about your job is that you could spend all that time and energy with people and end up without a sale. How do you deal with that?"

"It does happen, but not usually very often. And what can I do? If it doesn't work out, it sucks, but I can't focus on things like that or I'll go nuts."

The background noise disappeared, and I realized she must have shut off her car. "Are you home?"

"Yeah. Just pulled in."

"What are your plans now?"

I glanced at the clock and found myself almost hating how early it still was there, when it was growing later here. It made me a little envious that she still had her whole night ahead of her when I'd be going to bed soon.

"I need to work out, eat dinner, and I'll probably research new places to show them just to plan ahead."

I smiled at the thought that she'd continue working from home. Of course she would. We were cut from the same cloth.

"Do you want me to let you go?" I asked, understanding that even though my night was almost over, hers had just begun.

"I don't want to, but yeah, I should probably go," she said, her voice sounding sad. "Otherwise, I'll stay on the phone with you all night and accomplish nothing."

"Can't have that. Talk to you tomorrow?"

"I'd love that."

As she sighed into the phone, I could picture her face, and

suddenly I remembered something.

"Jules?"

"Yeah?"

"Send me a couple of those pictures of us together. Whichever ones are your favorite." It wasn't fair that she could look at us whenever she wanted and I couldn't.

"Okay," she said, her tone suddenly upbeat. "We take the cutest pictures together, by the way, so be warned. They might take over your life."

I laughed. "Warning taken." When I heard her car door slam in the background and she began breathing heavily, like she was carrying things, I said, "I'll talk to you tomorrow."

"Okay. 'Night," she said, and then she was gone.

Impatient, I stared at my phone, waiting for the pictures to come through. When they did, I wasn't disappointed. We didn't look cute together . . .

We looked fucking perfect.

UGH, I MISS HIM

Jules

HEARING CAL'S VOICE was part heaven, part hell. Listening to him speak, I could picture him perfectly, those damn lips moving and his gorgeous white teeth. The hellish part had been accepting that maybe I'd never hear that voice or see those lips in person again. The thought alone saddened me. But it was reality.

Maybe whatever this was between us would fade away eventually. I had no idea where we were headed, if anywhere, but talking to him only made me want him more. With each text he sent, he felt a little less out of reach, closer somehow. And I had to admit that I liked the idea, no matter how unrealistic it might be.

Genuinely liking someone had seemed so impossible that it rarely, if ever, even crossed my mind before meeting Cal. Now, whenever I wasn't consumed with a client's needs or desires, my thoughts were with him. The feeling was as strange as it was exciting.

And I was excited. Just talking to Cal made me feel good, happier than I'd been in a long time.

It had never occurred to me that I wasn't truly happy before I met him. I'd always thought that work was enough for me. It took a chance encounter to show me that life was about so much more than just work. Logically, I knew this already, of course; I just thought it would be impossible for me to find a guy who really understood me. And I'd been okay with that, had accepted that.

At least, I thought I had. Funny how one person could make you question the things you believed were true.

As I changed into my workout clothes, my phone rang. I glanced at it, noting Tami's name before answering it on speaker.

"Hey, girl," I said as I laced up my running shoes.

"Hey. I just wanted to check in, and A, see how the showing went today. And B, ask about hot Cal. Did you guys talk?"

"I called him on my drive home."

"You called him?" she shrieked, sounding outraged. "No, he needs to call you. Why, Jules? Why would you do that?"

Rolling my eyes at her melodrama, I said tentatively, "Because he asked me to call him after I got off work," wondering what the hell I'd done wrong in the land of Tam.

"Oh, thank God. That changes everything. Remember, he pursues you, Jules, and not the other way around."

I giggled as she laid down the law to me as if she were some sort of relationship expert. She wasn't and I damn well knew it, but I decided to play along.

"What about texting?"

"What about it?"

"Am I allowed to text him first?" I tried to stifle another laugh as I waited for her response.

"You're laughing, Jules, but this is serious. Texting depends."

"On what?"

"I don't know! Who texted first today?"

I bit my lower lip as I remembered waking up this morning to a text from him. "He did. I woke up to a message that read *good morning, beautiful.*"

"Ah shit. Text him anytime you want. Have his babies. Do it now," she said, doing a one-eighty so fast my head was spinning.

"You're horrible at this," I said, no longer holding back my laugh. "I have to go."

"Wait! What about the house?"

My laughter turned into an annoyed groan. "They didn't like it. It wasn't grand enough. I have to find them more options."

"That sucks. I'm sorry. When you do finally find them something *grand* enough," she said in a British accent, "we'll go out and celebrate."

"I can't wait. Seriously. How's work for you?" I asked, knowing she'd gloss over her day, as usual.

As a lawyer, Tami wasn't allowed to talk about the specifics of her cases until they were settled. I knew today would be no exception, but didn't want her to think I wasn't interested in her day.

"You know—same old, same old. Sell that house so we can go out and party!"

"I don't have to sell a house in order for us to go out," I reminded her.

"I know, but it's more fun when we act like we're only out because we're celebrating something. The guys love it."

"You're seriously crazy, but I love you anyway. Talk to you later."

I pressed END, wondering for the millionth time how I'd

gotten so lucky in the best-friend department. Tami was a certain kind of crazy, but she always had my best interest at heart, and I knew I could count on her.

TEAMWORK

Jules

WAKING UP TO a text message that read *good morning, beautiful* every day for the past few weeks had become a welcome routine. Although, really, how could something so sweet ever get old? Knowing that Cal had gone out of his way to make sure I had a message from him when I woke up each morning made me feel special and wanted.

The funny thing was, I sort of did the same thing for him. Every night before I went to bed, I sent him a text telling him good night, wanting him to know that he was the last person I thought of before I went to sleep.

Those texts quickly became a habit I couldn't imagine ending anytime soon. To be honest, I couldn't imagine *anything* with Cal ending anytime soon. If I had thought that this thing between us might fade away with time, I was sorely mistaken. It had been a few weeks since I left Boston, and my desire for him hadn't faded. If anything, it had grown with each conversation we shared, each message we exchanged.

He'd even sent me flowers. I had been shocked to get them, the surprise written all over my face so much that my coworkers had teased me for days and begged for the details. They'd been around when Brandon had dumped me, so they were excited at a new prospect on the horizon for me.

Cal had grown on me so naturally that I found myself subconsciously counting on him in ways I hadn't expected. Our connection grew out of us debriefing about our days and sharing our thoughts. Whenever something happened at work, I wanted to call him and tell him all about it. He always had great perspective and was willing to listen without seeming bored or irritated.

As much as I wanted to be surprised by his willingness to help me, I couldn't be because I felt the same way when it came to hearing about his day and his career. I wanted him to succeed, and if I could help him in any way, I tried to do it.

The two of us brainstormed together about how I could reach more clients, and how he could grow his clientele. Cal pushed me in ways I never knew that I needed, helping me think outside the box and solve problems in simple ways that were only complicated because I'd over-thought them. He wanted me to be better, and he was excited about the goals I had for myself. It was such an unfamiliar feeling to be cheered on in this way, but it was also exhilarating.

"Thanks for your help, Jules." Cal sounded genuinely appreciative about the advice I'd just given him for ways to bring in new business to his firm.

"Of course. You do the same thing for me all the time." I snuggled deeper into my couch and pulled a blanket under my chin.

"I know. It's just really nice to have someone in my corner who gets it."

"I was thinking the same thing the other night. I've never had someone care about my success before," I admitted.

It was true. I'd never dated someone who felt like a teammate or partner, and didn't know I needed one. My ex-boyfriend Brandon definitely wasn't on board with my workaholic tendencies, and didn't want to hear about anything work related when we were together. *You're off the clock, Jules,* he would say anytime I mentioned the dreaded four-letter word.

Brandon's attitude had created so much tension in our relationship. I'd been excited about my growth in the company and wanted to share it with the one person who was supposed to love me the most and want me to succeed. Not only was he not interested, he made me think there was something wrong with me, when the truth was there was something wrong with him.

Cal made a noise of disbelief. "I don't understand that. What about your ex?" he said, referring to a brief conversation we'd had about our exes.

"He hated when I talked about work."

"How could any man hate that?"

"Maybe because he wasn't as driven as I was. I never stopped, Cal. I was all work, all the time, no matter what day it was or what time it was. My brain never shut off."

After being conditioned to believe I was weird for so long, I felt obligated to look at things from Brandon's point of view, to imagine how he must have felt when he dated me. I definitely didn't give him the amount of attention I'd devoted to my job, not by a long shot. Maybe a man could only tolerate something like that for so long.

Cal made a sound, something that was part grunt, part huff. "I think that for people like you and me, Jules, we can't be with someone who isn't as driven as we are. It would never work."

"Why do you think I don't date?" I said with a laugh.

For as open and honest as we were with each other, there were certain topics I was still too nervous to broach with Cal, and his feelings for me was one of them. I was scared it was too soon to talk about feelings, especially since we'd only spent one weekend together.

"Because the guys in LA are idiots," he said without missing a beat.

My cheeks burning at his compliment, I blurted, "Then the girls in Boston must be stupid too."

Surely Cal knew he was a catch. Not that I wanted another woman to catch him anytime soon; at least, not until whatever this was between us had run its course. The thought of him dating someone else made my stomach churn.

When he let out a big laugh that ended in a yawn, I glanced at my mantel clock, noting it was well past midnight his time.

"I don't want to let you go," he said, "but I probably should."

"I know. It's late. Thanks for everything tonight. I feel like we should get matching baseball jerseys or something."

"Team Success," he suggested, and I laughed.

"I like the way you think."

"You should. It's the same way you think."

Touché, Cal Donovan. Touché.

"All right," I said as I threw off my blanket and sat up. "Go to bed. You're so distracting. I haven't even worked out yet."

"Slacker."

"Tell me about it."

"Talk to you tomorrow." He yawned again before saying good night and ending the call.

If I'd thought I was in trouble when Tami picked me up from the airport, I was in so much more trouble now. And the worst part?

I loved it.

———✦———

MY PHONE VIBRATED and the familiar blue smiley face stared back at me as my heart rate doubled and my thumbs couldn't press the buttons fast enough to respond. I always found myself racing to open Cal's text just to see what he had to say. No matter how many messages he sent me, my body reacted as if it were the first.

> DREAM LIPS: Are you home from work yet?
> JULES: Not yet. I have about another hour or so. Text you when I'm done?
> DREAM LIPS: Yes, please.

I smiled and put my phone away, then tried to focus again on the paperwork piled on my desk. It was crazy how easily a man could distract me, especially considering I'd never been the type to lose focus so easily before.

Apparently the right guy could throw you all out of whack and make you want to reprioritize everything in your life to make sure they fit into it. At least, that was the effect Cal seemed to have on me.

Shit. I really was in trouble. As the logical side of my brain nagged at me to resist this sort of behavior, to not behave how a typical woman might, my heart begged me to make room for him.

And for once in my life, I was siding with my heart over my brain.

LONG DISTANCE

Cal

E VER SINCE JULES had mentioned that we were sort of like a team, I couldn't get the notion out of my head. When she'd first joked that we should have matching jerseys, my gut reaction had been to shout *Team Success* into the phone as if it was the most natural thing to do.

I'd never had a teammate before. Sure, I had Lucas, but it wasn't the same. Before Jules, I'd never met a woman who seemed invested in my success, in me.

Scratch that. I'd definitely met women interested in my success, but only because they wanted to reap the rewards of my hard work. They didn't want to be part of what it took to get there; they simply wanted to share in the outcome.

Jules couldn't have been more different. She didn't care about my money; she had her own. She pushed me to better myself because that was what a good woman did for her man. And that was what a good man did for his woman.

Whoa. Where the hell did that *thought come from?*

I pressed my desk phone's intercom button. "Lucas?"

He poked his head in my cubicle a moment later. "You rang? And why am I always coming to you? My desk is right over there, you know. You could come to me." He rolled his eyes.

"Yeah, but you sit next to that asshole, and I don't want him eavesdropping."

Lucas agreed with a grimace.

The guy who sat next to Lucas was related to one of the owners in the company and had a reputation for ratting people out whenever it benefited him. I imagined that he would love the fact that my focus was now split between work and Jules, and he wouldn't hesitate to fill in the managing partners.

"I had an idea, and I wanted your opinion."

Lucas leaned against my desk. "Is this about Jules?"

I nodded.

"I'm all ears," he said and leaned in a little closer.

My mind spun. It was crazy how quickly I'd grown accustomed to Jules occupying my thoughts. At first, I'd tried to resist it, but I soon realized it was a battle I was never going to win. Thoughts of her moved right on in, unpacked, and made themselves at home.

When I dropped her off at the airport all those weeks ago, the idea of seeing her again seemed ridiculous. Hell, I honestly never thought we'd be talking every single day the way we were. Now I couldn't imagine *not* talking to her. She'd become part of my daily routine, easily the best part.

But I was going crazy only talking to her and not seeing her. What I had initially thought was a fun weekend fling had somehow turned into more, and I wasn't exactly sure when that had happened.

I wanted to see Jules again. No, I *needed* to see her again. I found myself longing to touch her. Thoughts like that would normally make me feel like a fool, but I didn't feel foolish when it came to Jules. It was as if my primal desire for her superseded any other emotion I might normally experience. All I thought about was how much I needed her in my arms again.

I drew in a long breath through my nose before exhaling slowly, watching Lucas for his reaction. "I was thinking about going out there to see her. Do you think it's a stupid idea?"

"Why would I tell you that's a stupid idea?" He gave me a look that clearly said *you're an idiot.* "I've been waiting for you to say it since she left."

"Be serious for once," I growled out.

Cocking his head, he studied me. "I am. You're just being stubborn."

"You're not helping."

"Helping? What do you want me to help with? Looks like you've got this covered. You want to go see her, so go. She probably wants to see you too." He dusted his hands off as if brushing away any concern, and said, "My work here is done."

"You're sure it's not a dumb idea?" I asked again, giving him one more chance to talk me out of it.

Lucas clapped me on the shoulder and gave it a shake. "It's not a dumb idea. It's the best idea you've had since she left. Go see your girl. I've got work to do. We can talk about this more later." Hooking his thumbs in his belt loops, he practically swaggered back to his cubicle, apparently pretty damn pleased with himself.

I leaned back in my chair and smiled, deciding I'd talk to Jules about it tonight. I hoped she would want to see me again as much as I did her, but she hadn't mentioned it.

Did that mean she didn't? I supposed I'd find out later when I talked to her if flying to LA was a good idea or the stupidest one I'd had lately.

THE DAY DRAGGED on, especially after the stock market closed with shitty returns. Clients always freaked out when the market took a nosedive, and I spent the majority of the late afternoon calming them down and reminding them that selling off their stocks now would only lose them more money in the long run. It was much smarter for them to hold on and wait for the market to come back up. It always rebounded, eventually. It might take years, but the majority of my clientele had that kind of time. They simply needed to be reminded of it.

When I closed out my e-mail and shut down my computer, I stood up and noticed Lucas was still in the office and on the phone. I walked over to his cubicle and waited for him to end the call, thankful that that nosy prick Jeremy had already left for the day.

Lucas hung up and spun toward me in his chair. "You're not second-guessing the trip idea, are you?"

Sometimes it was helpful how well my best friend knew me. Other times, like now, it was simply annoying.

"Maybe," I said, sitting on the edge of his desk the way he always did mine. "I'm not sure. What's the point of going to see her?"

My brain had been working overtime all afternoon. Was I being foolish for giving my heart what it so clearly wanted when my head knew there was no future in it? Was I setting us up for an inevitable fall?

Lucas frowned at me. "What do you mean, *what's the point?*"

"She's there," I said, throwing out one arm and then the

other. "I'm here. Maybe going out there and seeing her again would just complicate things."

"It's already complicated," he said with a snort. "You're just pretending it isn't."

Lucas had a point, but I didn't want to admit it. I thought about denying it, but he'd see through my bullshit anyway. He always had.

Pushing aside what he'd just said, I blurted, "Just tell me if I'm being an idiot."

"No, you're being a romantic for once. You're practically in a relationship with the girl already, but you can't see it. Or won't admit it."

Dropping my head in my hand, I closed my eyes and groaned. "We're not in a relationship."

"You are. And to be honest, it's perfect for you."

Confused, I squinted at him. "What are you talking about now?"

Lucas rolled his chair a little closer. "Seriously, think about it. You two talk every single night like you're a couple, but you don't have to rush home to her because she's not there waiting for you—"

"Does this story have a point?" I interrupted.

"Just listen," he said with a scowl. "You're way too busy right now for a chick who lives here. Could you imagine all the whining and the *Why don't you spend time with me? You're too busy for me. I need you. I miss you. Come over. Where are you?*"

Lucas's dead-on impression of a needy woman's voice cracked me up, and I had to stop myself from laughing.

"But with Jules," he said seriously, "you can't do any of those things, even if you want to. Instead, you can focus all your time and energy on work and volunteering, and it won't change your relationship with her at all."

I wanted to argue the point with him, but it did sort of make sense.

Warming up to where he was going with this, I asked, "What are you saying exactly?"

"I'm saying," he said, giving me an amused look, "that a girl who lives out of state is the perfect solution for a guy like you. It's the best of both worlds, a relationship without all the pressure."

"Shit, Luc. That might be the smartest thing you've said all day." I gripped his shoulder and squeezed.

"I take offense to that," he said, obviously joking. "I say a lot of smart things. You just don't hear them."

"So I'm not being stupid by going to see her?" I asked again for the third or maybe the fourth time, because apparently I had lost my balls somewhere on my walk over to Lucas's cubicle.

He rubbed his temples like my questions gave him a headache. "No. You're not. You want to see her, right? You miss her?"

I looked around the empty office to make sure no one was within hearing distance, but lowered my voice anyway. "I miss her like crazy. And yes, I'm dying to see her."

"Then it's not stupid, okay? So stop asking. It's okay to want to be with someone, Cal. It doesn't make you any less motivated or ambitious here." He waved his arm to indicate the almost empty office space.

"I know that," I snapped at him.

"Do you? Because I don't think you do."

At that, I had to take a moment to let his words sink in. Lucas might be right—I might be so married to my work that

I was afraid to let someone else into my life. Being taken seriously at work and having a personal life didn't have to be mutually exclusive. Plenty of successful people were married or had a significant other.

Lucas gave me an exasperated look. "Cal, if it's permission you want to follow your heart for once, I'm giving it to you. Do it. Book a flight. You've got some vacation time. Go see your girl."

"Why do I even ask you for advice?" I huffed as I pushed off of his desk.

"Because I'm your best friend, and I give good advice. Everything I say is golden and should be tweeted. And then retweeted," he added with a big grin.

Rolling my eyes, I walked away. "I don't even know what the hell you're talking about anymore," I said over my shoulder as I headed back to my desk to grab my things.

LATER THAT NIGHT, I fired off a text to Jules. I never knew how late she would be working since she tended to tailor her own hours around her clients' schedules and the availability of any houses she wanted to show.

> DREAM LIPS: *Are you home from work yet?*
> JULES: *Not yet. I have about another hour or so. Text you when I'm done?*
> DREAM LIPS: *Yes, please.*

Jules texted me right after I got out of the shower to let me know she was home. I dialed her number before I plopped down on top of my bed.

"Hi," she said, her voice breathy, and all it did was make

me miss her more.

"Hey. How was your day?"

"Busy, but good. Yours?"

"Same."

"I saw the market took a nosedive," she said, and I laughed because I knew she only started following the market to see how my day was.

"You did, huh? Stalking me again?"

"Just your market. You okay, though?"

"Yeah, it was fine. A few clients freaked out, but I calmed them down. It's a lot of repeating myself with them, you know? Reassuring them and hearing them out."

"I get it. I'd freak out if it was my money. I wouldn't want to lose it."

"That's why I'm there. I move it around to minimize the losses, and I monitor everything so there are no surprises."

She sighed. "It's so hot when you talk about work."

I laughed. "Sure it is."

"No, really. I mean it."

"Thanks, anyway." I hesitated a moment before saying, "I was thinking about something and wanted to run it by you so you could tell me if you're on board with it or not."

"Okay . . ."

She sounded a little nervous and apprehensive, which wasn't what I wanted at all, so I blurted, "I want to come out there and see you."

"Wait, you what?" she asked, her tone instantly changed into one of surprise.

"Is that the wrong thing to do? If it is, you can say no," I said, suddenly more unsure of myself than I'd ever been.

Shit. What if she didn't want to see me again the way I

wanted to see her?

"Say no? Are you crazy? It's not wrong at all. It's the great-est thing you've ever said. Come tomorrow. Come right now!" She laughed, that unselfconscious belly laugh that I loved, and said, "I miss your lips!"

Relieved, I released a pent-up breath. "They miss you," I told her, and then added, "I miss your body," before I could stop myself.

"It misses you too."

"So it's okay if I come out there?" I asked again, just so my ego could hear her say yes.

"Of course," she said, and I wished I could take her in my arms right then so she'd know just how much I'd missed her too.

"I can't wait to see you."

"Cal, I'm so excited! When would you come?"

Ready for that question since I had already looked at my calendar, I said, "I was thinking two weeks from this weekend, if it works with your schedule."

"Hold on. I'm checking," she said as her laptop keys clicked in the background. "That works for me."

"Good. Does from Friday to Sunday work for you?"

"Perfect."

"And do I fly into LAX or somewhere else?"

"Yep. In and out of LAX is perfect too," she said, and then practically yelled into my ear, "Cal!"

I laughed. "Yeah, babe?"

"I can't wait to see you. Really, you have no idea."

Grinning, I said, "I'm pretty sure I have some sort of an idea."

"You are so getting lucky this time," she told me, and my

dick instantly hardened at the thought of my touching her again.

When I quipped back, "Maybe I'll come out tomorrow," she laughed, but I wasn't joking.

My dick wasn't, anyway. He was seriously ready to jump on a plane tonight.

DEVIL IN PINK CONTACTS
Jules

I COULDN'T BELIEVE that Cal was coming out here to see me! Of course I'd wanted to see him ever since leaving Boston, but didn't know if it would actually happen. I had no idea what it meant for us, but at this point I couldn't have cared less. All I could focus on was the fact that I would get to see those dreamy lips again and feel his arms around me.

I dialed Tami's number after Cal and I got off the phone, knowing that I was far too excited for a mere text message. I needed someone to be crazy happy along with me.

"Hey!" she answered, the traffic noise in the background telling me she was driving.

"I just got off the phone with Cal, and guess what?"

"Um, he loves you? He can't live another day without your sweet loving? He's moving? What?"

I shook my head as she rattled off crazy answers that I'd all but asked for when I suggested she guess. "He's coming out here!"

She whooped so loudly, the speaker cut out for a moment before her voice returned. "Shut up! Oh my God, when? For how long?"

"He'll be here in two weeks. Just for the weekend." Lost in

thought, I absentmindedly tugged at the fabric on my comforter. It felt like a dream.

"Shit, Jules, are you dying?"

"I'm so freaking excited, I feel like I could do anything right now," I said with a laugh.

"That's adorable," she said, her tone sugary sweet.

"Don't tease me."

"I'm not. This is awesome. I can't believe I get to finally meet this guy," she said before stopping abruptly. "Wait! I *do* get to meet him, don't I?"

I hadn't thought about any of the logistics yet. Would it make Cal uncomfortable to meet my best friend? What if he thought I was moving too fast? I hated not knowing where we stood and didn't want to ask him in case it pushed him away. The last thing I wanted was for Cal to feel pressured and call this whole thing off.

"I don't know," I said, bracing for her reaction.

"You don't know? Give me one good reason why I can't meet him!"

"Because I haven't even thought about what we're going to do yet," I said. "What if meeting you freaks him out?"

"Why? Because I'm so awesome and hot? I know, it's intimidating."

I laughed. "Yes to all of those things. But what if he thinks meeting my best friend is moving things a little too fast?"

"If he thinks that, then he's an asshole, Jules. Seriously. I want to meet him. We'll go out one night. Either to dinner or to a club. Shit, two weeks, you said?"

When a tapping sound started up in the background, I scolded her. "Do not text and drive, Tami!"

"I'm not!"

"I hear you. You're the most distracted driver I know. Pay attention to the road!"

"Shut up. I was just looking at my calendar. And I was at a red light."

"Liar."

"Just be quiet. My calendar says we have that VIP party at Colossal. You invited me as your plus-one, so I have to come. And you'd better get Ron to make it a plus-two."

Shit. One of my clients, Ron, was a big-time nightclub owner in Hollywood, and he was hosting an invite-only event. We'd worked together on three separate properties over the years and had developed a friendship. He would definitely notice if I blew him off, although I was fairly certain he wouldn't be mad at me for it, but I didn't want to be the kind of person who promised she'd show up to a private event and then bail. At least I knew making my invite a plus-two wouldn't be a problem, so I was thankful that wouldn't be an issue.

"You're right. Looks like we'll hit Colossal on Saturday. And you guys will meet. Please don't embarrass me," I pleaded, and she giggled.

"Be thankful I don't own any pictures of you as a little kid, or I'd be busting that shit out. 'Oh, Cal, this was when she took the scissors and cut her own hair. Don't you like the way it's longer on the left side than it is on the right?'"

How the things that Tami thought about even popped into her head, I'd never know.

"I'm suddenly thankful I didn't know you in high school, Tam. Just don't wear your pink contacts. Please."

I rolled my eyes at the thought of her ridiculously colored lenses. The pink ones creeped me out whenever she wore them. The natural brown color of her eyes mixed with the pink and created a light red effect. She looked like the devil, or at least someone who was possessed by him. I had a hard time looking her in the eye when she wore them, always thinking that she was hexing me, or trying to figure out ways to steal my soul.

She laughed hysterically. "I won't, but that would be fun just to see you freak out all night long. I could chase you around the club, and Cal would think you were a lunatic." She kept laughing. "It's so tempting."

"I'll disown you and make sure you're on the no-entry list for all of Ron's clubs. I swear." I tried to sound serious through my own laughter.

"Don't blackball me in my own city! Okay, okay. No pink. I promise."

I let out a sigh of relief. "Thank you."

Her laughing finally stopped. "Hey, I'm almost at the gym. Can I call you back?"

"No, go on. I just wanted to tell you that he's coming out." Excitement rippled through me again as thoughts of Cal being here consumed me.

"And Jules?"

"Yeah?"

"I'm really happy for you."

I bit my lip, blushing like a schoolgirl. "Me too. Can't wait for you to meet him."

"He better not suck!" she said. "'Bye!" Then she hung up on me.

My best friend was insane. Certifiable.

It was hard to reconcile the crazy girl I knew with her alter ego who practiced law and won most of her cases. Unlike Best

Friend Tami, Lawyer Tami was neither fun nor happy. She didn't wear contact lenses in crazy colors, or mermaid-length extensions in her hair. No, Lawyer Tami was a bulldog who hated losing.

I only hoped she didn't pull her tough-girl routine on Cal when she met him. Then again, I was pretty sure he could handle her, and that she'd most likely melt at the mere sight of him.

Even she wouldn't be able to resist the power of those damn lips.

MY DAILY TEXTS from Cal now included a countdown. I opened my eyes the following morning to a message that read:

DREAM LIPS: *Good morning, beautiful. 13 days!*

Absolute giddiness surged through me as I responded.

JULES: *13 days!!!*

This was going to be the best and the worst countdown in history—the best because of what we were counting down to, and the worst because thirteen days suddenly felt like an eternal string of twenty-four-hour periods that would never end.

Thankfully, work kept me busy with house showings and new property listings that popped up every day. Staying busy kept my mind distracted and occupied so I didn't slip into a Cal-induced countdown coma. Or at least, it tried. He was a powerful force, that boy from Boston.

I'd kept in touch with Robin from the conference and

could practically feel her excitement when she responded to my email about Cal's impending visit. She wrote something inappropriate, reminding me that I was living for the two of us now, and not only did it make me laugh, but it made me miss her as well. She also offered me a job every other day, in case I wanted to "come land that man before she left her husband for him."

During a break between showing properties, I pulled into a liquor store parking lot and sent Cal a text. I hoped he would respond quickly so I didn't have to come back later.

> JULES: *Do you have a favorite bourbon, or do you love them all?*

Lucky for me, he responded right away.

> DREAM LIPS: *Blanton's Original is my favorite. Plus, I collect the tops. I know; I'm a nerd.*
> JULES: *The tops? No clue what you're talking about, but thank you! 'Bye!*

I wanted Cal to have something at my house that he loved, and I figured bourbon would be a good place to start. Plus, we had a little history with the stuff, and I'd grown a soft spot for it somewhere between learning to drink it properly in that hotel lobby and now. Not that I'd probably ever drink it on my own, but still.

With absolutely zero bourbon knowledge, I scoured the liquor store's bourbon aisle and found more selections than I ever knew existed. I found Blanton's almost immediately, the unique bottle a standout from all the rest. Instead of being tall, it had a rounded bottom that was both intricate in its design and stylish, while still looking classic.

Once I'd paid for a bottle, I tossed it onto the passenger

seat of my car and opened the photo app on my phone so I could scroll through the pictures of us together for the millionth time. As always, I smiled at how happy we looked. Those photos never got old, no matter how many times I stared at them before bed each night, or how many times I pulled them up during the day. They never failed to make my heart flutter and my pulse race.

Only thirteen more days until Cal would be here. How would I ever make it until then without going totally crazy?

I had to chuckle at the thought as I drove along the Pacific Coast Highway on the way back to my office. No, Cal and I hadn't known each other long, but it didn't seem to matter when I thought about how he made me feel. I could pretend I didn't look forward to our nightly phone calls, but that would be a lie.

And now I looked forward to them even more. Knowing I'd get to see him soon changed things for me. It gave all our communication a little more meaning, as if there was a light at the end of the tunnel. A light and a pair of dream-worthy lips.

My phone rang inside my car, startling me. I was surprised to see Tami calling at this time in the afternoon. She was usually either in court or prepping for it.

"Hey," I answered.

"Hey, yourself! I just got out of court."

"Already?"

"The judge is puking in her chambers. I've never seen someone's face turn green before, Jules. Sure, they make cartoon characters do it all the time, but I thought that was just for fun. I didn't realize it was a real thing."

"You're disgusting."

"I know. Listen, I wanted to come over. How late are you

working tonight?"

"I'm heading back to the office now, and I have a showing at three thirty. I should be home around five, at the latest."

"Okay. I'm just gonna let myself in," she said through a yawn. Tami not only knew the security code to get into my gated community, she also had the only spare key to my apartment.

"All right. I'll see you when I get home."

After Tami ended the call, I wondered if I'd find her asleep when I got home. She enjoyed pretending that the guest bedroom that doubled as my home office belonged to her. I always found new spare clothes of hers hanging in the closet after she'd spent the night, and some days it felt as if she'd all but moved into the guest bathroom with the amount of toiletries and makeup she left there.

I used to pray she'd leave her pink contacts so I could throw them out, but she'd only left the most ridiculous pair of turquoise ones once. That night when we'd gone out, guys had complimented her on her unusual eye color, asking who she took after in her family, her mother's side or her father's. *Idiots.*

Malibu didn't have much choice in the way of affordable rental units, and the majority of apartment complexes in the area were old and outdated. When I first toured my apartment complex, I fell in love on the spot. While it unfortunately didn't have an ocean view, the entire property had been landscaped to look and feel as if you lived in an island resort. The trees were lush, vibrant, and perfectly aligned with the benches, picnic areas, fountains, and hammocks that were scattered across the acreage, all to give the common areas a Zen-like feel.

My apartment was a two-bedroom unit that was almost as big as the house I'd grown up in. It wasn't that I needed that much space for just me, but when I first looked here, it was either that or rent an even larger three-bedroom. The frugal side of me wanted to walk out of there and say no, but the practical side reminded me that I could easily afford the rent, and that my options in Malibu were somewhat limited.

Plus, it would have been hard for any other rental space to compare to the features this one had. Considering the marble entryway, hardwood floors, stainless steel appliances, oversized terrace, and a walk-in closet the size of a normal bedroom, I couldn't resist. It was hands down the prettiest place I'd ever lived in my life. I loved coming home each day and walking through my door.

After showing my last property of the day and finishing up some paperwork, I headed home well before five. I glanced at the bottle of bourbon sitting on my passenger seat and smiled. *Thirteen days.* Driving through the privacy gates, I noticed Tami's BMW in a visitor's spot, and was thankful she hadn't stolen my assigned parking space like she sometimes did.

I took the stairs up to my third-floor apartment two at a time before bursting through my front door with a wide smile.

"Honey, I'm home!" I shouted.

"Hi, dear." Tami appeared from around the corner with a glass of wine already in hand. "Ooh, did you bring me a present?"

When she hustled over and grabbed for the bottle of bourbon I was holding, I stashed it behind my back, out of her reach.

"Hands off. That's for Cal."

"But Cal's not here," she pointed out, her natural brown

eyes sparkling with mischief.

"Since when do you drink bourbon?"

I nudged her with my hip before moving to put the bottle in one of the many empty kitchen cabinets. I honestly had no idea how anyone could possibly fill them all up unless a family of ten lived there.

She brightened. "Since right now?"

"Not happening," I said with a laugh. "It's a gift."

"Party pooper," she said with a pretend pout.

When I stuck my tongue out at her in response, she went to the fridge and poured me a glass of wine as a peace offering.

"Thanks."

I took a big sip of my wine as we stepped out onto my covered terrace, furnished with a patio furniture set that was not only gorgeous, but was well worn in since we sat out there whenever we could. I plopped down in one of the oversized chairs, tucking my feet beneath me, and Tami stretched out in the chair next to mine and propped her feet on a footstool.

"How are you feeling today?" she asked once we were settled in. "Even more excited than you were last night, or are you going to start freaking out?"

"Why would I freak out?"

"Because you've only known this guy for a month?" she said, her eyes wide. "And he's coming out here and he's going to sleep over in your personal space and stick his thingy in your thingy and who the hell knows how long it's been since that's happened."

Shaking my head, I stared at my best friend like the insane lunatic she was. "I just don't even know what to say to that." Rolling my eyes at her, I took a sip of my wine.

"You're seriously not freaking out at all?"

I shrugged, wondering if something was wrong with me. Should I have been freaking out that Cal was coming here? I didn't feel like that at all.

"Honestly, I'm just excited. And really freaking happy."

That answer made her smile. "I like that. I'm happy for you. And I'm really excited too. Cheers." She pushed her glass toward me and we clinked them together.

"Cheers," I said, and then leaned my head back against the pale blue padding and breathed in the evening air.

Even though I couldn't see the water from my place, the ocean was just across the main street. The only issue was that the street was wide and the beach access wasn't easy, no matter what the apartment complex brochure tried to lead you to believe. *Oceanfront, my ass.* Still, I could smell the salt in the air. The only thing that could make my terrace more perfect was being able to hear the waves crashing against the shore, but I couldn't, not even when there was no traffic and I strained to hear.

"You are going to have sex with him, right?" She pointed at my crotch. "It's not broken, is it?"

"How would it be broken?" I said with a laugh. "And yes, I planned on it."

I definitely planned on sleeping with Cal when he came out here. I hadn't done it in Boston because we'd just met, and to me, it had simply been way too soon. But we'd talked every day for almost a month since then, and somehow that made things different. I felt closer to him than I did then, and having sex was something I wanted to do, something I was more prepared for.

"Thank God." She winked at me. "Wouldn't want the poor guy flying all the way out here and going home with blue balls."

"Seriously. Where did you come from?"

"Bob and Lila Cheng. Why do you ask?" she said matter-of-factly as she mentioned her parents' names.

"Because sometimes I think you came from Mars. Or Pluto. Or some other planet."

"I'll let my parents know you think so." She gave me a sassy grin before tossing back the rest of her wine.

My phone rang and I moved to grab it, not quite sure who it might be. Tami peered over, and when she saw Cal's name, she whispered, "Does he call you every night?"

I nodded as I answered. "Hey," I practically purred into the line.

"Hey, babe. Guess what?"

"What?"

"Thirteen days," he announced excitedly.

I squealed. "I was just talking to Tami about that. We're super excited."

"Tami's excited too?"

Cal knew exactly who Tami was. I'd filled him in on more than one occasion about her and her antics, the same way he'd shared Lucas's latest dating disasters with me.

When I thought about, it amazed me how much we now knew about each other's day-to-day lives. It was incredible what you could learn about a person when you did nothing but talk to them on the phone, rather than see them. Seeing someone could be distracting, but if you took the physical stuff out of the equation, you were only left with the rest.

"I can't believe he actually *calls* you," Tami said, seeming flabbergasted by the very idea.

"What's she saying?" Cal asked, his tone amused.

"She said she can't believe that you call me," I told him.

"As opposed to what?"

"Texting? I don't know."

He huffed. "I'm a man, Jules. Tell her that real men know how to have conversations on the phone, and we use ours for more than just text messages."

When I lowered the phone and started to relay the message, my best friend groaned. "Oh, just give me the phone."

She pulled the phone out of my hand.

"Hi, Cal Not-Klein," she said, trying to sound composed and not tipsy. "I know. It's impressive. Guys really don't call anymore. They text."

My eyebrows shot up at how her voice completely changed. He'd already charmed her through the damn phone. I sat there, listening to the one-sided conversation and wondering exactly what Cal was asking her, or saying to her. My heart raced as I listened to my best friend chat up my . . . well, my Cal.

Tami giggled, said good-bye, and handed me back the phone.

Cal chuckled when I was back on the line. "She's a nut."

Laughing along with him, I said, "You have no idea."

"I'll let you go since Tami's there. Call me later if you want, or I'll talk to you tomorrow."

I didn't want to get off the phone. I never wanted to, but he was right. Tami was here tonight to hang out with me, so focusing on her was the right thing to do.

"Okay. Thanks for calling."

"Of course. And, Jules?"

"Yeah?"

"I miss you."

"Miss you too."

Raising his voice to catch my attention before I hung up, he called out, "And hey!"

"Yes?"

"Send me a picture of you and Tami right now."

"Oh my gosh. Done!"

"'Bye, babe."

"'Bye."

As I pressed END, Tami raised her eyebrows at me. "Oh man. I can't wait to meet him in real life."

"You're going to love him. He wants a picture of us, by the way," I said as I held my phone up high, fitting us both into the frame and making sure we looked good.

"I'd want a picture of us too," she said, smiling as she held her wineglass in the air.

Making sure the picture was hot enough to send, I fired off a text to Cal with the picture included.

Less than a minute later, he sent one back. When I held the phone toward Tami, she laughed at the picture of him mimicking her pose, holding a beer in the air and wearing a kissy face.

"Holy lips," Tami said as she pulled the phone out of my hand.

Shaking my head, I said, "You have no idea." I tossed back the rest of my wine and pushed off my chair. "Want more?"

Tami stood up as well. "We need food."

"Agreed," I said, rubbing my stomach as we headed inside.

I whipped us up some whole wheat pasta with olive oil, which was way more fattening than one would think, but oh so delicious. My excuse was that it went well with the wine. Tami tried to complain about the calories, but when I reminded her that she never gained weight, she quickly shut up and finished off her plate.

We picked out a romantic comedy to watch after dinner, and when Tami fell asleep on the couch all bundled up, I left her there and headed into my bedroom for some Cal-filled slumber. Dream Cal was extra hot, and so were his lips.

God, I couldn't wait to see him.

WHOLE DAMN ZOO

Jules

EIGHT DAYS. The next handful of days flew by much quicker than I ever thought possible. Cal and I had a phone conversation every evening, no matter how brief, discussing things from our favorite foods to places we wanted to travel.

Throughout the day, we texted, those texts growing more frequent as his trip neared. They usually were just quick messages like "I miss you" or "thinking of you," but that didn't make them any less sweet. Maybe it made them even more so. Knowing that I was in his thoughts as often as he was in mine was reassuring.

I was thankful that my job was a constant state of busy. I could schedule appointments as late into the evening as my clients would allow. Working during the weekends was usually a no-brainer since most people preferred looking at as many properties as possible, and their work schedules during the week made their free time limited. On Saturdays and Sundays, I was usually slammed all day long, but I was thankful for it. It helped settle my heart and keep my mind focused and on task.

Once I got home, however, it was a whole other story. My entire being tuned to Cal Donovan and how many days I had left until he would be here. There were eight, by the way, a number I couldn't forget since I still woke up each morning to a countdown text. When we reached single digits, I almost cried, not out of anything other than being genuinely filled with happiness. It was ridiculous, but I loved it and refused to fight it.

The feelings I had for him were both unexpected and unfamiliar, and their intensity took my breath away. Cal had been an exception to everything I'd ever thought I wanted, and I couldn't pretend that he wasn't. It wasn't in my nature to lie—not to others, and especially not to myself.

So when he called each night, I found it more difficult than usual to keep those thoughts and feelings inside instead of letting them fly out of my mouth. Cal was focused on work, and even though he was the one who had initiated his trip out here to see me, I didn't want to scare him off with my intensity.

My emotions and enthusiasm grew with each day that passed. I planned things for us to do while Cal was here, with options depending on how tired he was or what appealed to him more. I planned my outfits, down to which panty-and-bra set I would wear each day and night. *I'm such a girl sometimes.* And I even checked Cooper's hockey schedule to see if his team would be in town or not. They wouldn't be, which made me a little sad.

Asking Cal about his favorite foods the other night on the phone had been a ploy so I could have them on hand when he was here. He loved Italian and seafood, which fit in perfectly with the ideas I had. I wasn't the best cook, but I did have a few Italian specialties up my sleeve, thanks to my grandmother, and living in Malibu meant access to some of the best seafood restaurants around. This trip was going to be epic.

I hoped like hell my heart would survive this without falling for him completely.

I was doomed.

ONE DAY. When I opened my eyes that morning, I noticed the green light glowing on my phone that indicated unread text messages. The familiar dark blue smiley face greeted me as I swiped at my screen.

DREAM LIPS: One day!

I quickly typed out a response.

JULES: OMG. One day! I can't wait, Cal!
DREAM LIPS: Me either.
DREAM LIPS: Oh yeah. Good morning, beautiful.

Our countdown had been sweet, something to help pass the time, but now the reality was actually starting to sink in. Cal would be here tomorrow!

I sucked in a long breath as I took stock of my emotions, and to my surprise I still wasn't nervous or worried. I didn't question whether we'd get along or how things would be when we finally saw each other again after all this time. Maybe if we hadn't kept in touch the way we had, I might have felt differently, but all I knew was that I was extremely optimistic and filled with hope, a potentially dangerous combination, but there was nothing I could do to stop it.

Not that I'd tried.

Knowing that Cal was working and we normally never

spoke during regular business hours, I hesitated for only a second before calling him anyway.

When he answered with an enthusiastic, "Hey!" I hid my surprise. I was convinced that the call would go straight to voice mail and I would have to leave him a message.

"Hi! Sorry to call during work, but I'm just so excited to see you tomorrow, and that text got me all giddy!"

"Me too. I can't wait to hold you, babe," he all but cooed into the phone, and I wanted to melt into a puddle.

I crooned in a low voice, "I can't wait to be in your arms and have those lips on me. God, I miss those lips. I want them all over me." I felt almost breathless with my admission.

"Jules, you can't." He lowered his voice, and I struggled to hear him. "You can't say those things to me while I'm at work. You're turning me on."

I laughed. "Sorry. I'll let you go. I just wanted to tell you that I can't wait to see you. I'm so glad you're coming out."

"Me too. I'll see you tomorrow, but I'll talk to you later."

"All right. 'Bye."

I ended the call and hopped up to get ready for work, still on a complete Cal high.

That night, I ended up working late to show a couple a new property that had just been vacated and listed. When a house was empty, it was easier to schedule the showings because I didn't have to ask the owners to leave the property, or work around anyone else. I made myself flexible, willing to show a house at eight p.m. if that was what a potential buyer needed me to do.

When I finally climbed into my car to go home, it was almost midnight in Boston. I hesitated for a minute, debating whether I should call him or not, but said *screw it.* Of course, I woke him up. I had to laugh at how groggy his voice sounded, and was convinced that he wouldn't remember our conversation in the morning.

TODAY!

When I woke up to Cal's text the next morning, I realized I was wrong. Apparently his mind was a steel trap.

> *DREAM LIPS: Good morning, beautiful. TODAY! Sorry about last night. I was out of it. I can't believe I get to see you later!*

It was a little easier getting through work that day, knowing that he would be in the air and unavailable for my call. I envisioned him on the plane, wondering if he was the type to make friends with the people sitting next to him, or if he kept to himself.

I laughed as I imagined Cal chatting up some old lady as she knitted a scarf in the seat next to him, who would eventually decide that said scarf would look better on him than on her nephew. Cal would graciously accept it, of course, and wrap it around his neck with a smile. No one ever said I lacked imagination.

My heart thumping I drove to the airport that evening and pulled to a stop at the arrivals curb. To be honest, I sort of hated waiting for him there. It felt impersonal somehow, but it was a hell of a lot quicker than parking, going in, and trying to find him.

> *DREAM LIPS: On my way out.*
> *JULES: I'm in front of the door marked A-2. Charcoal Audi.*

As I stood beside my car and waited for him to materialize,

I tried to convince the excited butterflies in my stomach to settle down. When he finally appeared, still in his work suit, a duffel slung over his shoulder, I had to stop myself from sprinting into his arms and knocking him to the ground. Forget the butterflies—a whole damn zoo erupted inside me at the sight of him.

Cal scanned the cars before finding mine and I watched with satisfaction as a smile crossed his face and he picked up his pace. There was something about a well-dressed man, and there was definitely something about Cal. My entire body warmed as he neared. I pressed a button on my remote and the trunk popped open.

He strode straight for me, ignoring the trunk as he grabbed me and pulled me against him. No words were exchanged before his lips, my dream lips, took over. They were as soft and perfect as I remembered. I opened to his kiss, and it was as if no time had passed between us. We fell into a familiar rhythm, our mouths and tongues exploring each other in a perfectly choreographed dance.

Lost in that moment, it wasn't until a horn honked that I remembered where the hell we even were. I opened my eyes as we reluctantly ended the kiss, the zoo animals inside me running amok.

"Hi." His eyes bright, he gave me a big grin before tossing his bag into the trunk and closing it.

"Hi," I said, unable to hide my smile.

"God, I've missed you."

He pulled me close and kissed me again, his teeth tugging lightly at my bottom lip. As he did, everything inside me turned soft, especially my heart. It was a strange sensation, that moment when every last icicle in my heart melted and fell like summer rain against my rib cage.

"I missed you too. I can't believe you're really here." I ran my fingers across his five o'clock shadow, the prickle of his skin a welcome sensation. Then I lowered my hand toward his loosened tie and pulled at it.

He shrugged. "Didn't have time to change after work."

"You look hot."

"You look amazing."

When his gaze roamed over my body, I suddenly couldn't wait to have him naked later. Even though it had been far too long since I'd been with a man, I wasn't nervous. I wanted him and was more than ready.

"We should go." I moved toward the driver's side of my car as he got into the passenger seat.

I pulled into the snarled traffic as Cal's hand found the inside of my thigh and rested there, his thumb moving slowly. Instantly, I was transported to the night we met and our weekend together. Glancing at him, I still couldn't believe he was actually here. Sure, we'd been talking about it for the last two weeks, but having him in my car was almost too much. It was like a dream.

"What are you thinking about?" he asked with a grin.

"That I just can't believe you're here. And how exciting it is that I don't have to hear your voice on the phone anymore. I get to look at you while you talk. I feel like Boston was a hundred years ago."

"I was telling Luc that exact same thing the other day." He shook his head in disbelief. "That I still remember every single detail from our weekend together, but it feels like forever ago."

I smiled, knowing exactly what he meant. "Here's the deal. I wanted to take you to Moonshadows for dinner tonight, but

I was thinking that since we have such a crazy night planned for tomorrow, maybe we'd just stay in and I would cook, if that was okay with you."

"Babe, if it was up to me, we'd never leave your bed. But whatever you want to do is fine by me."

"You don't mind staying in tonight?" I asked again, thankful that he was okay with my last-minute change in plans.

His hand squeezed my thigh. "I prefer it, to be honest."

Yeah. I preferred it too. Tomorrow night at the club event would be hectic, and I'd have to share Cal with everyone we met and talked to. Tonight, I craved alone time with him.

"Maybe we can go to Moonshadows tomorrow for lunch. If we wait until then, you'll be able to appreciate the views. It's right on the water, but you'll enjoy it more in the daytime."

"Sounds great," he said, and flashed me another grin. "But honestly, I don't care what we do, babe. I'm just happy to be here."

"That makes things easier."

I smiled as I turned off onto the PCH. I wanted to point out the sights to him, but the sun had set a while ago. The highway was mostly dark, and he wouldn't be able to see anything anyway.

"So, you're cooking for me, huh?"

"Yes," I said as I kept my eyes on the road.

"What are we having?"

"You'll find out soon enough." I gave him a grin. "We're almost there."

WHEN I PULLED into my complex, I glanced at Cal and saw his eyes widen as the gate opened. The grounds of my complex were even prettier at night, filled with lights that twinkled in the trees.

"Jules, this place is gorgeous."

"Yeah. I love it."

After shutting off the engine, I popped the trunk and reached for my purse. Cal walked around the car and kissed me before hugging me tight. We stood like that, wrapped in each other's arms in the parking lot, not caring about anything or anyone else in that moment. Being with Cal made me feel like time had stopped.

He lightly smacked my ass before he grabbed his bag and reached for my hand, intertwining our fingers as I led the way.

"I'm on the top floor."

When I opened the front door, he stopped dead in his tracks and stared. "Jules."

"I know, right?" I knew he was seeing the place the same way I had when I first toured it. My apartment was spectacular. It truly was.

"It's unbelievable." His gaze wandered from the kitchen to the living room and back to the floors.

"I fell in love with it the second I walked in. Wait until you see the bedrooms and the bathrooms. They're ridiculous." I walked toward my bedroom as he followed, running his hand along my kitchen countertop.

We rounded the corner and walked through the doorway of my bedroom. The space was massive, with a fireplace in one corner and double doors that led to the terrace outside.

Cal's eyes widened even more. "You have a fireplace in your bedroom?"

I nodded. It was fun seeing my place through new eyes again. It reminded me exactly how I had first felt.

He shook his head. "I don't know if I can handle seeing anything else, Jules. Your place is ridiculous."

"Welcome to Malibu?" I wasn't sure why I phrased it as a question, but that's how it came out of my mouth.

"I guess."

"Put your bag anywhere. I'm going to start dinner."

"Hey," he said before taking me in his arms. "Thank you. For making dinner and for letting me come out."

"Of course," I said as if it took no effort or was something I did all the time.

"Wait, I have something for you." He opened his bag and carefully pulled out a brown paper box. "Here," he said, shoving it toward me with a grin a mile wide.

"What's this?" I said, the weight of it catching me off-guard. The nondescript box was heavy.

"Open it, Jules. You'll like it."

I pulled at the tape holding the box closed and it popped open. The mouthwatering smell hit me immediately.

"Oh my God, is this . . . ?" I opened the top all the way to reveal an entire Boston cream pie from the diner.

"It is." He pressed a kiss to my nose. "I thought you might be missing it."

"You have no idea," I said before scooping off a small dollop of the chocolate on top and licking it off my finger.

"Shit, Jules," he growled out. "I'll never look at that dessert the same way again."

I laughed before closing the lid. "Sorry. I'll put it in the fridge. But I'm so excited. Thank you."

"You're welcome. Would you mind if I showered? I'd love to feel clean again. Or would you like my help in the kitchen?"

I smiled, loving that he was thoughtful enough to offer,

even if he didn't entirely mean it. "Go shower. I already put a towel out for you in the bathroom. It's the blue one. 'Cause you're a boy."

"Thanks for noticing," he said and planted a quick kiss on my lips.

Before I put the dessert in the fridge, I grabbed a fork with the intention of only taking a small bite. But one bite turned into four, and I had to stop before I ate the entire thing. Annoyed at myself, I opened the fridge and shoved it way in the back as far as it would go, as if I was hiding it from myself.

The dessert now safe, I headed into the living room to turn on the fireplace and light a few candles. I stood for a moment, admiring the ambiance, and returned to the kitchen to warm up the manicotti I'd made from scratch the night before. It would heat up nicely in the oven along with the homemade garlic bread I'd whipped up.

Once I'd popped open a chilled bottle of wine for myself, I retrieved the bourbon from the cupboard where I'd hidden it from Tami the other night. Leaving it on the counter, I searched for one of the bourbon glasses I'd also bought. I wanted everything to be perfect.

"You bought me Blanton's?"

Cal's voice startled me, and I turned around to see that he'd changed into sweatpants and a T-shirt. Even dressed ultra casually, he still looked delicious.

I shrugged. "You said it was your favorite and I wanted to have some here for you." My gaze drifted the length of his body as he sauntered into the kitchen.

"Sorry I got comfortable," he said, referring to his clothes. "Hope that's okay."

"Of course," I said, then took a calming breath to settle my erratic heart.

He walked me back into a corner. "That was really thoughtful of you. The bourbon, I mean. Thank you."

He leaned close and pressed his lips to mine. His hands slid behind my neck, holding me still as he deepened the kiss. He hardened instantly, something his sweatpants couldn't hide, and I had to stop myself from moaning. As if reading my mind, he pulled back.

"See the top?" He pointed to the bourbon's stopper, shaped in the figure of a jockey riding a horse. "They spell out BLANTON'S, and I have all of them except the *L*."

I let out a small chuckle. "Aw, that's cute."

"Be quiet," he said before shaking his head. "Feel how heavy this is." He put the brass figural stopper in my hand, surprising me with the weight of it.

"I didn't peg you for a horsie collector," I teased as I handed it back to him.

"Horsie?" He scowled at me. "These are cool. Women don't understand. I might just hate you a little for that," he said, teasing me back.

"You don't."

"I might."

"You don't." I leaned up on tiptoe and pressed my lips against his dreamy ones. God, I'd missed them.

"I don't," he mumbled against my lips, then smiled. "Can I at least show you so you don't think I'm a complete nerd?" When I nodded, he explained. "Each stopper has a horse and jockey in various racing positions. When you collect them all, you not only spell out Blanton's, but you have the story of a winning race. See?"

I couldn't help but grin at his enthusiasm. "I get it. It's a good marketing gimmick."

"You did not just say that. It's more than that. Jules, you're breaking my heart here." He placed his hand over his chest.

"Tell me it's not brilliant marketing? It so is!"

He groaned in frustration and reached for me again, pulling me against him in a tight grip. "Admit it's awesome."

"It is." I grinned, enjoying torturing him. "Awesome marketing."

"You . . . ," he growled out.

"You," I echoed, pressing my body even more firmly against his.

As his hard-on pushed against my lower belly, I wanted to move against it, slow and teasing. There was a feminine power that came with knowing you caused that to happen, that having me close turned him on.

"We could skip dinner and just go straight into that ridiculous bedroom of yours," he said, nipping at my neck with his lips before moving to my ear.

I swallowed, trying to ignore the tingles his lips were causing. "Food first," I managed to get out, but I had no idea how.

Cal pulled away and smiled. "Food first."

He poured himself a glass of the bourbon, and I watched him drink it the way he had taught me to, breathing it in before sipping it.

"You can go sit down while I deal with this, if you want," I said, not wanting him to feel obligated to sit in the kitchen with me.

When he said in a low voice, "I'd rather be where you are," my heart practically melted into a puddle at my feet, just like the icicles had earlier.

Taking in his perfect smile and damp hair, fresh from the shower, I said, "I still can't believe you're really here."

"I know. Me either." He winked and gave me a lopsided smile.

Cal talked to me as I went through the motions of warming up our dinner. As he did, I had my back turned to him, and it was almost like having him on speakerphone. But each time I turned around and realized that he was really there, standing with me in my apartment, excitement would rip through me.

"What are you thinking about?" he asked.

"Your voice. I got so used to hearing it over the phone, you know? But now it's here. In person. It's just . . ." I paused as I pulled the pasta from the oven, feeling stupid as I said the words out loud. "It's weird. Like I have to remind my brain that I can open my eyes and enjoy the fact that you're really here, not thousands of miles away."

"I know exactly what you mean," he said, his gaze lingering on my mouth.

It warmed me from the inside out that he understood. I'd never been in a long-distance relationship before, or whatever it was that we were doing, so all of this was uncharted territory for me.

I set the pasta on the kitchen table next to the salad and the bread. A pair of white candles set in sand and shells adorned the table, giving it a warm glow. Our conversation all but stopped once we started eating; apparently both of us were hungrier than we cared to admit.

"Jules, this is delicious," he said between bites.

"Thank you. I'll tell my grandma you approve."

He nodded, trying to talk around a mouthful of food.

"Did she make it?"

I laughed. "No, but she gave me the recipe."

WHEN WE FINISHED dinner, I stood up to clear the table but Cal placed a hand on mine, stopping me.

"I'll get the dishes."

"You don't have to do that."

"I want to. Go shower or get ready for bed, whatever you need to do, and let me take care of this, okay?"

He could not be this perfect. "Are you sure?" I felt a little guilty, but the offer was more than appealing.

"Go." He pushed me away gently before saying, "Wait. Take this." He handed me my refilled wineglass, and I did as he asked.

When I emerged from the bathroom in my pajamas, I was only marginally surprised to find Cal lying on my bed with the TV on. His eyes locked onto mine and I looked away, as if I was shy all of a sudden. Glancing down at my tiny shorts and tank, I padded my way across the wood floors toward the bed.

Cal didn't look away, his eyes still firmly focused on mine. When I reached the bed, I snuggled as close to him as possible. He wrapped his arm around me and pulled my head onto his chest, the feeling oddly familiar after being away from each other for so long. He ran his fingers through my hair as I splayed my hand across his rib cage, drawing lazy circles with my thumb.

"Thank you again for dinner." He leaned forward and touched his lips to the top of my head.

I craned my neck to look up at him. "It was my pleasure. Truly."

e'd built up in anticipation of what was to come.
more. I just wasn't sure you would want to." He
fore admitting, "I hoped you would, but I didn't
esume." He rolled the condom onto his length
sing his attention on me. "You okay?"

course."

led his body over mine, pressing only the tip of
inst me. When I spread my legs wider, inviting him
ed in gently, only a little bit before stopping.

, Jules."

u all right?" I was nearly panting with anticipation,
aintain my composure when all I wanted to do was
hips against his length and take him all the way

ot even all the way in and you already feel like
said, his breathing sounding pained.

mission made my heart swell inside my chest until it
night burst, but I said nothing, not wanting to ruin
it.

ched himself inside me until he could go no further,
that ancient rhythmic motion. As he slid in and
the feel of it—of him—was incredible almost to the
verwhelming. Neither too large nor too small, he fit
s made for me.

ps moved in rhythm with his, meeting his thrusts in
unterpoint. I arched my back slightly, which made
different angle inside me, and I never wanted him to

feel amazing," I said on a gasp. "God, you feel so
e me."

g down, he pressed his lips against mine in the

And it was. It had been. I'd never been the type before, but I realized that I enjoyed taking care of Cal, doing nice things for him. Something about it made me feel good.

We tried to kiss but it was awkward, the angle all wrong. He moved from under me, his body and mine switching places before he hovered above me. I stared at his lips as they moved closer to mine, and closed my eyes. When our mouths touched, so soft at first, the air filled with the intimacy of it all.

"I missed you so much," he breathed into me, our lips never breaking contact.

"Me too. Every single day," I admitted, not caring if it was too much, too soon. It was how I felt.

He pulled away slightly, and the corner of his mouth lifted. "So honest."

He'd said that more than once to me before and I'd never questioned it, although I was always a little uncertain about what he might mean by it.

When I reached around his back, trying to pull him down on top of me, he lowered himself, careful not to crush me as he settled his weight on me. My hips lifted slightly, moved in their own rhythm, wanting this, wanting him.

"Look at me," Cal said, and I opened my eyes to a sea of hazel. "Are you sure?"

I nodded, and his lips crushed against mine as if he'd been holding back since he arrived at the airport. He kissed me deep and hard before moving to my neck and nipping at my skin.

"I want you so bad," he said, almost breathless. "But I'll wait if you're still not ready."

"Shut up, Cal. You know damn well I'm ready." I tried to sound tough, but I wanted him as badly as he wanted me, if not more.

It was all the permission he needed. He dropped next to me on his side, his arm wrapped around my back as he pulled me against him, his grasp firm. He kissed me everywhere, as if he was afraid I might change my mind if he stopped. And when his lips met mine, I lost all train of thought. I could only think of his mouth, his tongue, and what it did to the zoo that apparently lived inside me.

I watched as he moved his attention to my knit shorts, his fingers working the elastic from my hips. I scooted from side to side as he pulled them over my hips, and when he slid them down my legs, he left a trail of kisses behind.

Another moan came from him when he saw my black lace panties. His body settled on top of mine before he reached for my underwear, his fingertips brushing a light trail down my stomach first. After moving the material to one side, he slid his fingers in, touching and toying with my most private area, exploring it like it was a treasure map.

I waited for him to make some comment the way men normally tended to, but was relieved at his silence. His fingers inched closer toward my sex, and when he pushed one inside me, I sucked in a small breath as my body accepted it with ease. I moaned with the pleasure it incited in me, and he worked it slowly in and out before another finger. My back arched at the sensation, and he kissed my neck.

Reaching in the tight space between the mattress and my back, he tugged my tank top over my head. He stared at my bare breasts for only a moment before settling his mouth around one nipple, sucking it between his perfect lips. He worshiped my breasts, his mouth moving back and forth between them in equal pleasurable measure, licking, sucking, and nibbling. I clutched at his back, hitting the top of his

sweatpants, and I fumbled wit
wanting to stop what we were d
my toes to grip at his pants and tu

Cal wriggled them off and k
rather than touching me right awa
seeing him without pants for th
erect behind his boxer briefs, twit
it free. It looked beastly beneat
animal trying to escape its cage. I
a moment longer, but I also want
I gripped around its girth through
and down gently, trying not to hu

He moaned, closing his eyes
and I leaned in, my mouth claimin
mouth, obsessed with those lips.
them; they were my everything.

Cal grabbed me and tossed me
wearing nothing but our underwea
I lifted my hips, trying to grind on
against me, even with fabric betwee

"Don't move like that or you'll
warned.

I bit my bottom lip in anticipa
anymore," I said, practically begging

"You sure?"

"Cal—" I moved my hips agains

"Fuck." He reached for the fl
wallet to pull out a condom.

"Tell me you brought more th
sound playful, but the moment wa
emotions hung in the air around us,

the sweat
"I hav
stopped b
want to p
before foc

"Yes,
He se
himself ag
in, he pus

"Dam

"Are y
trying to
grind my
inside me

"I'm
home," h

His a
felt like it
the mome

Cal i
then beg
out of m
point of
as if he w

My h
perfect c
him hit
stop.

"You
good insi

Lean

sweetest, softest kiss. Our mouths seemed to move in the same rhythm as our bodies, the movements slow, sensual, achingly beautiful. Our foreheads touched, and we shared the same air.

"I'm close," he said against my lips.

I dug my fingers into his back, pulling him deeper inside me. "I'm there," I breathed out just before my body reacted, trembling against him as he held me even tighter. He finished soon after me as the waves of my orgasm continued to roll through me. We lay there for a few moments, breathing hard, and I refused to move, even after I came down from that high.

Eventually, Cal pulled out of me slowly, leaving me feeling empty and cold. He stood up from the bed in all his naked glory, and I watched as he disappeared into the bathroom before returning with a lazy smile on his face. He crawled back into bed and lay on his back, then pulled me against him. My head rested on his chest again as his wildly beating heart pounded in my ear.

"That was . . ." He paused, pressing his lips against my forehead. "I don't even know the right word to say."

I had been thinking the same thing. It wasn't just incredible, or hot, it had been so much more than that. Words didn't seem to do it justice.

"It was something, all right."

"Good something, right?" he asked, obviously fishing.

"It was more than good, Cal. It was epic."

"Epic," he repeated.

This had been exactly why I knew I couldn't sleep with him that weekend in Boston. If the sex would have been anywhere close to what we just experienced, I wouldn't have been able to handle it. There was no way that I could experience something that intimate and then leave him forever.

Yes, we'd stayed in touch since my trip to Boston, but I didn't know that would happen at the time. I had no idea I'd ever see him again, let alone spend my evenings talking to him. Now that it was done, I was so happy for the way things had turned out between us, that we'd waited until now.

"What are you thinking?" he whispered as he stroked his fingers through my hair.

I laughed into his chest. "I was just thinking how glad I was that we didn't do *that* in Boston."

His stomach muscles tightened as he leaned upward slightly. "Why's that?"

"Because I wouldn't have survived it. That would have wrecked me for all other men," I said, half teasing, half serious.

"Have I still wrecked you for other men, Jules?"

"Yes, Cal, you've ruined me for all others. But I'm prepared for it now. I wasn't ready for you last time."

Actually, that wasn't quite true. I wasn't completely honest when I said I'd been prepared—nothing could have prepared me for that. I hadn't had sex in a very long time, and what we just did was so much more than sex.

Cal had been inside me, a part of me, joined with me on a primal level that was as emotional as it was physical, and I already felt more connected to him than I was two hours ago. Sex brought people closer. At least, I'd always felt that it should. Being intimate on that level should bring you together, not tear you apart.

Knowing my feelings on the subject had been the exact reason why I hadn't slept with him in Boston. But to be honest, I was no better off now. He'd still leave in two days, and I was hopelessly addicted to him.

Cal stayed silent after my admission, the only sound his

heart pounding beneath my ear. I was almost asleep when he finally whispered, "You might have ruined me too."

It was so soft, I wasn't sure he'd meant for me to hear it or not, so I remained still and pretended to be asleep.

MALIBU DAYS

Cal

I'D FANTASIZED ABOUT being with Jules in more ways than I cared to admit during our time apart, but nothing, absolutely *nothing*, compared to the real thing. Her body was made for mine. She curved around me, bending and moving in ways I'd only dreamed about before now. And when she told me I'd ruined her for all other men, I didn't care if she was only saying it to placate me or my ego.

I needed to hear it. It was only fair that she be ruined if I was.

No matter what happened between us after this weekend, I wasn't sure I'd ever experience anything like that with another female as long as I lived. Don't get me wrong, sex almost always felt incredible to a guy, but there were times that it was simply . . . something more. Better somehow, more intense, more emotional. This was definitely one of those times.

I'd promised myself on the flight that I'd try to keep a level head, but one look at Jules waiting for me outside the airport and all levelheadedness flew out the damn window. I couldn't keep my head on straight when it came to her. Long-distance Jules was one thing. In person, she was a different beast altogether. I had even less self-control when she was in the same room as I was. My hands proved to me time and time again that they had a mind of their own.

I had no idea how I'd survive this weekend, but I resigned myself to having a good time and not reading anything else into it. Whatever this was between us, I wasn't going to try to label it or categorize it, because that wasn't realistic when it came to us. We still lived on opposite coasts, loved our jobs, and were determined to get ahead in them. Those were our priorities, and when this weekend ended, they still would be. This was supposed to be fun; nothing more.

When I opened my eyes the next morning, Jules's head was still on my chest. Our bodies had become hopelessly intertwined during the night, her leg draped around mine, my arm under her back, holding her tight. Her long blond hair was splayed over my body, and I instinctively moved to touch it. Everything about my reactions to Jules was instinctual. I did things before I even had the chance to think about them.

God, she was beautiful. Still naked, the sheet covering only parts of her soft skin, she looked like a painting. No wonder my head was such a mess when it came to her. Her beauty rivaled her brain; she was a double threat.

I didn't want to move, didn't want to wake her, but I had to take a leak. When I pulled my arm carefully from under her, she stirred and turned her head slowly to face me, those green eyes as gorgeous as ever.

"Morning," she said as she stretched her arms over her head and mewed.

"Morning." I bent down to kiss her forehead. "I didn't mean to wake you. I need to go to the bathroom."

"It's okay."

She smiled as I pushed out of the bed, still naked and

sporting some serious morning wood. When her gaze dropped to my groin and stayed there, I had to stop myself from making a smartass remark as I walked into her oversized bathroom. The thing was truly over the top, large enough to house a small family. Of people, not pets.

"Jules?" I shouted from the bathroom, not sure why my question couldn't wait.

"Yeah," she called out, her voice still groggy.

"How big is this place?"

"Almost eighteen hundred square feet. Why?"

"Cause it's huge," I said before walking back into the room. It was way too much space for one person, and even though Jules had it decorated comfortably, she couldn't use all this space.

"This was the smallest apartment," she said, still raising her voice. "The others are all over two thousand."

Jules hadn't moved from where I'd left her. Not really. She was still spread out facedown on the mattress, the white sheet only partly covering her naked body.

I wanted her, needed her. And if I thought I'd been drawn to her before last night, it was definitely stronger now. I never really equated sex with making you feel closer to someone before. It was just something people did, an act that didn't always require thought. A need to be filled, a thirst to be quenched. I suddenly felt like I'd been doing it wrong my whole life.

I eased myself onto the mattress, covering the back of her body with the front of mine as I leaned down, trying not to crush her. Kissing her exposed back, I swept her hair off to the side before kissing her neck and her shoulder. She tried to turn to face me, but she couldn't. I pushed up, giving her enough space to turn over before I lowered myself on top of her once more and took what I was slowly becoming addicted to. Her body.

We showered together afterward, taking turns washing each other and becoming orally acquainted. I briefly considered packing my bags and moving into this shower forever as I looked down and saw Jules on her knees, her head bobbing up and down. It was one of those images you hoped stayed with you until the day you died.

"We slept late," she said as she wrapped herself in a towel and tossed one at me. "How about we skip breakfast and do lunch?"

Reaching for her, I pulled her close, unable to get enough of her. I molded my lips to hers, loving the way she tasted, the feel of her warm tongue on mine.

"Not at all. Lunch sounds good." Food was food. I didn't care what meal we were eating, as long as we were eating something.

"Good. We'll go to Moonshadows then." She kissed my cheek. "The place I told you about last night."

"Sounds great."

❦

I HAD NO idea what to expect of Malibu. Getting in late last night meant that I hadn't even really seen the area at all. The highway was dark, the houses were dark, the ocean was dark. I'd seen a lot of blackness as we drove. My expectation of Malibu was that it would be pretentious, a super-rich area in Southern California filled with the type of people you saw on those awful reality TV shows. And *Baywatch*.

Jules changed into jeans and a pretty top, nothing too

fancy, and I took my cue from her as I dressed in jeans as well and a casual button-down. As we drove along the Pacific Coast Highway, I was blown away. Malibu was stunning, the way the road seemed to follow the coastline, dipping and curving with it, the ocean as blue as the sky. And the glimpses of mansions you could see from the road were nothing short of impressive.

"You sell any of these properties?" I gave a nod toward the passenger window as I squeezed her thigh. My hand always seemed to settle there.

"Not yet. Most of those have been owned by the same people for years. A lot of them buy those houses or the land, and they don't sell."

"I wouldn't either," I said as we passed a giant wooden gate that looked like something straight out of a movie.

"The funny thing is, the owners don't even live here full-time. The majority of those houses are rarely occupied."

I nodded, completely understanding. We had areas like that in Massachusetts, like Nantucket and the Cape, and of course, New York had the Hamptons. It was the same idea, and it all boiled down to people who had too much money to burn.

"I'd like to think that if I owned one of those places, I'd live there and enjoy it."

"I know. But most of them are in the entertainment indus-try, and it's easier to live closer to the studios. Malibu is beautiful, but it really is sort of a pain in the ass to get anywhere from here," she said with a small shrug.

"Yet you still live here."

"But I work here too. I don't ever have to leave."

"Touché," I said as Jules turned off the road. The building she pulled up in front of looked older than Jules and me combined.

She traded her car keys for a tag with the valet, then took my hand and led me to a wooden wall at the edge of the small parking lot. I looked down, surprised to see waves crashing against the rocks below us.

"Wow. This really is right on the water."

"I know. It's so cool." She smiled, making me smile in return before I pressed my lips against hers softly, not wanting to ruin her lipstick or get the shit all over me.

We walked around a small garden with a statue of Buddha and entered the front door. The lobby area was dark, even during this time of day. Jules said something to the hostess and we were led to a huge outdoor eating area with various seating options.

I glanced around at the other patrons, noting they all seemed laid-back, not dressed to impress. The majority were in casual clothes and baseball caps. Apparently they weren't pretentious like I'd imagined. I wasn't sure why it surprised me, but it did.

Jules chose a small table for two closest to the water and near the fire pit, which had been turned on, even though the air outside wasn't chilly, in my opinion. Maybe this was considered cold for California.

"Your waiter will be right with you," the hostess said before placing two menus on our table and walking away.

"What do you think?" Jules asked as we sat.

I looked out at the ocean, the birds diving into the waves and disappearing before resurfacing. "It's really pretty. And way more casual than I expected."

"Welcome to Malibu." She waved her arm as the waiter walked up.

"Welcome to Moonshadows. Can I get you started with something to drink?" He looked between the two of us.

"I'm good with water for now, thanks," I said, not wanting to drink yet.

Jules gave him a small smile. "I'll take an iced tea and a water."

When we were alone again, Jules continued. "It's definitely more laid-back than other places, which is why I love it so much. I hate snobby people. You know, the kind who throw their money in your face and want you to know how rich they are? It's obnoxious. Malibu isn't like that, for the most part. The guy dressed in a ripped T-shirt and worn-out Vans could be a freaking billionaire, and probably is, but you'd never know it."

"That's pretty cool. I like that," I admitted.

I'd never really thought about it that way before. Granted, I was surrounded by success and excess in my line of work, but not to the level she was talking about. At least, not on a consistent basis. Schmoozing was required in my business. While I didn't necessarily love that part of it, it was a necessary evil, and if I wanted to land big clients and make big money, it was something I had to do. But Jules had a point when she called it obnoxious.

"It's all just so over the top, you know?" she said. "Don't get me wrong, I have success and I want more of it, but it's not so I can walk around like I'm better than everyone else. Some of the other beach communities out here are like that. I can barely stomach going there when I have to."

I smirked. "What is it you don't like exactly?"

"All the fakeness. The fake people, the fake things. I prefer the people in my life to be authentic, you know? Wait, do I

DEAR HEART, I HATE YOU

sound crazy? I probably sound crazy."

Jules needed to stop talking. I needed to stop asking her questions. Because every damn thing she said made her more and more attractive to me, and I was already in over my head here.

"No, I get it. East Coast money is the same. The worst are the families that come from old money. They walk around like they're royalty, as if everyone should be grateful for their presence."

She nodded. "I just don't get it. Do I want money? Yes. Do I want nice things? Yes. But will I become a total bitch who looks down her nose at people? Never."

"You're secure." I reached for her hand. "You know who you are, and your priorities aren't all screwed up. Most people aren't like that, Jules. They have fucked-up ideas about what really matters. They get a little money and they lose themselves."

"I like that." She smiled as she mulled over my words. "They get money and they lose themselves. So simple, but so true."

Our waiter came back with our drinks and asked if we needed more time.

"Yeah, sorry. We haven't even looked at our menus yet," I said, feeling like an ass.

"But in the meantime, we'll take the sampler for two," Jules suggested before looking at me. "It's delicious. A bunch of seafood for us to share."

"Sounds perfect." I opened my menu, trying to concentrate on it, but all I wanted was to focus my attention on Jules. I loved talking to her, learning the way her mind worked, hearing the things she thought.

"What about you?" she asked, distracting me from the menu again.

"What do you mean?"

"When you get more money, are you going to lose yourself?" she teased.

"I'm already so far gone, I'm never coming back," I answered playfully before lifting her hand to my lips and pressing a kiss there.

"Be serious. What kind of guy are you when it comes to money?"

"The kind of guy who likes money and wants a lot more of it?" I shrugged. "I don't know, Jules. I like nice things too, like you said. I would love to own a few properties, and I like nice cars. But I don't want to turn into some pompous asshole because I can afford nice stuff."

"I don't think you will."

I raised my eyebrows. "Why not?"

"Because I think Cooper would kick your ass," she said with a laugh, referring to my little brother. "Plus, you spend a lot of your time volunteering. Pompous assholes don't usually tend to do that. Unless they're doing it for the press or having cameras following them around. Is that why you do it, Cal? For all the accolades?"

I shook my head, wondering what the hell to do with this woman. Part of me wanted to bend her over my knee and spank her.

"Yes, Jules. I spend my time teaching kids about math and finance for the fame that comes with it."

"Figures."

"What am I going to do with you?" I asked her rhetorically.

"You tell me," she said with a slight smirk and a shrug.

"I could think of a few things." I glanced around us at the busy lunch crowd. "But they don't involve a single one of these people."

Jules threw her hand in the air. "Check, please," she said before we'd even gotten our food.

I had to laugh. This woman was downright perfect.

NAPS ARE UNDERRATED

Jules

LUNCH WAS DELICIOUS, and I think Cal was impressed with not only the food, but with Malibu as well. I wasn't sure why I wanted him to love where I lived so much, but a part of me definitely did.

We were driving down PCH back toward my apartment when Cal asked if I could show him a property.

"Really? You want to see a house?" Surprised, I glanced at him before turning back toward the road.

"Yeah. Can we?"

I nodded. "Uh-huh. But you might have to act like you're a client if other people are there."

He gave me a devilish grin. "I can do that."

"I'm sure you can."

As I drove, my mind raced. What kind of property should I show him? Something in one of the few neighborhoods, or something over-the-top fancy?

"I already know what you're thinking," Cal said. "Show me something in an exclusive area. Is there anything?"

My mind immediately zeroed in on this house in The Colony. It was traditional Nantucket style, and I wondered if he'd be drawn to it because the style would be familiar.

"I have the perfect place," I said with my own devilish grin as I pulled toward a security gate. When the guard approached, I flashed my Realtor badge and signed in.

"So, Miss Abbott. Tell me a little about where we are," Cal asked, his tone professional.

"Well, Mr. Donovan, we are in a section of Malibu called The Colony. It's literally one mile of the most exclusive and sought-after beachfront properties. It used to be *the* place to be back in Hollywood's heyday. It was Celebrity Central; things happened here that we've watched on the big screen or read about in magazines."

As I gave him the spiel, I started to get excited at the thought of how much history the neighborhood held. "The beaches are private, and although the public can access it in places, for the most part, they don't. The homes typically range in price from fifteen to twenty million, but the property I'm showing you today is a steal at only nine ninety-five."

I pursed my lips to keep from smiling as I pulled in front of the modest two-story home. To be honest, it didn't look like much from the outside. This house, like most of those in the area, had been built in the early forties.

"This looks like the Cape," he said as he climbed out of the car.

I knew he'd think so. "It's Nantucket style in architecture, and was built in 1942. It has three bedrooms and three baths, and is roughly twenty-three hundred square feet," I said as I opened the front door. "There's also a two-car garage, and everything has been newly painted."

"Holy shit," Cal said as we walked through, no doubt stunned by the ocean view showcased by the floor-to-ceiling windows. "What a view." He walked straight toward the double doors and opened them, stepping outside onto the brick patio and deck.

When I followed him out, he turned and grabbed me by the waist and positioned my body in front of his. He wrapped his arms around me and we stood like that, my back pressed to his chest, staring at the ocean in front of us for who knew how long. Nothing mattered as long as he held me that way.

"The beach is private?" he whispered against my ear.

"Mm-hmm," was all I managed, the feel of his groin pressing against me more than a little distracting.

"What are the other features?" he asked, moving my hair to the side and running his lips along my neck.

"Um, the kitchen has all stainless steel appliances with warm wood cabinetry. There are two bedrooms and bathrooms on the main floor, and the entire upstairs is the master suite." I breathed out as he kissed me again. "It's floor-to-ceiling windows up there as well. The view is unbelievable, and . . . Oh hell, who cares?" I said before turning around to face him, my lips meeting his as my need for him continued to build.

"I can't get enough of you, Jules," he said between kisses, and I couldn't agree more.

"Let's get out of here," I suggested as we practically sprinted to my car.

As I navigated the PCH, Cal's hand didn't stay settled in its usual spot on my thigh. No, it inched closer to my sweet spot, his fingers brushing against me lightly, causing sounds to escape from my throat without warning.

"You're going to make me crash."

I glanced at him before reaching for his pants, and feeling the bulge there, squeezed lightly. The hard feel of him made my thighs clench, and even though I'd just had him this morning, it suddenly seemed like way too long ago.

He moaned as I continued to stroke the length of him, his fingers pausing in their torture campaign on my body.

I couldn't get home fast enough.

The stupid privacy gate wouldn't open quickly enough.

And I couldn't pull into my parking spot swiftly enough.

We raced each other up the stairs, one thing on our minds as I struggled to get the key in the slot.

"Jules," Cal growled out, pressing his body against my back as I fumbled with the key.

"That isn't helping," I warned.

The key finally slid in and I pushed the door open as Cal pulled my purse from my shoulder and dropped it to the floor, the contents spilling out around our feet. I'd get it later. Right now, his mouth was hot on mine, our bodies connected as he walked me backward toward my room, bumping us into the walls along the way. Heat spread between us, my body feeling like it was on fire with every touch.

As if his patience had worn thin, Cal scooped me into his arms in the hallway, his mouth still attached to mine as he walked me through the doorway and deposited me onto my bed. He unbuttoned his shirt, and I stopped breathing for a moment to watch as his glorious chest was revealed.

"Get naked, Jules," he demanded, his voice throaty.

I did as he asked, but he was distracting. I tried to take off my clothes without tearing my eyes from his body, but it was a challenge. When I removed the last article of clothing, I found Cal watching me with hungry eyes as he bit his bottom lip.

"Mine," I said possessively as I reached for him, pulling him down on top of me.

Taking his bottom lip between my teeth, I nibbled and

licked at it, loving how soft it was in contrast to the rest of his scruffy face. The feel of his bare stomach against mine caused my eyes to close for only a moment. When I reopened them, his hazel eyes were fixed on mine.

The look in his eyes combined with the feel of his skin on mine caused the zoo inside me to come to life. I wasn't sure what animals were in there, but they sure as shit weren't butterflies. Something much larger was wreaking havoc inside my chest. Probably a dinosaur. With large feet. Stomping around inside me like it owned the place.

The tip of Cal's length pressed against me and I literally ached for him, my need growing to an almost ridiculous level. I raised my hips up as I bit at his lip again, sucking and licking, running my tongue across it. He pushed inside me, and a moan escaped as I exhaled quickly.

"You okay?" he asked.

"God, yes," I answered, almost breathless as he attacked my mouth with his, our movements fueled by passion, by lust, by desire.

How could someone feel *this* good inside me? I'd liked sex in the past; it had always been fine. But that was just it—it had always been *fine*. It had never quite been like this.

Cal worked his hips, moving in and out of me as I bucked against him, the pressure building. I dug my fingers into his back, pulling him into me. Harder. Deeper. Faster. We came together, again and again and again, until I couldn't hold on anymore.

"Let go, Jules," Cal breathed against my ear, his back slick with sweat as he pressed a kiss to my cheek.

My neck arched back and I released a cry, my body convulsing as waves of pleasure moved through me. Cal mumbled something I couldn't decipher before his body jerked repeatedly and he collapsed on top of me, our breathing erratic and shallow.

"Still epic?" he asked with a smile.

"Oh yeah." I couldn't even toy with him at this point; my body was spent in the best way possible.

"You might kill me this weekend, woman."

"Not if you kill me first."

He slid over so he was no longer covering me completely, but parts of him still pressed against parts of me. I closed my eyes for only a moment, but when I reopened them, the room was dark.

Shit.

My eyes bleary, I glanced at the clock on my DVD player. It was a little after six. We still had plenty of time before we needed to be at Tami's.

Relieved, I closed my eyes again and reveled in the fact that I was all tangled up in Cal, in more ways than one.

CAL WAS OUT. I wiggled myself out from under him and plugged in my curling iron, pulled out my makeup bag, and hung up my outfit in the bathroom. It would take me longer to get ready than it would take him, so I figured I'd let him sleep a little more.

He looked gorgeous, lying there in my bed, wrapped in my sheets, his dark hair all mussed. I couldn't resist taking a picture of him with my phone. I realized in that moment that we hadn't taken a single photo together since he'd gotten here. I'd make sure Tami remedied that later. No need to keep staring at the ones from Boston every night when I could have new ones to look at.

"Hey." I shook his shoulder lightly and pressed my lips to his temple. "Cal?"

He grumbled before rubbing his eyes and blinking up at me. "Hi. How long was I out?"

"We both crashed, but you need to get up and get ready. Do you want a bourbon or some coffee?"

"Bourbon, babe. Always bourbon." He reached for my waist and pulled me on top of his lap before tangling his hand in my hair and pulling my mouth to his. "I love kissing you."

"You're telling me." I ran my finger along the curve of his bottom lip before taking it into my mouth and sucking gently.

"Better stop," he warned, and I laughed.

"We can't. We have to get ready. I'll go get you that bourbon." I smiled as I pulled out of his grasp.

"This is the night I'm dressing up, right?" he called out from the room.

"Yes!" I shouted back as I poured his drink and brewed some coffee for me.

A moment later, I walked back into the bedroom with both drinks in hand. Cal wasn't in my room, so I headed into the bathroom.

My jaw dropped open slightly when I saw him dressed in a navy suit and a crisp white button-down shirt. The shirt's top two buttons were undone, and I drank him in as he leaned toward the mirror and fussed with his hair.

"Wow. You look so hot," I said before handing him his bourbon.

"Is this okay for Hollywood?" he asked, meeting my eyes in the mirror.

"It's perfect. I'd better get dressed."

I grabbed my outfit hanging on the back of the door and slipped out of the yoga pants and tank that I'd worn while doing my hair and makeup. As I tossed my clothes on the floor, I noticed Cal's gaze on me. When he took a step toward me, I put my hand up to stop him.

"Don't come closer, Cal. I mean it. We have to get to Tami's on time."

"You should have gotten undressed somewhere else then, Jules. What do you expect?"

"Self-control." I narrowed my eyes at him as I took a tentative step back, and he sipped his bourbon, watching me through hooded eyes.

I stepped into my high-waisted black pencil skirt that fit me perfectly, hugging every curve on my body and stopping well above my knees. My black sleeveless blouse was beautiful, the material light and flowy as I tucked it in. Moving to the tub, I sat on the edge and slipped into my black heels with white pearl straps. To finish off the look, I pulled on a white dress jacket, which added the perfect amount of pop to the otherwise dark outfit.

Checking myself in the mirror one last time, I fussed with my hair, which now had long, loose waves in it, and touched up the contouring on my cheeks.

"You look stunning." Cal stepped behind me as we stared at our reflections in the mirror. We looked damn good together.

"Cal, we need a selfie," I said as I reached for my phone. Holding it in front of us, we both smiled as I took a picture.

"One more," he said as he kissed my neck from behind, and I took another. Damn it, if this guy wasn't going to be the death of me somehow. "You liked our kissing pictures from

Boston."

"Of course I did. I'm a girl," I said without thinking.

He stepped next to me and took my phone from my hand as he kissed my lips tenderly, but with determination.

"Now I have to fix my lipstick again," I complained half-heartedly when he pulled away.

"You're going to have that problem all night if you don't just leave it off," he said with a smirk, so I reached for the tube and plopped it into my clutch.

"Ready?"

"Ready," he said.

I looked him up and down, liking what I saw.

"I still can't believe you're here." I got all giddy again, as if this was somehow a dream I'd wake up from.

Cal chuckled. "I can't believe I get to meet Tami."

Shit. I prayed she wasn't wearing her pink contacts as I typed out a text and told her we were on our way.

HOLLYWOOD NIGHTS

Jules

I HEADED THE car toward Tami's house, not only excited because I was taking Cal to Hollywood, but also at the thought that he and Tami were finally meeting. I assumed they'd hit it off, but Tami could be a real ballbuster, and it would seriously suck for me if she hated him.

I glanced at Cal in his suit, his hair perfectly messed up in spikes, and decided he looked dapper. Stupid word, but it fit. Tami was going to love him.

"So, tell me everything I need to know about tonight." Cal settled into the passenger seat, his hand resting on my thigh, as usual.

"The guy who owns the club is Ron. He's one of my clients, and I've known him for years. He owns a handful of nightclubs in the area, all super successful. I don't know much about his background. I think his mom might have been an actress at some point, but I don't know for sure. What I do know is that all of his clubs are popular with celebrities, and are usually the clubs you see people stumbling out of in the tabloids."

"Is he a nice guy?"

"Really nice. Pretty normal, just super involved in his

businesses and making sure they're successful. But you'll like him. He's not a dick at all. I can't say the same for whoever else might be there tonight."

I shook my head. While celebrities were usually fairly normal people, some were total assholes with huge egos and bad attitudes.

"What's tonight's event about?"

"I think Ron said that some actor was starting his own line of tequila, so it's a promotional party for that, and maybe someone's birthday. I don't know exactly, to be honest. Whenever Ron invites me, I come because his parties are usually really fun, but they're also good for networking. Ron introduces me to everyone. He's great about that."

Cal nodded his head slowly, as if lost in thought. "That's really cool that he does that."

I reached for his hand on my thigh and squeezed it. "Don't worry. I'll make sure he takes you around too," I said before stopping short. "If you want. You can take out-of-town clients, right?"

A slow smirk appeared. "Yeah. I have clients all over the country. But that would be great, Jules. Thank you."

I shrugged. "Not a problem."

Knowing Ron, he would happily introduce Cal to anyone who might need his services. It was a long shot, since most people would most likely be set up already in the financial end of things, but you never knew what could happen. Plus, if I could help Cal, I wanted to. I knew he'd do the same for me.

Tami lived below Sunset Boulevard in West Hollywood. And while we could technically walk to the club from her place, I knew we weren't going to.

As I pulled into her short driveway, I looked at Cal.

"We're here."

"Cool place," he said as he glanced at the lighting in her yard. "Does she own it?"

"No. It's a rental, but the location is killer and it's not an apartment. Tami couldn't handle the whole shared-wall thing. Before she moved here, I thought she was going to murder someone if she didn't find a new place."

He reached for my hand as we headed toward her front door. Instead of walking right in, I knocked first and waited, not exactly sure why since it wasn't what I'd normally do.

"Come in," she shouted from somewhere in the house, and I turned the door handle and stepped inside.

Tami came flying around the corner from her bedroom and leaped into Cal's arms. He laughed and hugged her as she kissed his cheek.

"Oh yeah, did I forget to mention that she's crazy?" I pointed at my best friend who was currently molesting my . . . Cal.

"I already knew," he said as he set her onto her feet.

"Cal, it's so nice to meet you in real life," she said with a big smile that I was thrilled to see was genuine.

"You too."

As he took her in, he paused at her eyes, and I worried for a second that she had those damn pink contacts in. But when she glanced at me, I saw she was wearing the ones that made her eyes an unnatural shade of green.

"Your eyes," he said before looking at me and then back at her.

Oh Lord. If Cal complimented Tami's fake eyes, I might have to end whatever this was between us immediately. I begged him silently to not be that guy, to please be smarter than the rest, as he continued to glance awkwardly between us.

"Your eyes aren't real, are they?" he finally said, and I wanted to shout with joy.

Tami parked a hand on one hip. "What do you mean, Cal?"

"It's just . . . don't get me wrong, Tami, they're attractive, but they're not normal," he said, his expression wary as if he was afraid of offending her. "Contacts, right?"

She laughed. "Yes, they're contacts. I don't have green eyes. Mine are boring and brown and I get tired of them, so I spice it up. Speaking of, I need to finish getting dressed. Help yourself to whatever. I'll be right back."

When Tami was gone, I grinned up at Cal. "I freaking love you for not telling her how pretty her eyes are," I blurted without thinking. "Not love-love you. You know what I mean." I waved a hand, hoping I hadn't completely freaked him out.

He pulled me close and kissed the tip of my nose. "Your eyes are prettier. I love the color."

Inside, I moaned a private little sigh. I wouldn't have been surprised if all my bones had turned to sand and I slipped right through his fingers. Who knew I could be such a sap?

"You want a beer?" I asked as I pulled open her fridge.

"Yeah, sounds great. But I can get it."

"I know you can." I pulled out a bottle and handed it to him. "I'll be right back. I'm going to make sure she's actually getting ready and not texting, or we'll be here all night. You okay?"

He looked around her living room. "I think I'll manage."

I hustled into the bathroom. Tami still wasn't dressed, but was instead focused on clipping blood-red and neon-blue extensions into her hair.

"I hate to feed your ego, but those look fierce." I reached for one of the blue strands.

"I know." She smiled in the mirror before turning around to face me. "First of all, he's stupid hot and looks so good. A man who knows how to dress is such a turn-on," she said, her face serious. "Second, he's awesome, Jules. He let me hop into his arms and he knew my eyes were fake. What a keeper." She smirked at me before turning back around.

I wasn't sure how to respond so I just grinned, knowing my best friend would have more to say on the subject.

"How has the weekend been so far?" she asked. "Oh my God, Jules." Her eyebrows shot up as if she'd only just remembered something important. "How was the sex? Tell me right now!"

My cheeks warmed, and the mirror revealed I was blushing. "It was . . ." I glanced around, searching for the right word.

"It was what? Awful? Awesome? Amazing? Terrible? I'm dying here, Jules. Tell me." She frowned at me, contorting her lips in the mirror as she lined them and applied deep red lipstick.

"It was incredible," I said with a sigh. "I don't know what the hell I've been doing all those other times, but it wasn't that."

She tilted her head, her eyes meeting mine in the mirror. "Aw, you finally found a man who knows how to fuck properly. I'm so proud of you. And happy for you."

I bit my lip to keep from smiling. "You're so inappropriate."

"I know, but I'm right. Hand me my dress. You look

gorgeous, by the way." She started to slip out of her clothes but paused to call out, "Don't come back here, Cal. I'm getting naked, and I wouldn't want you to fall in love with me while Jules is standing right here."

I smacked her shoulder. "You're an idiot. Seriously."

"Stop trying to seduce me with your fake eyes and hot body, Tami," he yelled from the other room, and I giggled.

"I knew you wanted me," she yelled back, and I wanted to do a crazy victory dance at the easy way the two of them got along.

I touched up my lipstick in the mirror before giving Tami a once-over in her gorgeous red dress. "You look amazing."

"I'd look better with my pink contacts, but someone won't let me wear them." She rolled her eyes.

"Listen, devil woman, I'm doing you a favor. Don't you want to make friends?"

She pouted. "Not really."

Laughing, I said, "Let's go."

We walked arm and arm into the living room where Cal was sitting on her leather sofa, finishing off his beer. He set it down on a coaster when we appeared, his eyes widening.

"Jesus, you two. I get to walk in there with both of you on my arm?"

"Charmer." Tami winked. "Are you driving or should we call a car?"

"I don't plan on drinking much and they have valet. I can just drive. It will be easier," I offered.

Normally we'd call for a car, but usually I'd be drinking way more and didn't feel like dealing with the parking situation. This was different.

"Cal, take a picture of me and Jules, please?" Tami handed

him her phone as we posed. "Thank you."

"Will you take one of us?" I asked her, and she snatched my cell from my hand.

"Anyone ever told you two that you look perfect together? It's gross, actually," she said.

I stuck out my tongue, and she chose that moment to take the picture. When I started to complain, she held up her hand.

"I'll take more. Hold your horses."

"Oh, Cal loves horses. Don't you, Cal," I said, meaning the tops he collected from his bourbon.

He grinned at me before leaning down and kissing me thoroughly, ruining the lipstick I'd just redone.

"Told you not to keep putting it on," he said when he ended the kiss.

Breathless, I blinked up at him. I'd almost forgotten that Tami was there, taking pictures.

"Hello," she said, snapping her fingers at us. "Can I have one where you're both looking at me, please?"

Cal wrapped his arm around my waist and pulled me close. I leaned my head toward his shoulder, my arm around his back as I smiled.

"Perfect," she said before handing me my phone. "You owe me. You're going to die with how many I took."

I quickly swiped through them as excitement tore through me. She really had taken a bunch of candid shots, which was awesome, and I turned the phone off so I could look at them later. I mouthed *thank you* to her as we headed for her door.

"I like your place, Tami. It's really nice," Cal said as he held the door open for us.

"Thanks. It was a steal, and perfect timing. It's a first-time rental."

"The architecture is cool. It's so woodsy," he said before looking at me as we piled into my car. "I'm not the real estate guru, so I don't know what it's called."

I smiled. "It's an old Craftsman. All original beams and wood. It's a great house."

THE CLUB WAS about a five-minute drive from Tami's house, ten with Saturday night traffic. I pulled up to the valet in front of the building and gave him my name.

He nodded and opened my door for me, waiting as I carefully maneuvered out of the driver's seat so as not to show off my goods. Paparazzi swarmed us, and even though we were technically nobodies, a few flashes still went off.

Cal positioned himself between me and Tami, giving each one of us an arm. We walked up to the entrance, where an older gentleman dressed in black glanced at us before smiling, his earpiece and clipboard identifying him as the greeter. Ron preferred to used the same people at his events when possible. He said he liked the idea of having people be familiar and comfortable, believing it took the edge off.

"Jules." Razz smiled at me before giving me a kiss on my cheek. "Tami," he said, greeting her the same way. "And who is this, besides the luckiest gent of the evening." He extended a hand toward Cal.

"Hi, Razz," I said with a smile. "This is Cal. He's here from Boston for the weekend."

"You know how lucky you are, right?" Razz asked him, and Cal grinned.

"I'm aware."

Razz scanned his clipboard and crossed off our names

before adding the time next to it. Even though he knew us, he still needed to mark that we'd arrived, and for whatever reason, Ron liked to know when his guests showed up.

"All right, you three. Go have a good time."

"Is Ron already here?"

Razz cocked his head to the side. "Are you kidding? He's been here since five."

I laughed. "Have a good night, Razz."

"You too, doll. You ladies look stunning," he said as we headed through the door.

I loved this particular club because it was split up into sections. There was a dance floor that boomed with the bass from the DJ, but there were also separate sitting areas where you could actually conduct business or have conversations without shouting to be heard. There was something about a space that fit multiple needs that appealed to me.

As we walked in, a guy in a tuxedo approached us with a tray in his hand. "Tequila shots?" he offered.

Remembering that the party was to promote this particular brand of tequila, I took one and made sure Cal and Tami did too. It would be rude not to.

When the waiter slipped away, the three of us glanced at one another.

"I hate tequila," I said with a groan.

"Me too," Cal said, grimacing at his shot.

Tami rolled her eyes. "Well, I love it. Stop being pussies and try it, then give me the rest," she said before clanking her plastic shot glass against ours. "Cheers." She downed it without making a face.

"Like a pro," she said, still watching us. "Are you two going to stare at yours all night, or are you going to drink it?

It's actually pretty good."

When I sniffed my shot glass, my insides quivered. One bad tequila night back in college and I'd banned the stuff from my life until now. I didn't even care for it in a mixed drink, much less down it by itself.

"Just give it to me," Tami said before taking it from my hand and tossing it down her throat. "What's your excuse?" she asked Cal.

"Not a tequila guy, honestly," he said with a shrug.

"But you'll drink that bourbon shit all night, and that stuff's awful," she snapped at him before turning her back to us and moving through the crowd.

Cal grabbed my hand as we followed her. "I think your best friend hates me," he said sadly, and I laughed.

"She'll get over it," I promised.

Tami led us in the direction of the dance floor, which had women dancing in choreographed routines on top of elevated platforms. It was mesmerizing to watch them; they were awesome. I looked around the room for Ron, hoping to introduce him to Cal before it got too crowded or late.

"I'm going to head over to the bar over there. I see something I like." Tami pointed toward the corner and I nodded, noting the group of guys standing there.

"Isn't that . . ." Cal stopped himself from pointing at a couple dancing on the dance floor.

I followed his stare and smiled. "If you're thinking it's Quinn Johnson and Ryson Miller, then you'd be right."

Quinn and Ryson were one of the hottest young couples in Hollywood. They were both actors who also happened to live in Malibu together, and although I hadn't sold them their house, my boss had.

"Nice." Cal sounded composed, but I could tell he was impressed.

"Are you freaking out right now?" I squeezed his hand, now realizing that seeing celebrities like this would be a totally new experience for him.

"No. It's just a little surreal, is all. Lucas would shit if he were here. I can't wait to tell him I saw Ryson Miller. He's had a crush on him since he was like fifteen or so."

I laughed. "Who hasn't?"

Ryson was ridiculously hot and had that bad-boy appeal going for him. And Quinn was absolutely stunning in person, and was the one person who seemed to have tamed the beast that was Ryson, which made them even more adorable.

"Let's go into another room. I want to introduce you to Ron, if I can find him." I pulled Cal by the hand and walked away from the pounding music and beautiful dancers.

Leaving the groups of people behind, I took a left and walked us down a long, dark corridor.

"Is this where you murder me and leave my body in pieces?" Cal asked, squeezing my hand.

"No. That happens later. We'll dump your body in the hills so no one will find you. We have coyotes, you know," I said with a raised eyebrow.

"Reassuring."

Around a corner and up a flight of stairs, I found Ron chatting up a blonde on one of the many velvet lounges in the room. As I reached the top step, he noticed me and his entire face lit up.

"Jules!" he called out before saying something to the girl that I recognized as Tabbie James, an actress I'd met many times before. He stood up and made his way toward us, dressed to the nines in a black suit and tie. His brown hair and beard were longer than I'd seen them before, obviously growing out.

"Love the beard." I tugged at it playfully.

"You look hot as hell." He pulled me into a hug and kissed my cheek. "Is this the elusive Cal I had to add as your guest?"

"The one and only," I said as Cal stepped forward and shook his hand.

"It's nice to meet you, Ron. Thanks for letting me crash. This is a great place and a great party," he said sincerely, his natural charm coming out.

"Thank you. Glad you could make it. Cal, Jules tells me that you work in finance."

"I do."

"Do you think we could talk a little business?" Ron asked. "That is, if Jules doesn't mind. And if you don't mind talking work on a Saturday night, Cal."

When they both looked to me, I threw up my hands. "Have at it. I'll just go grab a drink." I gave Cal a quick kiss and watched as he followed Ron back toward Tabbie, who still sat alone on the lounge chair.

Although I knew Cal was a little excited, he looked at ease and totally in his element as he shook her hand and made himself comfortable, looking back and forth between her and Ron. His demeanor was all business, and it was hot to watch. He talked with his hands a lot, something I hadn't noticed until now, and it was adorable. *He* was adorable.

I smiled to myself as I made my way over toward the bar, hoping they had something more than the featured tequila available.

The bartender smiled as I approached. "What can I get

you?"

"Tell me I don't have to get tequila," I begged, and he laughed.

"We're supposed to only serve the tequila. We have a bunch of specialty drinks featuring it, but I can get you whatever you want. I have a full bar back here."

I let out a sigh of relief. "Thank you so much. Can I just get a vodka cran, and do you happen to have a good bourbon?"

"Of course." He smiled, his dimples on full display. "Any vodka preference?"

"Yes. Belvedere or Cîroc."

"You got it," he said before pouring and mixing my drink. "Any bourbon preference?"

"I actually don't know a thing about it. But he likes Blanton's, if that helps," I said.

The bartender frowned for a moment. "We don't have Blanton's, but I have something comparable that he'll like."

"You're the best. I'm going to tell Ron to keep you forever."

He smiled again. "I'd appreciate that. It's actually my first time working at one of his events."

"I really will put in a good word for you."

"Thank you."

I paid for the drinks, left him a tip, and walked over to where Cal was still sitting, deep in conversation.

"Sorry. I don't mean to interrupt; I just wanted to bring you this." I offered the bourbon to Cal, who smiled and kissed my hand after taking the drink.

"Thanks so much, babe."

"I'm going to go find Tami. Take your time. It's nice to

see you again, Tabbie," I said as I smiled at her.

"You too, Jules. Thanks for letting us borrow him," she said, batting her fake eyelashes.

"No problem."

"Jules." Ron reached for my wrist and pulled me toward him. "I have a couple people I want you to meet. They're thinking about getting a summer home, and I suggested Malibu."

"You're the best. Thank you." I kissed his cheek. "By the way, that bartender over there was a sweetheart. Don't let him go."

He glanced toward the bar. "I'll make sure I talk to him before I leave for the night. I got your boy here. Go have fun."

Knowing Cal would be tied up for a while, I headed back downstairs and toward the dance floor, where I assumed Tami still was. When I walked into the room, which had grown exponentially more crowded than when I'd just left it, I saw Tami right where I expected her to be—standing in the center of a group of guys, her arm around one of them. No doubt he was complimenting her on her exotic green eyes.

I walked over, and her face split into a big smile when she noticed me. I had to bite my tongue to keep myself from commenting on how red her face was from drinking.

"Jules! Guys, this is my best friend, Jules, and her—" She looked past my shoulder. "Where's Cal? Oh my God, did you ditch him? Jules, I liked him. Where is he? Did you send him back to Boston?"

I grabbed her shoulders and squared her to face me. "He's talking to Ron and Tabbie about work stuff."

"Seriously? What kind of work stuff?"

"I don't know, but Ron asked him if he worked in finance,

and then said he needed to talk to him."

"Interesting," she said before sipping whatever she was drinking.

"I thought so too." I swirled my drink around, making the ice clink against the glass.

We hung out there together, chatting with the guys, who apparently worked at one of the studios in town, and doing some people watching. Tami was flirting with one of the guys, and if I knew my best friend, which I did, she planned on taking him home later.

Feeling like hours had passed, I told Tami I was going to check on Cal before leaving her in the arms, literally, of her future one-night stand. She stood on her tiptoe and whispered something into his ear before she motioned for me to come back.

"What?" I had to practically shout my question over the noise of the crowd.

"I don't need a ride home. Okay?"

Not happy with the situation, I studied the guy. He was tall, built, and looked sort of sweet with his hipster glasses perched on his nose.

"Are you sure?"

She cocked her head. "I'm sure."

"Please be safe." I turned toward the guy, whose name I had already forgotten. "What's your name, and where do you work again?" His face paled slightly before he answered my questions, and I gave him an evil smile. "Good. You kill her, I turn you in to the cops."

"Uh . . ." He shot an uncertain glance at Tami, who glared at me.

"She's joking."

I leaned close to whisper in her ear. "I'm not. You need to be more careful, please. There are crazy people in this world. Probably here at this party, as a matter of fact."

She sucked in a breath and a crease formed on her forehead. "You're right. I'll text you later when I get home, and I'll call you tomorrow."

Confused, I asked, "Are you leaving already?"

"No. Not yet, but soon."

I shook my head and left to check on Cal. I had no idea how much time had passed, but it felt like forever. As I turned down the long corridor, I spotted him coming toward me.

"Cal!" I quickened my pace.

He opened his arms and pulled me into a hug before kissing my lips. "I think I just got hired to handle Tabbie's finances," he said with an incredulous look on his face.

"Seriously?" I asked, completely surprised.

"I'll tell you about it on the way home."

"Okay," I said, super excited for what all this meant for Cal.

Then a director I recognized tapped Cal on the shoulder and asked if he could speak to him. Cal cast a glance at me before I stepped aside with a smile.

I made my way back through the crowd toward Tami, who forced me to dance with her for the next hour. My body dripped with sweat as we shook our asses and danced like no one was watching.

When someone gripped my waist and turned me toward them, my hands instantly balled into fists and my body turned rigid.

"It's just me," Cal said as he released me, and I threw myself into his arms.

"Sorry I'm sweaty."

"It looks good on you." He kissed my cheek. "My little salt queen."

"Gross," I said with a mock snarl as the guy Tami had picked for the night approached her.

Tami turned to us. "We're leaving. I'll talk to you later, girl. 'Bye, Cal. It was nice to meet you." She gave him a hug and whispered something into his ear. He bit back a smile before turning serious and nodding his head.

We watched her walk away with her guy before I asked, "Did you want to stay and mingle some more?"

"No." He pulled me close and pressed his lips against my forehead. "I'm ready to go whenever you are."

I wanted to be home in that instant. Why hadn't someone invented a transportation machine yet?

"Now. I'm ready to go now," I said, and he smiled.

"Good. I'd rather all this sweat on your body have come from the things I'm doing to it."

My thighs quivered as I sucked in my bottom lip and pulled him toward the exit. The evening air was cooler than I expected, and when it hit my sweat, it made me shiver. Cal noticed and wrapped me in his arms, tucking me against his side as we waited for the valet to bring my car around.

"So, spill. I'm dying here," I said as soon as we were alone in my car.

"Jules, that was insane. Apparently, Tabbie just fired her finance guy. She found out he was stealing from her," he said, and I nodded my head. "Ron did too."

"That's right," I said as recognition dawned on me. "Bernard. He was stealing from a lot of people out here. It's been a big deal." I couldn't believe that I hadn't put two and two together. It had been all over the news for the last couple of weeks.

"Right. So she was telling me about this and how she needs a financial advisor, but she doesn't trust anyone in Hollywood right now since Bernard had come so highly recommended. She said she'd like to use someone outside of Hollywood, not wrapped up in the business. I have a call set up with both her and Ron on Monday to finalize the paperwork, but I also have to follow up with twelve other people." He sounded excited and dumbfounded. "Twelve, Jules."

"Cal, this could be huge for you. You could corner a market with this."

The wheels in my head were turning. If Cal got one celebrity, it wouldn't be long before word of mouth got him more.

He laughed. "Lucas is gonna flip."

"Poor Lucas."

"I'm surprised he didn't make me bring him with me on this trip."

"Aw, you should bring him next time," I said without thinking, and when Cal didn't respond, I wished I could suck the words right back.

It was so easy to forget that he wasn't my boyfriend, or that what we had was still new and not set in stone the way I sometimes felt it was. Cal and I come a long way since we'd met in Boston, but we still hadn't discussed what any of it meant.

And for whatever reason, I was too nervous to be the one who brought it up.

LAST DAY

Jules

MY PHONE HAD been blowing up all morning, and as much as I wanted to continue ignoring it, I knew that I couldn't. I looked over at Cal, who watched me through sleepy eyes, even though it was almost noon. We'd stayed up half the night, drunk on the possibilities about his potential new clients and our desire for each other, each one fueling the other.

"I have to take this, I'm sorry."

"Don't apologize," he said as he rubbed my back and dropped a kiss on my bare shoulder.

I sat up on the bed and answered the call from one of my coworkers, who filled me in on the properties she'd been showing to one of my clients all weekend. They wanted to make an offer on one, and she asked if I wanted to jump in and handle the deal or if she should just take care of it. I glanced at Cal and handed the reins over to her, knowing that meant I'd have to split the commission.

In that moment, I didn't care about the money. My time with Cal was limited and I didn't want to spend it working, even if it came at a financial loss. I would always make more.

When I hung up, Cal pulled my body against his and spooned me.

"Work stuff?" he asked, running his fingers through my hair.

"Remember those clients I told you about? The ones who've been really hard to please?"

"Yeah."

"They're finally putting in an offer on a house."

"That's great. Do you have to go? You know I don't mind." He continued stroking my hair as I turned to face him, our mouths mere inches apart as his hazel eyes looked at me with concern.

"No. I handed them off to one of my co-agents for the weekend. She took them out last night and this morning. She's going to handle everything."

The muscles in his chest tightened as he moved to sit up. "What do you mean?"

I pushed myself up too, narrowing my eyes at him. "What do you mean, what do I mean? Which part has you confused?"

"You've been working with these clients for weeks, Jules. I don't want you to miss out or get screwed out of your commission just because I'm here."

"I'll still get commission. And I made a choice. I wanted to spend this weekend with you. I work pretty much every weekend, all the time. I work late at night almost every day. I'm at my clients' beck and call, basically." I reached for his hand and squeezed it. "I don't get to see you, ever. So if you're coming into town for the weekend, then yes, I'm going to hand off my clients to a co-agent, and I'm going to be okay with that."

I had no idea what Cal was thinking, but it was obvious the wheels were spinning in his head. Work had always come first for me, but being with Cal had changed that. It wasn't that he had replaced my career, but I definitely found myself wanting to make room for him, to share my time. There had to be a way to balance being successful with being in a relationship. Hell, people did it all the time, every single day. It was just that before meeting Cal, I'd never wanted that balance before, never sought out how to have it.

But I did now.

And I hadn't expected him to be upset about it.

"What's the matter?" I asked, my voice shaky.

"I hate the idea of you giving things up that you've worked so hard for, just because I'm here."

"I'm not giving anything up. You're reading way too much into this."

Cal seemed upset, and I wanted to calm him down. I knew now exactly what he was doing and thinking. A guy like Cal would look at what I'd done and interpret it as my taking a step backward in my career instead of forward. He would never want to be responsible for something like that.

"Please don't read into this," I practically begged him. "I know you are. It's nowhere near as big of a deal as you're making it out to be."

He stared at me, but his eyes looked right through me, suddenly making me feel invisible. He was questioning my decision making, and I could tell he felt guilty about it in some way.

When he asked, "Do you want me to head to the airport now," I freaked out.

"Don't you dare. We have to leave in a couple hours, as it is. Work can wait. I know that you and I don't normally believe in that kind of thing, but this weekend, right now, I do. I believe that while you're here with me, my work can wait." I hoped I sounded as convincing as I felt. I needed him to see reason, to understand. "Do you understand that? It's one client, Cal. Just one property. There will be others."

"Okay, Jules," he said with a forced smile that didn't reach his eyes. "If you say so."

But it was too late. Something had changed. I could see it in his eyes, could feel it in the air.

He scrubbed at his face before lying down and staring up at the ceiling.

Moving next to him, I pressed a soft kiss to his lips. "Did you want to go to Santa Monica? Maybe we could have lunch and walk around Third Street before you have to go."

"That sounds nice." He nodded, his eyes slowly moving to meet mine.

"Then you'd better get up," I said before hopping up from the bed and making my way toward my walk-in closet to get dressed.

"Should I pack my things? We aren't coming back here before the airport, right?" he called out.

I poked my head out from around the door. "Right. We won't be back."

As I said the words, it made me sad to know that when I came back to my apartment later, I'd be alone, without Cal.

THAT LITTLE SHIFT between us lingered as I drove toward Santa Monica. I hated how much I sensed it and wished I was wrong, but I knew that I wasn't.

Even with Cal's hand firmly planted on my thigh where it belonged, his disappointment, or whatever it was that he felt, was still there, hanging between us like a foul odor I couldn't swat away. A woman knew when a guy was off. We noted little things like facial expressions, tone of voice, and gestures, and I was no exception. I read into everything Cal said and everything he didn't say.

He did, however, hold my hand a little tighter than usual as we walked along the shop-lined street after eating.

"Is it always like this?" he asked.

I glanced around, unsure what he meant. "Like what?"

"This many people?"

I glanced around, trying to see it through his eyes. I was used to the crowd of people shopping and milling about on Third Street. I'd rarely seen it empty.

"Pretty much, yeah." It was one of the reasons why I had preferred living in Malibu. Santa Monica always seemed crowded, no matter the time of day or night, but Malibu wasn't that way at all. "You like it or not?"

"It's interesting. I prefer where you live, though," he said before kissing my cheek.

I smiled at him. "Me too."

"I need to run in there," Cal said, pointing toward a shop with souvenirs in the window.

"Lucas?" I guessed.

"Yep." Cal shook his head. "He's like a child. I can't come back without a present for him, or I'll never hear the end of it."

"I was kidding. But you know, you did see Ryson last night, and you didn't get a picture of him for Lucas," I reminded him.

"I couldn't take a picture of Ryson last night, but I really wanted to," he admitted with a smirk.

Cal searched the whole store for the perfect California gift for Lucas. He settled on a Santa Monica Pier snow globe that featured sand instead of snow, a key chain in the shape of California with Lucas's name on it, and a mug for the office.

"I think he'll love them all," I said.

"He'd better."

Cal's impending departure dampened the mood, both of us growing more silent as our remaining time ticked away. I didn't want him to go, but knew that he had to.

Knowing the reality of our situation didn't lessen the hurt. I wished he could stay, even though I'd never admit it, especially not now. I didn't want to do anything else that might push him away. We'd had such a great weekend up until that phone call this morning. It had been damned near perfect.

The airport was close and traffic was light, meaning our time was ending even quicker than I'd anticipated. The dread in my chest grew heavier, weighing me down as I neared the exit for LAX. It seemed silly of me to feel this way, but I liked Cal, probably more than even I realized.

As I pulled the car up to the curb at the departures, I schooled my features, not wanting my face to reflect my sadness.

"Don't be sad," Cal said, telling me I'd done a shitty job of hiding it. He pulled my hand to his lips and pressed a kiss on top.

"Wait," I said before he opened the door. I pulled out my phone and opened the camera app. "It's like tradition now," I said.

I smiled as he pressed his head against mine. When I'd taken a few pics, he reached for my chin, holding my face in place as he kissed me, his tongue gently sweeping inside my mouth.

I'm going to miss those damn lips and that tongue, I thought as he pulled away and opened the door. I popped the trunk before following him outside.

"I don't want you to go," I said, pouting as he pulled his duffel bag from the trunk.

"I don't want to go either, babe. This sucks." He pulled me into his arms tightly, as if he didn't know when he'd get the chance to do it again. Hell, neither of us did.

"I hate this." My voice was muffled against his chest as he patted my hair.

He pressed his lips against the top of my head. "I'll call you when I land."

My eyes started to fill as I silently berated myself. I refused to cry simply because Cal was going home. After all, that's where he lived, and I needed to accept that.

Giving him a trembling smile, I said, "Have a safe flight."

He kissed me again, but this kiss was rougher, more desperate, filled with want, desire, and unspoken promises. "I had a really great time this weekend. Thank you for everything."

My cheeks warmed. "Thank you for coming out. It was so much fun."

He stood behind my car, holding his bag awkwardly, as if unsure of how to walk away from me. I fidgeted in place, not knowing how to let him go. I sure as hell didn't want to.

Cal drew in a sharp breath and grabbed me again, pulling me tightly against him. "I really hate this."

"Me too." I kissed his mouth, my heart shattering. "So much."

Studying me with a pained expression, he said, "I'd better go or I might never leave." He gave me one last quick kiss and turned away quickly, as if afraid he might change his mind.

God, how I wanted him to.

Once he disappeared from my view completely, I climbed back into my car and had just started to pull away, but the ping of an incoming text message made me slam on my brakes.

DREAM LIPS: *I miss you already.*

With tears in my eyes, I tapped out a response.

JULES: *Come back.*

LOSING IT

Cal

WALKING AWAY FROM Jules at the airport was fucking brutal. It was one thing to let her leave me back in Boston, but being the one who had to get on a plane after a weekend that amazing absolutely sucked. I wanted to turn around, get right back into her car, and tell her to take us home where I could make love to her for hours.

But I didn't. I couldn't.

I had to walk away, had to get on that plane, go home, and get back to work.

I also really needed to focus less on Jules and all of this long-distance shit, but there was little chance of that happening. I wondered for a minute how the hell I'd allowed myself to get sucked into something like this—a situation with no happy ending—before I fantasized about her naked body underneath me and forgot all about reality.

As soon as I landed, I called her to tell her I made it back home safely. She sounded tired, but her voice was sweeter than usual. We had bonded this weekend, on every level. As much as I might have wanted to convince myself otherwise for my sanity, I knew it was true. The only difference was that I was better at hiding it than she was. Jules had opened up to me so easily, so quickly, her feelings always so transparent and honest, but I tried to keep mine at bay.

Crawling into my bed alone that night after having Jules in my arms was just one more thing I added to the suck column of this whole thing. I'd been perfectly fine my entire life without having her next to me in bed, but now it felt ridiculously empty and cold.

Shaking my head, I reached for my phone and scrolled through the new pictures she had texted me of us. I'd just left, but she already felt worlds away.

WHEN I WOKE up the next morning, I texted Jules as usual, but also added that I missed her before I could talk myself out of it. There was a quiet battle starting to brew between my heart and my mind, and Lord only knew how I'd survive once the war finally broke out. I tried not to think about it as I got ready for work, preparing myself for the numerous questions that would inevitably come from Lucas.

Work was pretty standard, with the exception of my calls with Tabbie and Ron back in California. They both signed with me for a trial year, and I sensed that this was only the beginning of my celebrity client list. I planned on blowing their minds in that year and being someone they could depend on so thoroughly that they couldn't imagine not having me in their life, let alone making any financial decisions without consulting me. My bosses were ecstatic about the new additions to our client roster, and teased me about a prospective partnership coming about sooner rather than later.

Lucas wandered into my cubicle and perched on the edge of my desk, pouting. "I can't believe you saw Quinn and

Ryson at a party in Hollywood. Hell, I can't believe you went to a private party in Hollywood without me. Life isn't fair."

First thing this morning, I'd told him briefly about the party and my new clients before telling him I'd give him all the details after the stock market closed. He had freaked out, the way I knew he would when I mentioned Ryson's name, forcing me to threaten to pound on him if he didn't calm the hell down.

"It was from a distance," I said. "They were dancing. It's not like I talked to them or anything." I tried to play it cool as if it were no big deal, but we both knew that it was a pretty big damn deal.

Lucas crossed his arms over his chest, studying me. "You leave for the weekend and come back with two new clients, one of whom is an actress. A pretty big one too. How does this shit even happen?" When I just shrugged, he said, "I know how. Jules. Jules happened. Why couldn't she love me instead of you?"

I laughed. "I think we both know the reason for that."

"She could change me," he joked, mocking all the women who'd said those words to him in the past, wrongly thinking that his gender preference was simply a choice he'd made. "How is she, by the way?"

"Great, I think."

"You think? You don't know?"

"I haven't talked to her yet today. I assume she's good."

"You suck at being a boyfriend."

Bristling at the criticism, I said, "Then it's a good thing I'm not anyone's boyfriend now, isn't it?"

"Deny, deny, deny," he said in a singsong voice, and I wasn't sure why, but it bothered the hell out of me and made me uncomfortable.

"Go away." I shoved his ass off my desk, but he stubbornly stood there, refusing to leave.

"No."

I groaned. "What do you want?"

"I want to hear about your weekend," he insisted, raising his eyebrows. "The details."

I wasn't sure how I felt or how in depth I wanted to get, so I kept it vague. "We had a great time. That's all, Luc."

He raised his hands in the air in surrender. "Okay. You don't want to talk about it. I'll let it slide, for now. But . . ." He tilted his head, giving me an expectant look.

"But what?"

"Where are my presents?"

I bit back a smile. "What am I, your dad?"

"Don't act like you didn't bring me back something. We always bring each other gifts. You might be a shitty boyfriend to Jules," he said with a smug grin, "but you're a great one to me."

Resisting the urge to punch him, I opened one of my drawers and pulled out the bag from the souvenir shop. "Here," I said as I tossed it to him.

"I knew it!" He dug in like a kid at Christmas, pulling out each item before oohing and aahing over it. "Thank you."

"You're welcome, you big baby. Now get the hell out of my cube."

WHEN JULES CALLED me later that night, my heart leaped into my throat at the sound of her voice.

At the risk of sounding girly, I admitted, "I hate only

being able to talk on the phone with you after just being with you."

"I was just thinking the exact same thing. It's so much better seeing you face-to-face," she said, and her words made me smile.

"How was work?"

"Good. The deal went through and they got the house, so everyone's happy."

She sounded so pleased, it simultaneously made me happy for her and upset on her behalf. I was glad the deal went through, but still upset that she had to share her commission after doing the majority of the work for weeks.

"Wait! Did you talk to Ron and Tabbie today?" she asked.

"I did."

"And? Don't leave me hanging. What happened?"

"They signed with me for a year."

"That's so awesome! Congratulations. That's huge. I'm so happy for you."

"Thanks, Jules. And thank you for the introductions. I couldn't have done it without you."

"I didn't do anything but introduce you. You did the work of convincing them you're trustworthy. I'm really excited for you," she said, and I could tell that she meant it.

"Thanks, babe."

"I miss you," she said, the sadness in her voice stabbing at my heart.

"I miss you too."

Whatever we were to each other hung in the phone line between us, begging to be defined. I refused to acknowledge it, and I prayed to God that Jules wouldn't ask me to. I simply wasn't ready to go there, no matter how strong my feelings for her were. That fight silently raging inside me had primed a battlefield for war.

We ended the conversation like we always had in the past, and I forced myself to go to sleep instead of overthinking it like I tended to do.

THE REST OF the week flew by pretty much the same way. I'd set up five more calls with Hollywood's royalty, signing two of them after a detailed conversation. This new clientele fired me up more than usual, and I found myself wanting to work even harder and more effectively. I'd always taken pride in my work, but something about this was different, maybe because they were celebrities and had ridiculous amounts of money. I wasn't quite sure, but I knew that I wanted to impress them. I wanted to make a difference and be their go-to guy.

If I'd thought I couldn't stop thinking about Jules before I'd flown out to see her, I was seriously delusional. Because this was something else entirely. I thought I'd made the right choice by going to see her, but now I wasn't so sure. I was a fucking mess when it came to her. I'd turned into the kind of guy who couldn't get through the day without wanting to book another flight back to see her, which was no good for anyone, least of all for a workaholic like me.

Seeing her for two and a half days hadn't been enough. Would any length of time ever be? Missing her physically hurt, and I didn't have time or room in my life for that kind of pain. I needed to focus, but all I saw was her. Jules's face was everywhere, and I was losing my damn mind over it.

For most people that would have been a good thing, but not for someone like me. She consumed my every waking thought even more than she had before my trip, and I couldn't have that.

It wasn't like there was a future between us, so what the hell were we even doing? I'd believed that with her living all the way across the country, I'd be able to maintain some sort of balance. But I was so wrong. Distance had absolutely nothing to do with how I felt when it came to her. No matter where I was, I missed her.

I didn't want to, didn't want to miss anyone. That longing made me feel weak and vulnerable. I'd seen men walk away from work for their families, and I had never wanted to be one of them.

The fact that she'd let a coworker take over her clients while I was there gutted me. I hated to admit it, but that bothered me more than I'd let on. As much as I wanted to get over it and be nonchalant about it like she'd been, I couldn't. That little nugget stuck in my brain, reminding me at every turn what she'd walked away from for me.

Unable to let it go, I picked up the phone and punched Lucas's extension. "Luc, can I ask you something?"

"Of course," he said, and I could see the top of his blond head from my cubicle.

"Should I be freaked out that Jules handed her clients off for the weekend to another agent?"

"You mean, when you were there?"

"Yeah."

"No. Why would that freak you out? You were in town for two days, man. Of course she'd hand her clients off."

Lucas's reaction was nonchalant, as if her actions made perfect sense. And if they did, why couldn't I get past them?

"That's just it, Luc. I don't want her doing shit like that

for me. What if she expects me to do that for her?"

I tried to imagine putting my work after Jules, and I couldn't. If I had a client with a last-minute request, or who called me freaking out about a purchase, I'd explain to Jules that I needed to handle it and she'd have to deal with it. Always. I could never imagine my clients not taking priority in my life.

Lucas took on a patient tone. "She doesn't expect you to do anything. And she made a choice. That was her decision. It was one client. I'm sure she has a ton of others."

"But if she could give that one up so easily, what does it mean for the rest? I'm no good for her. This is no good for her." I kicked at the leg of my desk, frustrated with how this was eating at me.

"I really think you're reading too much into this."

"That's what Jules said too."

"Then why don't you just believe her?"

"Because it made me nervous," I said, but that was only half true. The reality was that it had scared me shitless listening to her conversation that morning.

He groaned, and I saw him lean back in his chair and cup his free hand behind his neck. "I know what you're doing. Don't sabotage this, Cal. I've never seen you this happy."

"I'm not sabotaging anything. I'm looking at things realistically, which is more than I can say for you."

"Me? This isn't my relationship."

"Yeah, but you're acting like it's totally normal, and we'll live happily ever after at some point."

"Why can't you?" he asked, and I wanted to hit him over the head with something hard.

"Because we don't live in the same state!" I growled out,

then lowered my voice, trying to maintain the composure that I was slowly losing. "And we never will. It's the same issues that have been there since day one. Nothing's changed."

"Except your feelings," Luc pointed out, and I bristled.

"Those don't matter. It's not about that."

"Why not? You're not a robot. I know you have a heart in that chest of yours somewhere."

"I'm just saying that regardless of how I feel about Jules, nothing changes the facts of our situation. It's pretty black and white. She's there and I'm here. That's never changing, so our feelings don't do anything except make this situation worse. It's wrong to keep this up. We're not being rational."

Lucas's other line rang. "I have to take that. I'm not done talking about this with you. Don't do anything stupid," he warned before hanging up.

I definitely hadn't thought this whole thing with Jules through properly. I didn't even weigh the consequences of what my going out there might do. For once in my life, I'd been impulsive, and I was all messed up over it.

I had to stop this. My focus needed to be trained on one thing and one thing only, and hers needed to be as well. Our situation wasn't good for either of us—surely she had to know that too.

Lucas walked past my desk and signaled for me to follow him. Sighing, I got up and trudged after him.

"Tell me what the problem is again," he asked once we were alone in a conference room.

"We're living in a damn fairy tale. This isn't some movie where things work out in the end. I'm not moving California and she's not moving here, so what the hell are we even doing?" I started pacing, chewing on my thumb.

"Why can't you just enjoy each other and see where it goes?"

"Because I can't stop thinking about her. She's all fucking consuming."

"That's not a bad thing, man," he said, and then sucked in a little gasp. "You're falling in love with her."

"Shut up."

"You are."

"I'm not," I argued, even though I damn well was, and that was the biggest problem of all. I couldn't be in love with someone I had no future with. That was beyond idiotic, and I'd always prided myself on being smarter than that.

Lucas rolled his eyes. "Okay, let's pretend that you're not. Didn't you have a good time when you were there?"

Memories of our night in Hollywood and spending time at her apartment flashed through my mind. I hadn't just had a good time with her; I'd had the best time.

"It was almost perfect."

"Then don't throw it away because you don't have it all mapped out."

"It's not about mapping it out, Lucas. You're not listening to me." Damn if I'd let him turn this into some Hallmark movie with a happy ending. "I'm trying to be realistic, and what we're doing isn't. There's no future with us. The longer we drag this out, the worse it will be for both of us."

Lucas crossed his arms over his chest and gave me a point-ed look. "I think it's a little late for that, don't you? If you're this torn up about things, how the hell do you think she feels?"

His words hit me like a sledgehammer to the gut as all the air escaped me. "That's what I'm talking about, though. Stopping it before it goes any further is the best thing for both of us. I'm not just thinking about me here. I'm thinking about Jules as well."

"I'm not sure she'll agree with your assessment," he said as he blew out a breath. "Matter of fact, I bet she fights you on it and convinces you not to end things."

"By what rational reasoning? Seriously, Luc, what argument could she possibly make?"

He shrugged. "I don't know. She'll probably say that she can come back out here next, and you guys can see each other once a month or so. That's what I would say."

My temper rising, I practically snarled at him. "Until when? We'll do that for how long? To what end?"

Everything Lucas said, I'd already thought about. It still led to the same ending. No matter how many times Jules and I saw each other, the fact remained that neither of us was ever going to move. Not when we had these careers that we'd worked so hard for. None of what we were doing made any logical sense.

Lucas shook his head, clearly losing his patience with me. "Just date long-distance forever. I don't know. You're making this really difficult."

"That's the thing." I ran my fingers through my hair. "I'm trying to make it really simple. By ending it."

His mouth twisted into a wry half smile. "I'm telling you she won't let you. There's no way that girl will let you walk away that easily. Brace yourself for one hell of a fight, my friend."

Lucas was right. Jules would absolutely fight me on this, and I wasn't sure that I'd be strong enough to stand my ground against her. As long as she had a say in things, I was screwed. She'd try to convince me that what we had was worth fighting for, but she wouldn't be thinking rationally. Jules would base all her decisions on her emotions, on the way she was feeling. I needed to be the voice of reason when it came to us, the logical one.

THE NEXT MORNING when I went to send her my usual text greeting out of habit, I stopped myself. I needed to put some emotional distance between us, as if the physical miles weren't enough.

But by the time I made it to the office parking lot, I found myself typing out a good-morning message to her. I couldn't even go a single day without texting her. I had to try harder.

Tomorrow, I'd try again.

Breaking things off would be the best thing for both of us. It would hurt at first, but it would hurt a hell of a lot more down the road if we kept doing this. Our end was inevitable, so why delay it? One day she'd thank me for making the harder choice when I did instead of stringing her along for months.

The war inside me was coming to a head—shots had been fired and I was going down. There would be no saving me now, no saving us.

I knew what I had to do.

DISAPPEARING ACT

Jules

C AL HAD BEEN a little different the past few days. It wasn't anything overly noticeable, but I sensed something was off. His tone seemed a little more cautious, and the things he said were the same, as if he was holding back somehow. But instead of asking him about it, I pretended everything was normal.

What was it about Cal's complex mind that scared me? Was I really that afraid to hear the answers to my questions? And if so, when had I become that kind of woman? Apparently, ever since I'd met Cal. Not only had I opened my heart up to love again more easily than I'd ever thought possible, I was suddenly scared to death to lose it.

That didn't mean that I liked this newfound side of myself, because I didn't. It seemed pathetic to avoid asking the tough questions just because I was afraid of the answer. Cal had become such a beacon of light in my life that I hated the idea of it burning out. Somewhere deep inside me, I feared this would end, and I wasn't ready for it. So I stuck my head in the sand, believing that as long as I denied that anything was wrong, we could keep whatever this was between us going.

Even an e-mail from Robin wanting a play-by-play of Cal's

visit refused to break me. I wrote her back, giving her the CliffsNotes version of our weekend together, which included that I had finally "given it up"—her words, not mine—and avoided all talk of the weirdness between him and me. Robin responded by sending me a video of her doing a happy dance in her bra to a Taylor Swift song.

When I woke up today and there was no text message from him, I worried for only a minute before convincing myself it wasn't a big deal. I stared at my phone and our last text message exchange, rereading the words from the night before. He was probably just busy, I rationalized as I rolled out of bed to get ready for work. Even though the lack of a morning text was odd, I wasn't too worried.

AFTER TWENTY-FOUR HOURS without a word from Cal, I became concerned. When texting was your main source of communication, going a full day without it meant that you weren't talking at all. That would be fine if it was normal for us, but twenty-four hours without talking at all wasn't our norm. I tried to minimize it, to pretend it wasn't a big deal, but it nagged at the back of my mind.

And when I woke up the next morning and there was still no text from him, a shiver of concern crept through me.

What if something happened to him, or worse yet, what if he was dead? Would anyone think to tell me? Did anyone even know I existed? Of course his brother knew, and so did his best friend, but would either Cooper or Lucas think to contact me? Cal could be dead on the side of the road, and I'd never know if no one told me.

Shaking my head to rid myself of my morbid thoughts, I

pulled up Facebook and saw that Cal had been active within the last four minutes. I sighed, relieved that he was still alive, but confused that he wasn't talking to me.

What the hell did that mean?

I tried not to read too much into it as I got ready for work, assuming that I'd hear from him eventually. He'd apologize and explain to me why he'd been silent. I wouldn't be upset with him, of course, because I understood how time consuming our lives could be. And it wasn't like the world ended if we didn't talk every single day.

Right?

Right.

I sent Cal a text asking how he was, and waited for a response. Sometimes it took him a while to get back to me, depending on how his day was going, so it wasn't unusual when I didn't get a message back right away.

But when minutes turned into hours, my what-the-hell-is-going-on meter started to ping. I constantly checked my phone for that familiar blue smiley face to appear, but it never did.

I was too nervous to call him, thinking that I wouldn't be able to handle it if he ignored my call the same way he was ignoring my texts. One after another, I sent a handful of texts that all went unanswered, as well as a single e-mail on social media that still sat there unread.

Agonizing alone in my apartment, I flipped through our time together in my mind, dissecting the last time we had talked. I mentally raked through all our recent past, looking for anything that could give me a clue as to what was happening between us. But nothing made any sense. Nothing added up.

We'd had an amazing time together when he was here.

When we spoke on the phone a few days ago, he told me how much he missed me and wanted to see me again. How could things have changed so quickly? In the course of three days, he'd gone from missing me to wanting nothing to do with me?

Why?

What reason could he have?

My heart ached, and I found myself wishing that I'd stayed closed off to love if this was how it was going to make me feel. Feeling nothing was a thousand times better than feeling this pain.

Determined to get an answer, I fired off another text, asking if he was alive. I meant it to be funny and assumed he'd respond right away with some smartass response. But he didn't.

My next step was to call Tami for reassurance, knowing she'd be home from work by now.

"What's up?" she chirped.

"Cal's not talking to me," I said, pressing my hand to the ache growing in my chest.

"What do you mean? Like you pissed him off or something?"

"No. I don't know. It's just he hasn't called or texted me in three days."

She turned serious, adopting her lawyer tone. "Have you called or texted him?"

"I haven't called, but I've sent a couple texts."

"No response?"

"No."

"When was the last text you sent?"

"A few minutes ago."

She stayed silent for longer than was comfortable, making

me wonder what she was thinking. Finally, she said, "That's weird, Jules."

"That's it? That's all you've got?"

Damn it, I wanted answers. I'd already known that it was strange. But what I didn't know was why he was doing this. And I wanted someone to tell me.

"I just don't know what to say," she admitted. "Did you guys get into a fight?"

"No."

"Are you sure?"

I huffed out, "I'm pretty sure I'd know if we'd gotten into a fight or not, Tami."

"Sorry, I just don't understand."

"Me either," I said sadly.

A rustling sound came from the background, and she said firmly, "I'm on my way."

"I want to be alone."

"I know you do. Be there in twenty."

Groaning, I knew that arguing with Tami was no use. She'd just come over anyway whether I wanted her there or not. But the truth was that I needed her, and I was grateful for the times when she was more stubborn than I was.

"Thank you," I said before hanging up.

I MANAGED TO hold in my emotions long enough for Tami to walk through my front door and take me in her arms. The second she hugged me, I allowed the tears I'd been holding back to fall.

"It's okay," she said, wiping my face for me.

"It just doesn't make any sense," I said, hating how pitiful and whiny I sounded.

She walked into my kitchen, pulled out a bottle of wine, and opened it. With a full glass in each hand, she led me toward the couch in my living room and we settled in.

I took a sip as I waited for her to grill me like I knew she would. The lawyer in her would want as many facts as possible. The woman in her would too.

"Is he still online?"

I nodded. "That's almost the worst part. Seeing that he was just active minutes ago, but knowing he isn't responding to me."

"What do you replay the most?" she asked, and I was lost. I had no clue what she was asking.

"Huh?"

"In your head. What memory do you see the most often?"

"Oh," I said, thinking it was an odd question. "It's the little things. Like the way he looked at me when he dropped me off at the airport after we first met. Or the way he introduced me to his family. How excited he got that I'd had his favorite bourbon here for him. Mostly the little reactions, bits of time. They twist me up inside."

Tami stared at me as I spilled my guts onto the living room floor. I still had no idea why she'd asked that particular question. Maybe she was just curious. Or maybe this was the lawyer in her at work, putting together all the details to create a fuller picture in her mind. I had no idea.

"You said the rest of the weekend here was good, right? Nothing happened on the last day before he left?" She narrowed her eyes at me.

"Nothing," I said, then stopped short. "Except he got upset when he heard that I'd allowed someone else to take my clients out."

"He got upset?"

"My clients wanted to make an offer on a house, and I told Ashley to go ahead and handle it. Cal didn't like that."

Tami smiled. "I can see that."

"But it can't be that. We were fine right after he left. He even mentioned wanting to come back out."

"I don't know, Jules, but I will tell you this. That boy was into you. He liked you. A lot."

My heart warmed with her words, the heat slicing through the pain and softening it a little, giving me a reprieve. "You really think so?"

"I saw you two together. I took those pictures that I know are still on your phone. I know you can see the way he looks at you. And vice versa."

"I thought we were happy. At least, *I* was. I know he lives across the country and it probably was going to end at some point, but I didn't care about that right now."

"Did he know how you felt?" she asked before she took a long sip.

"We never even talked about the distance. It was this thing between us that neither of us ever brought up."

Tami rolled her eyes. "That's healthy."

"I know, but it didn't seem necessary to focus on it. In reality, we'd just met. What would be the point of talking about something neither of us was going to change?"

"Did you want to change it?" she asked.

"I don't know. It was too new to think about something like that. I have no idea."

"For as often as you guys talked, you really didn't communicate well, did you?"

I shrugged. "I guess not. To be honest, I was scared to ask him certain questions."

"You? Scared?" She all but guffawed at me as she lifted her drink.

"I know, it's embarrassing. But there was a part of me that was terrified to hear his answers. What if he called things off? I wasn't ready for that." I winced as my thoughts sliced through me.

Tami's expression softened. "I'm sorry, Jules. I know this is hard for you."

"It's just ironic. I didn't want to ask him things to scare him away, but he's still gone."

"Finish your glass." She pointed at my wine, and I downed it. "Time for something stronger."

Leaving me on the couch, she headed back into my kitchen and mixed a concoction that was sure to leave me feeling horrible the next day.

"What is this?"

"A lot of vodka. A splash of cran. You'll like it." She laughed.

I took a sip and almost spit it all over my couch. "I need more cran. Seriously, Tami, how can you drink like that?"

"I'm a professional," she said, her cheeks turning pink already.

"Why are you getting me drunk again?"

"So you'll feel better."

I rolled my eyes. "I think it makes it worse."

Quickly, I reached for my phone. I typed out a text to Cal before Tami could ask me what I was doing, and before I could stop myself.

JULES: Where are you? Why aren't you talking to me?

Tami's eyes grew wide. "What did you just do?"

"Nothing," I lied and put my phone under my butt.

"Do not text him!"

"Too late." I shrugged as I waited for my ass to vibrate, signaling his response.

"Well," she huffed, "don't do it again."

"How can he just ignore me? I mean it, Tami. How can he get texts from me and just act like I don't exist?" I groaned and leaned back into the cushions.

"I don't know. I have no idea what that boy is thinking."

Feeling vulnerable, I moaned. "This sucks so bad."

"Are you hurting?" she asked, her tone serious.

"Yes. Very much."

Although I was hurting—my heart aching, my mind unable to make sense of things—I still held on to the tiniest sliver of hope that Cal would come back, or that this was all some silly misunderstanding. One phone call from Cal could fix all of this, and believing that alleviated some of the pain.

I wanted it to be true. I wanted to believe, because believing he would come back to me was a hell of a lot easier than accepting that he'd walked away without saying a word. How could I accept that when nothing about it made any sort of sense?

"I'm sorry you're hurting. Do you want me to stay the night?" Tami asked, already knowing the answer.

Needing her near, I nodded. "Thank you."

"It's a good thing I keep clothes here," she said with a smile.

WHEN THE WEEKEND rolled around, Tami refused to let me sulk in peace and insisted we go out to get my mind off of things.

As if that were even possible.

She tried to convince me that the best way to get over a guy was to get under another one, but we both knew that wasn't my style. At least she'd gotten me to laugh.

As we wandered down Third Street in Santa Monica, I tried to push aside the memories of Cal's last day here. How had my personal space become littered with thoughts of him? If he wasn't going to be in my life, then I didn't want him in my city.

We chose a bar, headed inside, and I grimaced at the giant chalkboard that read OVER FIFTY TYPES OF BOURBON!

Bourbon.

Two months ago, I most likely would have ignored the sign or not even seen it. Now the word triggered something so deep inside my heart, I thought it might stop beating. It was so stupid, the way I associated Cal with the liquor, but it was tied to a memory, a minuscule speck of time that had come to represent so much more.

Bourbon had once made me feel happy and brought a smile to my face. Now all it brought me was pain associated with loss, and I never wanted to drink it again.

I hated bourbon.

I hoped it all burned to the fucking ground.

Sorry, Kentucky.

Rolling my eyes, I chose a small two-person table farthest from the bar and sat down.

"We're eating, right? I'm starving," Tami said, concern pinching her features.

"Yes, we're eating. Stop looking at me like that."

"Like what?" She tilted her head, staring at me with aqua-colored eyes today.

"Like you're afraid I'm going to fall apart at any second."

"I don't think that. I'm just still sad for you, is all." She reached across the table and squeezed my hand.

"Let's drink first, be sad later," I said with a smile.

Our waiter appeared, and we ordered drinks. When he walked away, I gave Tami my full attention.

"Tell me what's going on with you. Distract me."

She waved away my question. "You know there's nothing going on with me. All work, all the time. And then random guys who mean nothing the rest of the time."

"I can't wait to see the guy who knocks you on your ass and steals your heart."

She gave me a wry look. "To be honest, you're not making me want that anytime soon."

"Pretty sure you won't have a choice in the matter," I said with a small smile. Tami truly in love was going to be something to see.

"Trust me. I'm aware."

Our drinks arrived and we toasted each other before downing them way too quickly.

"I need bread," I warned, "or it will not be a pretty night."

Tami snorted. "I need more than bread." She waved our waiter back over, and we ordered food along with our next round of drinks.

I downed my third lemon drop before reaching for my phone, which I'd placed on top of the table.

"Oh no, you don't. Give me your cell!" Tami practically yelled before prying the phone from my grasp.

"Why are you taking my phone from me?"

"Because you're drunk," she said matter-of-factly, as if that was a perfectly acceptable answer.

"And?"

"And drunk Jules equals drunk texting with Cal. You'll hate yourself tomorrow if you cave and text him tonight."

She was right, so damn right. But that didn't stop the desire from churning within me. I wanted to text him. I missed him so much, I felt it in every part of me, especially my stupid heart.

"How can he just walk away from me and not care?" I asked Tami again, as if she'd have new insight into the same question I'd been asking since he left.

She shrugged, her eyes sad. "I don't know, Jules. I'm sorry. None of it makes any sense to me."

"Me either. I just . . ." I stopped and sucked in a deep breath. "I miss him, and I don't understand how he doesn't miss me. Was everything he said to me a lie? It has to have been, right? Otherwise, he'd be just as miserable as I am right now."

"Do you think it was a lie?" she asked before sipping her cocktail.

"Yes." I shook my head. "No. I don't know. I don't want it to have been lies because then that just means I'm a fool on top of everything else."

"You're not a fool."

"But I believed him without question. Every single thing he said to me, I totally bought into and believed because I felt the same way."

"That doesn't make you a fool, Jules."

Tami might have been trying to make me feel better, but it

wasn't helping.

I had believed every word Cal said and texted me over the past two months. My heart would skip when he told me he missed me, that he couldn't wait to see me again, or that he couldn't stop thinking about me. I never even thought for a second that those words might be untrue. Until now. Now it was all I thought about, how his words had to be lies.

I didn't understand what he had to gain by lying to me, but it was the only thing that made any sense. If everything had been a lie, then of course it would be easy for him to walk away and never speak to me again.

"I wish I had the answers for you." Tami lifted her glass to me before downing the rest of her drink.

"Me too."

I wish someone did. The not-knowing part was slowly and painfully killing what was left of my heart.

As my brain tried to come up with scenarios that made sense, a new possibility occurred to me. "Maybe he met someone and didn't want to tell me. If he met someone else, he would probably just move on and not want to tell me about it."

Tami raised an eyebrow at me. "Is that what you would do?"

"No! Of course not. But I'm not looking for anyone else; I don't want to date anyone else. I really like Cal. I don't want to be with someone who isn't him."

She toyed with her drink, seeming deep in thought. "I don't think he met someone."

My eyes widened, my heart suddenly a fraction more hopeful than it was two seconds before. "You don't?"

She looked up at me and shook her head. "I don't. I don't

think that's what happened at all, and I'd be surprised if it had."

"I wish I could read hearts," I all but slurred as I downed the last of my drink.

The waiter paused at our table and looked at me with raised eyebrows, but I shook my head. I wanted another lemon drop, but I certainly didn't need one.

Tami laughed. "Don't you mean minds?"

"Why on earth would I want to read minds? No. Hearts. Hearts don't lie. Okay, well, maybe they do. But you can't talk yourself out of feeling the way you feel in your heart the way you can in your mind. Hearts feel things whether you want them to or not. They aren't logical, trying to make sense all the time. They just do."

"So you'd read Cal's heart if you could?"

"In a heartbeat. Pun intended." I laughed at my own joke. "If I knew how he felt about me, then I'd be okay with his silence. It would at least ease some of the pain, or help me get over it altogether. If I just knew what was going on in there." I jabbed at my chest with my finger.

Tami shrugged. "You should just ask him how he feels."

"I can't."

"Why not?"

"'Cause you took my phone."

"I didn't mean tonight!" she exclaimed. "No. I take it back." She pointed at me, looking all bossy and lawyer-like. "You don't ask him anything. You don't reach out to him, you don't text him, you don't tweet him, you don't call him or send him an e-mail, or Snap-whatever. Nothing, you hear me? That was a bad idea from me. Don't you dare contact him ever again."

"I hear you," I said, nodding at her.

"You aren't going to listen to me, are you?"

"Who knows. I clearly enjoy the torture of putting myself out there and getting nothing in return."

But it wasn't about the torture, really. I wanted answers. Hell, I wanted something from him. Anything was better than the silent treatment.

Cal had grown on me way quicker than I'd ever anticipated, and felt his absence like a loss in the worst way. The pain in my chest reminded me how undead my heart truly was with each beat it sputtered out. It had simply been an organ that existed inside me for so long, feeling nothing, and now all it brought me was a constant ache.

"You know, I wonder what's wrong with me," I said, my heart spilling out of my mouth.

"What do you mean, what's wrong with you?"

"Let's just say that everything he said to me was a lie."

"This again?" Tami leaned back in her chair and groaned.

"Yes, just listen. Say he lied about everything. Then how messed up is my truth meter if I had no idea the whole time?" I glared at her, begging her to help me make sense of my heart.

"Because he wasn't lying?"

"If he meant the things he said, then where is he right now? How could he walk away so easily like I never existed and ignore me?" My eyes welled with tears, and I swiped at them before any dared to fall.

I had meant every single thing I'd said to Cal since I met him. Everything I had confessed to him was said with a full heart, and I'd believed everything he had said back to me. I'd smiled when he contacted me, every part of me jumping for joy.

But now I simply felt like a fool, as if somehow I should have known better. If he misled me, why hadn't I sensed it? Why didn't I know this could happen?

Because my heart is stupid, something inside me whispered.

Stupid heart. *I hate you.*

"Can I trust you not to do anything dumb?" Tami asked as she held my phone just out of my reach.

"Yes," I snapped as I reached for it, but she pulled it away.

She grinned as she handed it to me and I grabbed it, quickly scanning for any text message notifications. None appeared, not even from work.

I glanced at Tami and typed out a quick message.

JULES: *Say something, Cal. Please. Anything is better than this silence.*

Tami's eyes grew huge. "Shit, what are you doing?"

I pressed SEND on the message before anything could stop me, even myself. But when he didn't respond, all I wanted to do was go back in time and take it back.

Damn it.

I had no self-control when it came to him and my lust for answers, especially when I'd been drinking. When I was sober, I could at least talk myself out of texting him, but drunk, all bets were off. It was as if I came unhinged and let control fly out the window.

But Cal had answers that I wanted. And drunk Jules was apparently relentless, and a little needy.

"Nothing," I tried to lie.

"What the hell did you just send him?"

I shook my head. "Don't be mad. It was the last one."

"The last one? Yeah, right." She rolled her eyes.

"It was. I mean it," I said, trying to convince her.

Cal had been silent for too long, too many days in a row. It was sad, how even when you expected the disappointment, it still hurt, still stung. It was a feeling I didn't want to get used to.

I was such a sap, still holding on to a thread of hope, no matter how small that thread was. There was always a chance that he'd respond to a text after I'd sent one. But as minutes turned to hours, and hours turned to days, it was obvious that he never would.

How could he walk away so easily? How could he ignore me like I didn't exist? And why did he want to? What happened? The questions compounded inside my mind as the answers never came. How was I supposed to get past this when I had no idea what went wrong?

It was all well and good to involve your heart in love again when things were going well. But holy hell, when things went bad . . . I found myself wishing I'd never even cracked open the door to peer outside. Life had been so much easier feeling nothing for a guy, although it was far less satisfying.

That was the trade-off—you could close your heart to love forever, but you'd miss out on all the good that came with giving and receiving love. You had to decide if it was worth the risk.

And was it?

I'd like to say that I'd made the choice, that I had consciously decided the risk was worth the impending pain, but the truth was that the choice was made for me. There was no other option when it came to Cal. I'd been all in since the day I first met him in that hotel lobby.

Who we loved wasn't always a choice. Sometimes it was an

irresistible pull, a gravitational force, something we couldn't see or control that drew us toward another. Sure, we could try to fight it. But in the end, love always won because it didn't fight fair. It had a secret weapon, a tool of sheer force to use against us—our heart.

And once that son of a bitch got involved, you could say good-bye to reason.

BRUTAL SILENCE

Jules

EACH NEW MORNING, I woke up with a twisted sort of renewed positivity that restored my depleted hope from the night before. Would Cal be able to go another twenty-four hours without talking to me? That's what my brain wondered, the question my heart always asked. I was convinced it would be an impossible task.

But by the time I fell asleep each night, the answer was always a resounding *yes*. Apparently he could.

I hated feeling this way, so insecure, so vulnerable and weak. The feelings might not be familiar but they consumed me, infusing every thought or heartbeat that wasn't otherwise distracted. It was awful. I missed Cal so much that I constantly checked my phone, hoping a text would be there. I still wanted that. After more than a week of his silence, I shouldn't have wanted a text from him so badly, but I did.

How could a man walk away from a woman with no explanation and expect her to go on with her life as if nothing had happened?

Everything changed when someone did something so inconsiderate to you. There was no closure, no way to properly grieve the loss because you didn't know what the hell went wrong, or what you could have done to fix it. And therein lay my most soul-crushing problem—the fixing-it part. Oh, how I still wanted to fix whatever had broken us. Or at least know what the hell had happened.

It seemed there were two kinds of people in the world. First, there were those who simply accepted things that happened without question. Those who could watch someone walk out of their life and would shrug their shoulders before moving on. The ones who could let things go easily.

Then there were the kind of people who fought to save relationships, who demanded answers when things went south. The people who, when they realized they didn't want a relationship to end, held on with both hands, clinging to it as if their life depended on it.

I realized that I was the latter type. At least, when it came to Cal and my stupid heart, I was. I didn't let go easily, didn't accept well. I fought for truth, for reasons, for answers. For my heart. Who knew that I'd be such an advocate for that organ when I'd spent so many years hating it?

Each morning when I opened my eyes, I ached when I remembered that he was gone. The first thing I did was check my phone, the lack of a text notification or missed call just another stab to my already bludgeoned heart.

How much pain could one heart handle? I knew the answer: all of it. It could handle every single ounce that life doled out, and you couldn't do a damn thing to stop from feeling it.

I admonished myself for being so sad over the turn of events. In the grand scheme of things, I shouldn't be feeling this level of sadness for someone I'd only known a couple of months. It wasn't as if Cal had been in my life for years. He hadn't, and that was almost the worst part—how much I physically felt his absence, as if a part of me was now suddenly missing. But then I remembered that our hearts didn't care about logic or time.

My heart didn't play by rules that my mind made up. It didn't follow silly timelines or measure its feelings based on the number of days it had known someone. No, hearts simply *felt*, whether you wanted them to or not. And they didn't bother explaining themselves either. My heart longed for Cal, it missed him, and no matter how hard my brain tried to logically talk my heart out of those feelings, my heart refused to listen.

Silly brain, it would say. *You know nothing.*

All my heart did was remind me how easily it had opened back up after being closed for so long. I had no idea that it wouldn't take a miracle for my heart to breathe back to life. Cal had done that so easily before leaving me to crash and burn all alone. And I had no idea why.

I searched my mind, questioning every feeling, every emotion, every second of longing. What did I want? I wanted Cal to come back. I longed for him to tell me that it had all been a mistake, that he was wrong, and beg for my forgiveness. At this point, I'd have taken any of it.

The bottom line was that I was really, truly sad. I hadn't felt sadness like this in . . . well, I wasn't sure how long. I wore my sadness like a blanket, wrapped around my body for comfort. No part of me was left unburdened by the weight of it. I carried it all, felt it all, and moved through my days enveloped by it.

I was thankful that work was busy and that I had clients booking me out the next few nights in a row. Work was the only thing that seemed to keep me distracted, and saved my sanity. My sadness blanket was cast aside when I was busy working, my mind occupied, my thoughts busy. There was no time for sadness. No time for thoughts of Cal.

But the second work stopped, my brain began spinning with questions and pain. I became a woman obsessed. Obsessed with his Facebook page, stalking it, checking it constantly to see what had been updated. Had he accepted any new friends, posted any new pictures, gone out with any girls?

My behavior was awful, and I hated the way it made me feel, but I couldn't stop. My curiosity was a sickness, and there was only one cure.

Clicking on the UNFRIEND button quicker than I ever had in my life, I deleted Cal from my friends list and breathed out a sigh of . . . something. It wasn't quite relief, but I knew that eventually it would be. Hell, part of me wondered why he hadn't unfriended me first. My need to be involved in his online life would go away as soon as I could no longer access it.

I wished the questions that plagued my mind and heart would shut off as easily as my computer did. Unfortunately for me, my body was not a machine; there was no on-off switch. It would simply take time for me to heal, but I'd be lying if I said I was a patient person. I wasn't. And I hated feeling this sad about everything.

Tami checked in on me daily, sending me texts of encouragement and letting me know she was there for me and my broken heart. She offered to fly to Boston to repeatedly run over Cal with a rental car, but I told her she'd be no good to me in jail. She begrudgingly agreed to stay put and allow him to live, which made me laugh.

"You know, you weren't nearly this devastated over Brandon," she reminded me one night as I shoveled lime Jell-O into my mouth.

"Trust me, I'm aware," I said into the phone, hyperaware of the vast differences in those relationships.

"It's just interesting."

"How you can take the emotion out of every single thing, I'll never know. I always thought my heart was dead and cold, but maybe you're the one with no heart?"

"I have a heart. I just don't allow it to do its job."

I let out a laugh that ended in a sigh. "I used to be much better at that part."

"Do you wish you'd never met him?"

Tami's question stopped me short. The spoon with the Jell-O balanced precariously in front of my mouth. Practically dropping it into the bowl, I chewed on my bottom lip instead. The answer had come straight from my gut the moment she asked, so I wasn't sure why I hesitated in my response.

"No."

"Really? You don't? I figured you would."

"I probably should wish that, but I don't." I didn't believe the words as I said them. I didn't wish that. And I didn't think I should either.

"But he hurt you. If you'd never met him, you wouldn't be going through this right now."

I nodded, even though she couldn't see me. "I know, but it's more than that. Yes, I'm hurting right now. And yes, I don't understand what happened or why, but before meeting him that night, I honestly thought I was broken inside. I figured that I was going to be one of those women who sacrificed love for work, and I was okay with that. I wanted success more than I wanted love—or at least I thought I did. But meeting Cal that night showed me that I wasn't dead. My heart wasn't hollow or numb. He taught me something about myself that I didn't know, so I can't wish that away. I'm grateful to him for showing me that."

"You're so mature. It's annoying." She huffed out a long breath.

"And on that note—" I said through a yawn.

"Okay. I'll talk to you tomorrow. Feel better. Heal your stupid heart."

"I'm trying."

"I know. I'm just so mad at him," she said with a groan.

"Get in line," I shot back, although anger wasn't the main emotion I felt. At all. I wished it were, because then I'd hurt less.

After Tami hung up, I scrolled through the pictures of Cal and me as I lay in my bed, my comforter wrapped around me. It was a habit that had at first made me happy and giddy. I'd look at them and smile before closing my eyes and falling asleep each night. Now I looked at them and wondered what the hell had happened and where we'd gone so wrong.

One day I wouldn't need to look at them anymore.

One day they wouldn't make me feel anything.

One day I'd forget they were there altogether.

One day I'd delete every single one of them.

Today was not that day.

IT HAD BEEN three weeks and four days since Cal had gone silent and I still wanted him, still longed for him, and still missed him. I wished the feelings would go away, but they weren't fading.

I didn't want to feel this way, but my heart refused to

listen to reason. Absolutely refused. It mocked me daily, reminding me that something was missing and that we were no longer whole. As if I needed the reminder.

I didn't. I felt the loss with every breath.

Surprisingly, my mind liked to remind me that something was missing as well. I figured at least one of them would be on my side. When your heart and mind joined forces and worked against you, it was a wonder how a person could function at all without falling apart. The two of them warring against each other was one thing, but having them team up on me was something else altogether.

It was brutal, to say the least.

Fuck you, heart.

Fuck you, mind.

I knew what I'd lost and didn't know how to get it back. But what really pissed me off the most was the fact that neither of them were helping me get past this. Shouldn't I have been over him by now? Why wasn't I well on my way to post-Cal living? How was it that I was still counting the days since I last heard from him?

I should be angry and bitter; I should hate him. But I felt just the opposite because I didn't stand a chance when my heart and mind worked against me. Or because I was weak. Or in love.

And I didn't want to be either of those things because I wanted to be strong and a force to be reckoned with. Who the hell reckoned with a weak woman who cried every night over some guy who most likely wasn't even worth her tears?

This pity party needs to stop, I yelled at my mind, and then I gave my heart a stern talking-to.

Neither listened. They never did.

So I drowned them out with alcohol before realizing that alcohol lowered all my defenses and it made me miss him even more. I almost sent Cal another text before I had the gumption and self-awareness to stop myself. Thank God. I didn't need any more reasons to dislike myself lately.

My cell phone pinged, signaling a text message, and I grabbed for it too quickly, knocking it to the floor. Groaning, I reached down and picked it up, seeing the dark blue smiley face staring back at me.

One dark blue smiley and my heart leaped into my throat with hope and fear. My thumbs were clumsy, fumbling as I tried to press the button to read the text. They were as desperate as my heart was.

I miss you.

My phone pinged again.

I was an idiot.

And again.

I'm so sorry.
Can we talk?

Texts came through at a rapid-fire pace, filled with apology and want. But they weren't from Cal. They were all from Brandon, my ex-boyfriend.

Disappointment ripped through me like a hurricane. These messages stabbed me in the heart, each one assaulting me as it arrived. The words were all things I wanted to hear, but from the wrong guy.

All the right words. From the wrong guy.

Right words. Wrong guy.

Wrong guy.

Wrong guy.

The texts kept coming, the blue smiley face taunting me each time he appeared, and I was suddenly struck with violent urges that included smashing my phone with a hammer.

"Stop fucking smiling at me," I yelled at my phone, but it pinged again to torment me.

I scrolled through the options and changed my ex's icon to a black frowny face. I laughed at myself as it appeared, feeling victorious, as if I'd just won some secret battle. Battle of the text notification icons.

Take that, cell phone. You shall no longer smile at me! Only frowns from you!

I didn't respond to Brandon. I had nothing to say to him, and I couldn't have cared less about his feelings in the midst of my own. But when his texts turned into calls, I groaned and typed out a quick message.

> JULES: I don't think there's anything to say at this point, Brandon. It's been a long time. I've moved on.
>
> BRANDON: Moved on? You have a new boyfriend? I thought you didn't have time, Jules? What the hell? Who is he?

Damn it. I'd said too much, hoping that it would make him go away, but I should have known that it would only wound his pride. How could I shut this down as quickly as it had come about?

> JULES: I just meant that I've moved past us. I'm still just as focused on my work as ever, probably even more so. I would really rather not rehash the past.

I pressed SEND and prayed he'd buy into my line of bull-shit and go away.

> BRANDON: *You don't even want to talk this out?*
> JULES: *There's nothing to talk about.*
> BRANDON: *So you don't want to see me?*
> JULES: *No. I'm sorry, but I don't.*

I should have felt worse about being so blunt, but I lacked the desire to be anything else. The last thing I wanted was to rehash anything with Brandon, someone I hadn't sincerely thought about in forever, if not longer.

> BRANDON: *You always were selfish. I don't know why I bothered. Forget that I sent these texts.*

A year and a half ago, that message would have stung, even if it had been true. Today, it elicited absolutely no reaction from me. I didn't care that he called me selfish. I didn't care if he believed that I was. All I wanted was for Brandon to go back to wherever he came from and leave me the hell alone. I wanted him to stop texting, to stop calling, and to not want to see me.

And then it hit me—what if that was exactly how Cal felt about me?

WELCOME, BITTERNESS

Jules

WHEN I TOLD Tami about Brandon texting me, she almost had a coronary on the phone. She was proud that I nipped the situation in the bud so easily, and that Brandon had literally gone away as quickly as he had tried to reappear.

When I asked her if I was too mean to him, she laughed and said that while she had always liked Brandon, she knew he wasn't the right guy for me. Then she reminded me how lazy and unmotivated he was, and how if I ended up with someone like him, I'd be a miserable shrew by forty who spent her nights plotting ways to get away with her husband's murder.

She was the best. Mostly because she was right and I didn't want to go to jail.

After weeks of Cal-induced pain, I started to feel differently. I realized that my heart hurt a bit less than it had the day before. The disappointment of Cal being gone was no longer this crushing weight that lived inside my chest. I considered that progress.

And then I got pissed.

Really pissed.

Why the hell had I been chasing Cal? Sending him texts

that he didn't respond to? Pining over him like I had nothing else better going on in my life? Why was I the one doing all the reaching out when I wasn't the one who left in the first place? And if I was doing all the running, then who the hell was running after me?

I shouldn't have to chase after a guy to make him want me. And I shouldn't have to remind or convince him that I was what he wanted. He should already know that, without question. So why the hell was I treating this guy like he'd hung the moon, when he'd so clearly done anything but?

I really needed to get my head on board with what my heart clearly had already started to figure out. When was the last time my brain was the one left behind? Usually my heart was the last one to catch up, but not this time.

With a sharp intake of breath, I made a decision—there would be no more chasing after Cal Dumbass Donovan. My running shoes were off and tossed in the garbage where they belonged.

The once stabbing pain in my heart had lessened to more of a dull ache. It was still a constant presence, but it was much more tolerable than what I'd been experiencing. Originally I thought I was going to have to fill the hole in my heart with something else to get the hurt to stop, like binge-eating copious amounts of dark chocolate or Taco Bell nacho cheese.

Turned out that, thankfully, neither were required. Time had been the only remedy I needed. Even the lingering question of why he left lacked the emotion that was usually tied to it. I found myself almost not caring about the answer at this point.

Almost.

The indifference vanished quickly and was replaced by

anger. I wallowed in my anger, relished it. It made all the hurt stop. Being mad was a relief, but I had to stop myself from grabbing my phone and texting him things like "Fuck you!" and "You're a coward!" And by stop myself, I pretty much meant that at least once an hour I had to talk myself out of berating him via text message or e-mail.

Anger, how I loved you. Until I started feeling like a fool. He'd made a fool out of me and he probably enjoyed how stupid I was every time I'd sent him a text, all but begging him to reach out to me. I hated myself after each one I sent, but it was pure torture to not know what the hell had happened between us. I kept hoping he'd finally tell me something, give me anything to work with, some sort of logic to process.

But that never came.

So he gave my heart no choice. It had to get pissed to survive.

Opening up the message window in Facebook, I scrolled to our messages. The last one I sent him where I had been pathetic and fairly drunk still sat there unread. Unread, even after all this time.

I started typing, all my anger coming off my fingers like venom from a snake bite.

You're a total prick face, you know that? I mean, WTF, Cal? Where the hell are you and why don't you give at least ONE fuck about my feelings? How can you just disappear on me like this and NOT CARE AT ALL? I'll never understand that. I don't get it. How are you so okay when I'm nowhere near it? Did it all mean nothing to you? Because that's the only thing that makes any kind of sense. Unless you're just a complete fucking ass-face, which I haven't ruled out yet. I hate you. Have I told you lately how much I hate you? Because I do. You suck. I hate you. I hate you. I fucking miss you. I hate that I miss you.

I stared at my words, my feelings typed out so disorderly like word vomit across the computer screen. I pressed the BACKSPACE button, watching as each word vanished.

I'd never intended to send him another message he could ignore; it simply felt good to yell at him, to get my emotions out of me and into the open. Even though it felt like I was yelling into the wind, never to be acknowledged, I still needed to release the words.

It was in moments like these that I still couldn't believe we would never, ever speak to each other again. It seemed so unfathomable to me that this had happened. My mind sometimes refused to wrap itself around it all, like the reality was just too much to comprehend.

Reaching for my phone, I typed out a text message.

JULES: You're such a fucking coward. I never pegged you for being so weak. I'm glad I got out when I did. I don't miss you. I hate you.

I wanted to press SEND—God, how I wanted to press that button. Whatever had happened, he should have been man enough to just tell me. I was a big girl, I could have handled it.

My finger hovered over the SEND button on my phone. I was tempted to deliver the words that would give me a moment of sick satisfaction, but I ended up pressing DELETE instead.

Any communication from me at all made me the weaker of us, and I was tired of playing that role.

FIVE WEEKS, ONE DAY

Jules

FIVE WEEKS AND one day, that was how long Cal had been gone from my life. I only knew this because I checked the calendar at work today and actually counted how long it had been since he'd disappeared. Somewhere between the routine of going to sleep at night and waking up each morning, I'd stopped keeping track of the days.

I no longer looked at the pictures on my cell phone either. One night before bed, I'd transferred them to a storage album online where I kept copies of all my digital photos. I'd kept two of my favorite pictures of us in my actual phone gallery, but I'd stopped looking at them.

And when I did happen to see them in my gallery, they elicited nothing from me. My breath no longer caught in my throat, my heart no longer stuttered, the wind no longer felt knocked out of me.

They had simply become memories, a part of my past, which seemed strange now. I had been so sure that that particular time would never come, that I'd always be affected by Cal's leaving, but I had been wrong. It no longer hurt, and for that I was grateful. As time passed and I realized that he was gone forever, a feeling of contentment had settled over me, or maybe it was acceptance. It happened so slowly that I hadn't even noticed it until it was all that I felt. I had finally accepted that Cal was gone . . . and I simply didn't care about the rest anymore.

It was blissful to be free of the hurt.

"So, there's this restaurant and bar re-branding on Beach tonight, and we got invited," Tami singsonged in my ear as I drove home from an evening house showing. "I know it's last-minute."

"Sure," I agreed all too quickly. "Let's go."

"Wait. Sure? You'll come without me forcing you to? Oh my gosh, are you finally over that dickhead completely?"

I couldn't help but bristle at the term. Even with everything that Cal had done to me, I didn't consider him *that*. Sure, I'd had my moments when anger consumed me and I hated his very existence, but I didn't feel like that anymore. Every emotion tied to him felt like I'd experienced it so long ago, even though it really hadn't been that long at all.

"Do you want me to come out with you or not?"

"Yes, yes. Sorry. He's not a dickhead." She faked a cough. "Meet you there?"

"I just need to change," I said as I glanced down at my pants suit. I looked fine, but it wasn't what I wanted to wear out to a bar in Santa Monica.

"See you in a bit," she said before giving me the exact location on Beach Street.

I was actually excited and looking forward to getting out of the house for something not related to work. I'd been burying myself in house showings for weeks now, and I needed a little reprieve.

After rushing home to change, I pulled up in front of the

restaurant and was thankful they had valet parking for the evening. The last thing I wanted was to deal with parking and walking numerous blocks in the heels I was wearing. My yellow sundress dipped low in front, emphasizing my cleavage as I waltzed into the bar like I owned the place. I felt as good as I looked, and I reveled in that fact.

Tami waved at me, grabbing my attention immediately as I weaved through the crowd toward her seat at the bar.

"You look hot," she said. "And I ordered us both a drink from the themed menu. Here's yours."

She pushed an orange drink toward me. I picked it up and sniffed at it before taking a tentative sip.

Taking in her bright pink irises, I said, "New contacts?"

"Less devilish, right?" She winked and I laughed.

"At least these are truly pink. How many compliments did you get before I got here?" I knew damn well that guys would compliment her on her eyes, no matter what ridiculous color they were.

She rolled her eyes. "Just two. One from the guy at the door and the other from the bartender."

"Oh, Tami, your eyes are amazing," I said, mimicking a delusional male's voice. "I've never seen anyone with neon pink eyes before."

"Jealousy doesn't look good on you." She grinned at me as I let out a howl of laughter, but then her smile faded. "So, I'm sorry to bring him up, but I have to know. Are you totally over everything? I'm only asking because you actually seem okay." She placed her hand on mine. "And I mean that in a good way. In the best way."

I nodded. "I know you do. And I am over it, as much as anyone can truly be over something like that. I've given up the notion that I'll ever hear from him again. Which is a little weird to say out loud, but it's true."

"And you're okay with that?"

"I can't make him want to talk to me. And I shouldn't have to. So I don't know if I'm okay with it as much as there's nothing I can do about it. I've finally accepted the reality of the situation, and I have to move on." I shrugged. "It is what it is."

"I still don't understand what happened, though," she said, pouting.

"Me either. But honestly, I don't even care to know at this point. It doesn't matter anymore." I sipped at the orange cocktail. It was really good, the citrus flavors hitting my senses immediately, but not in a bitter or overly sweet way. It was the perfect balance of flavor. "This is delicious, by the way."

"You don't care about why he left? Really?" She cocked an eyebrow.

"I'll never know why. And honestly, I don't need it anymore. I wanted it desperately for so long, you know I did. But I literally woke up one morning and just . . . didn't care."

"I would have gone off the deep end, I think." She looked up at the ceiling as if lost in thought. "Like right away."

"I'll tell you one thing. When you have absolutely nothing to work with, you tend to jump to a lot of conclusions. You make a lot of things up. My mind is not my friend in situations like these."

I thought back to the worst-case scenarios my mind had dredged up back then. At the time, I wasn't sure if my mind was trying to test my resilience or break me completely.

Each scenario was more hurtful than the last—he was dead, he hated me, it was all a joke, I was a bet, he was a con artist, he was married (to someone a thousand times prettier, smarter, and more awesome than I was, of course), he had secret wives all over the world, he was a pathological liar, I was a game, he was gay, I was a challenge.

"I would have reacted the same way." She smiled. "Probably worse, though, because I definitely would have started sending shit to his office. Like dead mice, rotting dog crap, or those disgusting flavors of jelly beans, but in different packaging so he would think he was getting all popcorn-flavored or some shit. You know, the usual psycho ex-girlfriend stuff."

I laughed. "I wouldn't have let you do that!"

"I would have done it anyway."

Tami was right; she would have. And I wouldn't have been able to stop her. Cal should be thankful I wasn't like Tami in that regard.

"I guess in a way it still sucks, but it doesn't hurt anymore. So I'm happy for that."

"I'll drink to that." She held up her almost empty glass to mine, and we clinked them together.

"Cheers," I said with a smile that mimicked how happy I finally felt inside. It seemed like a lifetime since I'd felt anywhere close to normal.

"You really do look great," she added as she finished off her drink.

"I really do feel great."

"Great enough to"—she glanced around at the quickly crowding space—"take someone home tonight?"

I practically choked on my drink. Leave it to Tami to turn everything into an opportunity to have a one-night stand.

"No. I mean, yes, I feel great. But I don't want to meet

anyone right now. I'm not interested in getting involved."

"Who said anything about getting involved?"

"I'm not interested in general."

She blew out a long, loud breath. "This again."

"Seriously, Tami, you're one to talk. Please sleep with someone more than one time and get back to me, okay?"

"Ew, no one wants to do that," she said, her face scrunched as if she'd bit into something sour.

I laughed. "Actually, yeah. They do."

"Who?"

"Most people do, actually."

She grinned as she waved the bartender over and tapped the top of her glass. "I know. I'm just not ready for that kind of commitment."

Like me, Tami was motivated to succeed and build a name for herself in her career. It was why she kept men at arm's length, but she'd never admitted it to me before.

I nodded. "I know you're not."

"You and I are really similar when it comes to guys and work," she said, echoing my thoughts. "The biggest difference is that I don't deny myself sex the way that you do."

"Because I can actually go months without having it and not feel like I'm going to die."

Her jaw dropped open as if I'd said the most ridiculous thing in the world. "How that happens, I'll never understand."

As the bartender returned with two fresh drinks before placing them in front of us, I stared at her and her pink eyes, knowing that tonight she'd eventually find a guy to go home with, and I'd go home alone. But I'd be okay with that because I was finally okay.

Again.

CHICKENSHIT

Cal

DROPPING JULES HAD been a chickenshit move, and I knew it. But that still hadn't stopped me from doing it. I stopped calling, stopped texting, and did my damnedest to remove her from my brain and heart completely.

But it hadn't worked.

Nothing worked.

Cutting her out of my life hadn't stopped her from existing in it; I was already too attached to her. She'd wormed her way into my heart, and no matter how much I tried to pretend it hadn't happened, it had. I felt her there.

Each day that I ignored her, the place where she lived in me ached more. The pain hadn't lessened with her absence—it had only grown.

When Jules had told me that day about handing off her client to her coworker, my chest had ached for her. The last thing I'd wanted was for her to sacrifice anything work-related because of me. But she had done it anyway, willingly, and I figured she'd eventually hate me for it. I didn't want to be someone she ended up hating, so I made a horribly stupid decision and stuck by it.

And now she probably hated me anyway. She had to, by

this point.

Shit, even I hated me.

How the hell I'd gone this long without talking to her was beyond me, but as each day passed, it seemed more and more impossible to pick up the phone and fix the mess I'd created. What kind of an apology would be enough? How could I ever make her understand why I'd done what I had?

When you knew something had an expiration date, what did you do? If you were me, you apparently ran away like a coward and tried not to speak to the love of your life ever again. Like a goddamned idiot.

How could she not see what I was doing? How could she not see that I was driven by fear and insecurity?

Jules was smart. Eventually she would figure it out.

DAYS TURNED INTO weeks, and eventually a month passed. If I thought it would get easier to be away from her, I was dead wrong.

Jules was apparently a hard habit to break, and it hit me that I didn't want to. I'd spent so much time trying to fight what was happening between us, trying to talk myself out of having feelings for her. What I should have been doing was figuring out how to fit her into my life instead of forcing her out of it. I should have been thankful I'd found someone so amazing, not freaking out because of that fact.

I had been so stupid, so incredibly selfish and immature, and I didn't know how to fix it. How could I repair what I had so willingly broken? Lucas had given me a stern talking-to on more than one occasion, and I was convinced that if he had access to Jules's phone number, he would have called her and ended this fiasco weeks ago. The weaker parts of me had wanted to let him, but I couldn't do it.

And now we sat in a bar, drowning my sorrows as it all crashed down around me.

"You gonna finish off that bottle?" Lucas asked as he pointed to the Blanton's sitting across the bar.

"Probably. You got a problem with that?" I glanced at the bartender before signaling that I wanted another.

"No. Just figured I'd help you out. Be a team player and all."

A team player.

Jules had been my teammate and I'd cut her loose. Removed her from the team without warning, took away her jersey and all but burned it.

"How considerate of you," I said sarcastically, sniping at my best friend who didn't deserve the attitude.

Lucas gave me a hard look. "You know, you've been a real dick since you fucked up with Jules. I just wanted to point that out in case you wanted to do something about that. Go apologize to her. Make things right."

"How am I supposed to do that? It's been too long, Luc. I might have been able to fix it after a few days, but not after this long."

He scowled at me. "How do you know? You haven't even tried."

When the bartender refilled our glasses and sat the empty bottle between us, I reached for the horse stopper and pulled it off.

"You gotta be shitting me."

"What? Which letter is it?"

"The *L*," I said before practically throwing it at Lucas's

chest.

"That's the one you need. Now you have them all, right? I mean, if the bar lets you keep it, which I'm sure they will," he said with a smile, and I nodded. "Why aren't you excited? You've been looking for that damn top forever."

"I don't fucking want it anymore, okay?"

The truth was, I didn't want it because it reminded me of Jules. And that stupid *L* that had seemed so important at the time only served as a reminder of everything I'd lost. Who cared about a stupid bottle top when I didn't have Jules anymore?

"Like I said, you've been a real dick, Donovan," Lucas said as he sipped his bourbon.

"I need to get out of here." I tossed more than enough cash on top of the bar before stumbling out the doors and opening a car app on my phone.

Lucas appeared behind me. "You calling a car?"

"Yeah. You coming or what?"

"I'm gonna stay for a bit longer. Text me when you get home so I know you're not dead or in jail," he said before walking back inside.

I forced out a quick laugh. Lucas and the damn bartender had been flirting all night. It hadn't annoyed me before, but now it pissed me the hell off.

The car pulled up and I got inside, giving the driver my address as I fidgeted in the backseat.

I didn't know what the hell to do anymore. I couldn't live like this a second longer, not like this, not without her. Dialing Cooper's number, I prayed he wasn't at a game. I hadn't even looked at his schedule before calling, and I needed his advice.

"Hey," he answered, out of breath.

"Hey. You busy?"

"Not for my big bro. What's up? How's Jules?" Leave it to Cooper to ask how Jules was. Of course he'd ask.

"That's actually why I'm calling," I said, the bourbon sloshing around in my all but empty stomach.

"Okay," he said, his voice wary.

"I fucked up, Coop. I fucked up real bad."

"Shit, Cal, what'd you do?"

His tone was so concerned, I couldn't help but wonder what he thought it was that I might have done. Shoving that aside for the moment, I said, "I got scared."

"And you pushed her away?" he asked, finishing my sentence for me.

"Not exactly. I took myself out of the equation."

"I'm not following."

"I stopped talking to her," I said, the admission crushing me. The guilt I'd been carrying on my shoulders fell down around me like boulders once I said the words out loud.

"You stopped talking to her? Like you stopped returning her phone calls or what?"

I cleared my throat. "I stopped everything cold turkey, Coop. Didn't return texts, calls, e-mails. No explanation. No nothing. I basically disappeared."

My driver, who'd been acting like he'd been ignoring my phone conversation the whole time, caught my eye in the rearview mirror and shook his head in disgust.

"What the hell, Cal? That's awful. Why would you do that to her?"

The last thing I needed was my little brother yelling at me over shit I already knew. I didn't need to be chastised; I needed help.

Lowering my voice, I said, "Because I'm an idiot, okay? I was wrong. I made a mistake. I screwed up. I need to know how to fix it. If you'd done this to Katherine, what would you do to make her forgive you?"

"First of all, let's be clear that I'd never do that to Katherine," he said, his voice stern, angry even.

"Yeah, we already know you're the perfect brother. Got it. Help me, please."

"I wouldn't apologize over the phone or through a text, that's for sure. I'd make sure I apologized face-to-face," he said, and I nodded along. That was a good idea, the in-person part. "And I'd do whatever it took to make her forgive me. Whatever it took, Cal."

That one would be tougher, and I knew it.

"What if she won't? Forgive me, that is?"

"If she's what you really want, you can't let her say no. And then you figure out what it will take to win her back, and do that."

"Thanks, Coop."

"Keep me updated."

"I will."

I ended the call and ignored the glances my driver shot at me in the mirror as I went about formulating a plan of attack. I had no idea where Jules's head was, not to mention her heart. She could despise me by this point, and I wouldn't blame her if she did, but I needed to convince her otherwise.

I had no idea how to go about doing that, but I sure as hell was going to try.

HE'S HERE

Jules

M Y ARMS FILLED with all of my things, I pushed my way through the apartment complex door with my hip and ran straight into a solid wall of . . . *chest?*

My morning coffee spilled and the client folders filled with paperwork I had been holding fell to the ground. I watched as the sheets scattered before muttering *shit* and rushing to grab them. Squatting, I started gathering them before hearing, "Let me help you."

My heart thumped once, maybe twice, before it stopped beating altogether. Apparently, even my heart had a self-preservation mode. My breath hitched as a golf-ball-sized lump instantly formed in my throat.

How could four stupid words cause such an intense physical reaction?

My gaze moved slowly from his black shoes and followed the length of his jeans up past the formfitting black T-shirt before landing on my demise, the one thing that captured me in the first place, those horribly stupid perfect lips. I paused on them a little longer than I should have, and when I locked onto Cal's hazel eyes, I had to stop myself from falling to the ground completely.

"What are you doing here?" I asked, my tone as annoyed as I could muster through my surprise as I shoved the papers into a rough stack.

"I came for you," he said matter-of-factly, as if that simple declaration would wipe away the last several weeks of emotional hell I'd been through and make it all better.

His response was such a shock, I couldn't hold myself up. Stunned, I dropped to the concrete and pulled my knees up to my chest as his words repeated inside my head.

I came for you. I came for you. I came for you.

"Why?" My emotions warred within me, contradictory, conflicting, and almost too much for me to bear.

Cal sat down across from me, mirroring my position but not touching. "Because I messed up, Jules. I messed up so bad."

I tried to swallow but my throat felt thick, and my heart thumped loudly against my chest as if it couldn't fit in there a second longer.

My mind warned me not to trust him so easily, no matter how hard my heart battered against its cage. *We believed all of his pretty words before*, my mind said, *and look where it got us— heartbroken, discarded, and ignored.*

Staring unseeing at the papers I'd dropped a second time, I said flatly, "Yeah, you did. Why are you here?"

It took everything in me to hold on to my resolve and not jump into his arms. Seeing him in front of me, I was still so very attracted to this man. But I'd finally gotten angry at him, and I'd been grateful for that emotion at the time. But now that he was sitting across from me, I felt anything but anger.

And that pissed me right off. I shouldn't melt at the mere sight of him. Not after what he'd done. I shouldn't even warm in his presence.

But I did.

He ran his fingers through his messy brown hair before he pinned me with his gaze. "I'm here to tell you I'm sorry, to make things right. To fight for you."

When he reached out to touch my leg, I jerked it away. I couldn't let him touch me. Not yet. My anger simmered just below the surface, and I held on to it like a lifeline. Being mad made me feel strong and powerful. It was all I had.

"To fight for me?" I said with a choked laugh. "What a joke. You threw me away, wouldn't even respond to my messages. Hell, you wouldn't even *read* them on Facebook. What kind of an asshole—"

"This asshole," he said, cutting me off. "Me. I know; I fucking know, Jules. I was wrong. I was an idiot. Please let me explain. Hear me out."

Glancing down at my cell phone and noting the time, I shook my head. "I have to go. I'm late for an appointment."

I pushed off of the ground and wiped the seat of my pants off with my hands before I scooped up my papers and headed for my car.

"I'm not going anywhere," Cal yelled at my retreating back.

"Sure you're not," I shouted over my shoulder without looking at him, unsure of what I'd do if I had to face him again.

Only once I was in the privacy of my car did I allow the few tears that had formed to fall. I refused to let him see me cry. I'd cried enough over Cal in the last several weeks; I wouldn't give him the satisfaction of knowing he still affected me.

He didn't deserve my tears.

DIDN'T GO WELL

Cal

I WATCHED AS Jules got into her car and wiped at her face with the back of her hand. Before that moment, I hadn't thought that I could feel any worse, but knowing that I made her cry proved me wrong. I sank even lower, feeling more like an asshole than I had five minutes ago.

Then her window rolled down and my heart flipped inside my chest as she turned to look at me.

"How could you go all that time without saying a single word to me? You ignored me." Her voice shook as she continued. "Your silence was a thousand times worse than anything you could have said to me. It was your indifference that gutted me the most."

Had I completely ruined her, ruined any chance of there being an *us* ever again?

I jogged over to her car, not wanting her to leave, desperate for her to hear me out. I should have brought flowers. But here I was, running toward her car emptyhanded like the insensitive jerk I was.

"I wasn't indifferent; I was never indifferent. I was stubborn and fighting with myself every day to prove that I was stronger than the pull you had over me," I admitted, needing her to know the state I was in without her.

"But why? All you did was hurt me. You had to know that you were hurting me." Her green eyes looked pained, and I hated that I was the one who put the hurt there. I should be the guy who took her pain away, not the one who made her feel it.

I couldn't pretend like I didn't know. I thought about lying to her, saying whatever would bring her the most comfort, but she deserved the truth. She deserved so much more than that after what I'd pulled. So I swallowed my pride around the lump in my throat.

"Yes. I knew I was hurting you."

"And you did that willingly. You made a choice to hurt me. Every single day for weeks, you consciously chose that." Her eyes filled again and I thought it might break me.

"I didn't want to hurt you," I tried to explain, but what could I possibly say that would make this okay? "I didn't want to hurt you, Jules, I just knew that I was. I put my ego and pride over your feelings. Hell, I put them over my own feelings."

"But you did hurt me."

"I know."

"How do I know you won't do that again?"

When she tore her gaze away from mine, I felt instantly lost. I hated what was happening, hated that I'd hurt her and she despised me for it. I deserved it, but I couldn't stand what I'd done.

"You don't. Nothing I say will mean a damn thing right now."

"Then why are you here?" Her jaw clenched as she glared at me.

"Because I want to show you how sorry I am. I want you back."

Jules narrowed her eyes. "You made me feel like I didn't matter. Do you have any idea how that feels? I met you and you mattered to me, Cal, more than anyone I'd met in a long time. And then you made me feel like I never existed, like you could live without me. Easily."

If she only knew the whole reason I was here was because I couldn't live without her. I knew that now.

"You always existed. There wasn't a single day where you didn't live inside me. I noticed everything you did. Every single thing you said. Every post you put on social media, I saw it all. Until you unfriended me. That was a torture of its own kind, but I knew I deserved it."

"You let me sit there and believe you didn't care."

"I know I did, and I was wrong. I was an idiot. I'm so sorry, Jules."

She sucked in a quick breath, the pink coloring her cheeks telling me loud and clear that her temper was rising. "You know what, Cal? Fuck you and your *I'm sorrys*."

I blinked at her in disbelief. "What?"

"I want you to leave." She pointed toward the exit of her complex and shot me a look that could kill weaker men.

I didn't blame her. I'd have to show her I knew how wrong I'd been. I'd have to prove to her that she could trust me.

"Can we finish this conversation, at least? Please, Jules."

"This conversation is over. You wrecked me. I opened my heart to you, and I trusted you. I believed the things you said to me, the way you made me feel, and then you disappeared on me. You have no idea what the past five weeks have been like for me. No idea. Because if you did, you would have stopped what you were doing by day two."

She glared at me, trying to be strong, but I could tell she was as broken as I was.

"Don't walk away from me, Jules. Please don't," I begged. I wasn't above it at this point.

"At least you know I'm going." She shoved my hand off her car door and stepped on the gas, leaving me and my broken heart in her rearview mirror.

I had hurt her more than I realized. I'd been hurting too, but it was nothing compared to what I'd put her through. I hadn't expected this level of pain. I should have known better, but I was an idiot. That much, at least, was clear.

That did not go as planned. Pulling out my cell, I dialed Lucas, who had been waiting for an update since the day I told him I was coming out here.

"How'd it go?" he said instead of hello.

"Like hell."

He laughed. If I didn't know any better, I'd think my best friend thought this situation was funny. And it was anything but funny.

"Well, what'd you expect?" he asked.

"I don't know, but not that. I thought she'd at least be mildly happy to see me. Maybe give me a smile," I admitted. "There was no smiling, Lucas."

"Bro, you didn't speak to the girl for weeks. Thirty-seven days, to be exact. That's a long-ass time when you're separated by the entire country and can't run into each other at the gym or the grocery store. She texted you and e-mailed you and you didn't respond to any of it. So you, what, thought she'd go jumping into your buff arms the second she laid eyes on you?"

When he laughed again, I found myself wishing he was sitting next to me so I could punch him. "Stop fucking laughing," I growled out, which only made him laugh harder.

He finally finished his laugh attack, and his tone turned serious. "You hurt her."

"I know. That's why I'm here."

"It's not enough that you're there. It's a nice gesture, don't get me wrong, and it's way better than a phone call or a text apology. But she's going to need more than just you showing up on her front porch saying you're sorry. You're going to have to convince her that she can give you her heart again. Look what you did to it the last time she gave it to you."

I tried to swallow, but couldn't. Lucas's words struck more than a single nerve inside me. It felt like he struck every one.

"You're good at this," I muttered.

"I know."

"So, what do I do? How do I convince her to give me another chance?"

He blew out a long breath into the line. "You've got to figure that one out on your own, but I will tell you this. Don't give up, no matter what she says. It's only been five weeks. There's no way her heart's completely changed course in that time. Trust me."

"Trust you? You don't even date girls!"

"No, I don't. But that doesn't mean I don't have experience with feelings and emotions. People are people, Cal. Don't be a prick."

I groaned. "You're right. I'm sorry. I'm just in a shitty mood, man. I don't want to lose her." My heart was literally aching inside my chest. I wanted to reach inside and yank it out just to get it to stop.

"Then don't stop fighting. Even when she tries to make you, Cal. If she pushes away and you run, you lose. You'll only prove her right if you do that."

"Prove her right?"

Lucas let out an exasperated sigh. "If she tells you to go away and you do, then all you've done is show her again that she wasn't worth it. You can't take no for an answer. You can't let her push you away. You have to be stubborn."

I nodded as I listened, and everything fell into place in my mind. "You're right. That's sort of what I was thinking anyway. I'm good at stubborn."

"No shit," he agreed too easily.

"Thanks, Luc. Talk to you later."

I tucked my phone in my pocket and began pacing back and forth on the sidewalk in front of Jules's apartment building.

How the hell was I supposed to prove anything to her when we didn't even live in the same state? I couldn't stay out here forever, but this was one war I refused to lose.

I'd have to start all over and win her back from scratch.

WHAT DO I DO?

Jules

I PRACTICALLY PEELED out of my parking lot, leaving Cal behind in my virtual dust. Or maybe I kicked up real dust and hit him in the face with it. I tried not to care, but oh how I cared.

Pressing the button on my steering wheel, I prayed to whoever was listening that Tami would be able to take a call from me. I needed my best friend.

"Hey," she answered. "I have court in thirty-five. What's up?"

"He's here."

"He, who? What are you—" She stopped and made a weird sound that reflected exactly how I currently felt inside, twisted up and short of breath. "Cal? He's where?"

"He was at my apartment just now."

My heart raced inside my chest. My emotions were spinning like a roulette wheel, not knowing which one to land on. I felt so many things all at once; too many, in fact.

"Holy shit, Jules. What did he say? How did he look? How do you feel?"

I tried to suck in a deep breath, but my lungs failed me. "I don't know. He said he was sorry. He looked really good, which is beyond irritating, to be honest."

She whistled into the phone. "I bet. And you?"

"I'm a mess."

"How did you feel when you first saw him?" she asked in her lawyer voice, as if I were a client up for questioning against the opposition later. Hell, maybe I was.

I settled my mind, searching for the answer. "I was confused at first, you know? Like my brain couldn't comprehend how he was standing in front of me when he was supposed to be on the other side of the country."

"It's Wednesday. What the hell is he doing here on a Wednesday?"

Good question. I hadn't even thought about the fact that he was all the way out here during the middle of a work week.

"I don't know. That is weird, though."

"It is. We'll come back to that. So your head was confused; I get that. But how did your heart feel?"

"Like it grew a thousand sizes in that first second. Him being here . . . it's what I wanted for so long."

"And now?" she asked, and a tapping sound filtered through our connection. Tapping her pen against her desk, probably.

"I'd just given up hope of it ever happening. I'd accepted our fate."

"But you still have feelings for him, don't you?" she asked through the sound of a pen scratching against paper.

"I honestly thought I didn't," I said as I slowed my car to a stop on the highway.

"But seeing him changed that?" The pen stopped scrawling, telling me she was focused on my answer.

I navigated around some traffic once the light turned green

before taking a right. "Definitely. Seeing him made me realize how much I'd been lying to myself."

"You weren't lying, Jules. You had no other choice."

"Thank you." Her words made me feel marginally better. "So, what the hell do I do?"

"I have no idea. Just don't give in too easily. I mean, if you want to forgive him, make him work for it. Don't forget how heartbroken you were when he disappeared."

"I could never." I couldn't forget the way his leaving made me feel if I tried. All I knew was that I never wanted to experience that kind of pain again. "I could never forget that."

"I'm sorry, Jules, but I need to go. I'll call you later and check in. Love you, and good luck," Tami said before ending our call.

Pulling my car through the privacy gate and onto the stunning ocean-front property I was scheduled to show, I sat for a minute longer, my brain reeling, until my heart rate finally returned to normal.

I would get through today, hopefully sell a house, and deal with Cal later. He could not be my priority today. I sure as hell hadn't been his in weeks.

With a determined breath, I got out of my car and went to work.

PULLING INTO MY assigned parking space after work, I noticed Cal immediately. His large frame was hunched over as he sat on the staircase leading up to my apartment, a bouquet of red roses and a familiar-looking box at his side.

I could have called security or the management company and had him escorted off the property since it was a private, gated complex, but I didn't. Part of me didn't want him to leave. In fact, my ego actually perked up a little at the knowledge that he was here for me. It wanted that, reveled in it.

Plus, today had been a good day at the office. I'd sold a beachfront condo and gained two new clients in the course of the afternoon through referrals, so my mood had lifted.

Cal pushed to his feet and picked up his things as I turned off the engine and opened the door, his strides toward me quick and purposeful. He approached me with the enormous flower arrangement in his arms as he balanced it with the box.

"Why are you still here?" I asked, hoping I sounded indifferent, when I was anything but. I was filled with feelings, with emotions that had no name.

"I waited. This is for you." He handed me the box.

It was a dirty move, bringing me a pie from the diner when I was still so angry at him. Refusing to even look at it, I set it on the hood of my car.

"And these." He handed me the bouquet of roses.

I reached for them but didn't smell them, even though I wanted to bring them to my nose and breathe them in. I let them fall to my side as if they were the least interesting thing that had been given to me all day. Truth be told, they were ridiculously gorgeous, some of the biggest, deepest red roses I'd ever laid eyes on, but I refused to admit that. I refused a lot of things when it came to Cal right now.

"Thanks for these. So, why did you wait for me?"

I studied him, noting that his hazel eyes looked tired. My heart begged me to jump into his arms, to pull him upstairs and fall into him the way I had so easily in the beginning. But I had to fight against my stupid heart, because giving in to him without a single thought was what had gotten me into trouble in the first place.

Cal's gaze burned into me. "I wanted to talk to you. I need to talk to you."

I considered saying no, telling him to pound sand as I locked him out of my apartment and my life. But if I did, I'd only be putting off the inevitable. Cal had flown all the way here for a reason. I couldn't imagine that he'd walk away so easily this time.

"So talk," I said as I placed the roses on top of the pie box.

"Can I come up?"

I folded my arms across my chest, refusing to move as I leaned back against my car. I couldn't give him any ground. If I gave him an inch, I'd give in entirely, and I had to at least attempt to make him suffer for all the pain he'd caused me.

After all, the man had hurt me without reason. Disappeared without a trace. His silence had been so deafening, so soul-gutting in its loudness. His quiet had been louder than any words he'd ever spoken.

"No," I said firmly. "We can talk right here."

He shifted on his feet, clearly uncomfortable.

Good.

"Okay. We'll talk here," he said as he looked around.

I waited for him to say something, still half in disbelief that he was standing right in front of me after all this time. He looked so damn good and I hated him for that, but couldn't really blame myself for thinking it. Being attracted to Cal had never been the issue.

"I fucked up, Jules. Worse than I've ever fucked up before." His hand ran through his hair and my eyes were instantly drawn there, focused on the way the strands formed into messy spikes.

In that moment, I wanted answers more than anything. My need for them came rushing back despite the fact that I'd stuffed them away and tried to convince myself that they no longer mattered. Why not get closure if he was offering it?

"Just tell me why you did it," I said. "Why'd you stop talking to me? Aren't we too old for that type of shit?"

Cal spread his feet a little further apart and stuffed one hand firmly in his pocket. "I thought I was doing us both a favor," he said with a deep sigh before looking me dead in the eyes.

"A favor?" I snorted out a disbelieving laugh. "What kind of favor could you possibly be doing for us?"

Oh, hell no. Not only was he confusing me, he was started to piss me off.

"I got scared, okay? We both knew that this thing between us was temporary." He wagged a finger between us. "Hell, Jules, you even said once that you had no plans to move out of LA, and I said the same thing about Boston. So I started thinking about what the hell we were doing, or what the point was. Why was I falling in love with someone I could never have?"

My heart stopped and lurched once before kicking back into its proper rhythm. *Love?*

"So you decided that going radio silent on me was the answer?"

"I didn't know what to do. I thought you'd be fine, eventually anyway. You're just as busy as I am with work, so I figured you'd bounce right back, forget all about me."

"Bounce right back? I've never felt about anyone the way I felt about you," I admitted, my emotions getting the best of me as my voice shook.

"Felt?"

I bristled. "Yes. Felt."

"As in past tense?" His brow furrowed.

"As in past tense." I repeated the lie with a shrug as his gaze dropped to his feet.

"I deserve that."

"You do."

God, I couldn't do this. I couldn't be here with him right now, my head swimming in thoughts, my heart drowning in them.

His eyes found mine again. "I thought I was making a decision that was the best for both of us. I really thought," he started, but stumbled on his words as if he hadn't had thirty-seven days to practice some sort of speech. "I just—"

"You chose for me," I blurted, interrupting him. "You made a decision about us without even asking me for my input." Furious, I glared at him. "You don't get to tell me how to feel, or how to act, or take yourself away from me when it was the last thing in the world that I wanted. I had no idea what we were going to do about the future or where we were headed, but I knew that I wasn't ready for us to end."

The pain in his eyes deepened. "I thought I knew what I was doing, but I was wrong. So wrong. I'm so sorry, Jules. I wish there was a better word than sorry, but I don't know one."

"I wish it was enough, but it's not. You really hurt me, Cal. I'm okay now, but I wasn't. I wasn't okay for a long time."

It was part lie, part truth. I had been okay until I laid eyes on him today. Seeing him had thrown everything in me for a loop. I wasn't okay, but I refused to admit that to him.

"Well, I'm not okay," he said. "I haven't been okay since the day I let you get away. I'm unsteady without you. I thought I knew what I wanted and when I wanted it. But then you came along and made me question everything without even trying. Just your existence had me feeling strung out."

He stopped short and rubbed his eyes with the heel of his hands. "I don't want to do this without you. I get that you're okay now, but I'm not, and I won't be if you're not by my side. I know that now. Hell, I knew it then, I just tried to fight it. Please give me another chance. I'm not saying I'll never make another mistake or screw up ever again, because I am a guy, but I can promise that I'll never leave you. I'll never be that stupid with your heart again."

"How? How can you promise me that? You can't promise something like that!"

What bullshit. That promise was nothing but a bunch of pretty words. Even if he meant them when he said them, no one could make a vow of that magnitude.

"I can, because I know what it's like to try to live without you, to try to pretend that I don't need you. You make me a better man, Jules. I'm better when I'm with you."

"But nothing's changed; we still live in different states. I don't plan on moving, and I'm sure you don't either. Why come here if nothing about our *temporary* situation has improved?" I asked, unable to hide my bitterness.

"Because I don't think we're temporary anymore. Look, Jules, I'm not sure what the future holds for us, or what the hell we'll do about it, but all I know is that I want one with you. My life's not the same when you're not a part of it. Trust me, I tried. It didn't work out so well."

"I don't know." I tore my gaze away from him and hugged myself, trying to keep a hold on my emotions.

This was exactly what I had longed for. I'd wanted Cal to come back to me more than anything, but now that he was here, wearing his heart on his sleeve, I was terrified to trust him again. He'd not only crushed my heart when he walked away, he'd done it so easily.

"I know you don't trust me," he said, his expression earnest. "I know you don't think you can. I'll show you. I'll prove it to you."

I studied his expressions and gauged his tone of voice, wanting to forgive him, to believe him, but I refused to be naive. I couldn't be stupid with my heart again. I wasn't sure I'd survive another blow from him.

Shaking my head, I said, "I don't know how to get past this. It might seem stupid to you, but what you did to me was heart altering. You threw me off balance. You let me fall off a cliff and you weren't there to catch me. You left me alone when all I wanted was for you to be there."

"I know." He winced. "I know I ruined things, Jules. I acted like a complete idiot. You have no idea how badly I wish I could take it all back."

"But you can't," I snapped.

"No, I can't. But I want to. I would give anything to rewind time and do it all over again."

"Yeah? What would you do differently?"

"I wouldn't leave you. I'd talk to you when I got nervous instead of becoming a stubborn, bullheaded pig. But mostly, I'd never let you get away from me. And I'd do whatever it took to make this work."

God, could I ever relate to the talking part. There had

been things that I was nervous about that I'd never addressed with him. I'd kept those questions inside, locked away, afraid of the answer. I'd been cowardly too. The only difference between us was that I hadn't run away.

My eyes pricked with the beginnings of tears I didn't want him to see. Turning my head, I swiped at my eyes quickly and willed them to stay dry. I needed all my strength in these moments with him.

"I have to go, Cal. I appreciate that you're here, truly." I grabbed the roses and the pie from the hood and took a step away. "But I have a lot to think about."

"Can we just start over, please? Let me take you out on dates. We can get to know each other again. I'll come out here every weekend. I'll do whatever you want me to. Just tell me what you need from me, Jules. Please tell me what I can do to fix this."

My arms full, I tried to shrug. "I honestly don't know. I don't know how to fix this."

Cal started to say something else, his mouth opening before he snapped it shut. As I walked up the stairs and away from him, he didn't try to stop me or ask me to stay.

When he shouted, "I miss my teammate," I almost tripped over my heart as it fell from my chest. I hesitated for only a second, my steps faltering before I continued through my front door and closed it between us.

Leaning against it for a moment, breathing hard, I had two questions on my mind.

How could Cal erase the space he'd so willingly created between us?

And did I want him to?

WIN HER BACK

Cal

THIS WASN'T GOING to be easy. Not that I'd expected Jules to go easy on me, but I had hoped she would be a little more willing or easier to sway.

Leave it to me to think that way. I had to put myself in her shoes. She wasn't the type to give away her heart, but she had so quickly opened up and given it to me.

And what had I done with it? I was careless and thoughtless. Instead of treating her like the absolute gift from heaven she was, I treated her as if she were replaceable, someone I could easily get over and never speak to again. It was an immature move on my part, among other things.

How could I take that back? Why wasn't time travel a real thing yet, so I could stop myself from being a complete and utter idiot?

I scrawled out a quick note, telling Jules I wasn't giving up and that I'd be back for her later, and slipped it under her windshield wiper. She'd probably throw it in the trash.

I didn't want to leave, but Malibu was lacking on the hotel front, and I had early morning meetings scheduled in the Hollywood area tomorrow. Even still, I'd have camped out on Jules's stairs all night long if that was what it took for her to forgive me.

It was probably better that I gave her some space, even though it was the last thing I wanted to do. The possessive caveman in me wanted to crowd her, make sure there was no space where I didn't exist to her, but she'd probably knee me in the balls. Figuratively and literally.

So I begrudgingly drove away in my rental car with no idea where I was going. All I knew was that according to my GPS, Hollywood was much farther away than I remembered.

MY MEETINGS AND appointments the next day ended up taking longer than I had anticipated, and I was running late. Not to mention, the Los Angeles traffic was something I could never have prepared for. And the rain seemed to make it all worse. Yes, apparently it did actually rain in Southern California, and everyone who said otherwise was a liar.

Things had gone well today, and even though I was being a bit presumptuous in what I'd accomplished, I didn't care. I was convinced that I had made the right decision, and I'd wait however long it took for Jules to feel the same way. I wasn't going anywhere ever again, and she needed to know that.

By the time I reached Malibu that night, it was well past seven. I considered giving her an extra day to think over everything, but I couldn't do it. Staying away from her was the exact opposite of my intentions.

I punched in the code at the gate, which I'd memorized from my first visit here, and pulled inside the complex. I breathed out in relief at the sight of her car. Thankful she was home, I parked my car and hopped out. As I took the steps two at a time up to her door, I knocked on it before I froze at the realization that she might not be alone.

I hadn't even asked if she was seeing anyone, had I? Discomfort surged through me as I realized I couldn't remember. *Shit.* This was the one time in my life I hadn't thought through every single detail, and I swore it might kill me. With no other choice at this point, I held my breath and waited for her to answer.

When I heard the sound of her walking across the floor, I started breathing again. The door creaked as she leaned against it before she barely pulled it open. She must have checked to see who was there through the peephole.

"I thought you'd gone back home," she said, her tone cool.

She had to know better than that. "I told you I wasn't leaving."

"You've said a lot of things." Her long blond hair fell in front of her eyes, and I had to fight my instincts to run my fingers through it.

"Can I come in?" When she hesitated, staring at me, I said, "Please?"

She closed her eyes briefly before pulling the door open all the way and stepping back to let me in. I looked around at her place, thankful to be a part of it again, even if it was only for the moment.

I headed toward the couch in her living room, hoping she wouldn't argue. "Can I sit?"

She nodded instead of speaking, making me wonder what was going on in that pretty head of hers.

"Have you thought about what I said last night?"

Her green eyes met mine and locked on. I figured she'd look away, but she didn't. Pulling out one of her bar stools, she sat down, her gaze still focused on mine.

"It's all I've been able to think about." Even when she hated me, she couldn't stop being emotionally honest with her thoughts.

"And?"

"And I still don't know what to do."

She was stubborn, maybe even more so than I had been. I didn't blame her for it; it was just killing me to sit there and accept it.

"How do you *feel*?" I asked, emphasizing the emotion in our situation. "What does your heart say? Right now, in this moment, what is your heart telling you to do?"

Yes, I was pushing her, but I had to. I needed to break through.

"My heart's on a time-out," she answered, her tone indifferent, but I knew better.

"A time-out?" I chuckled at her response.

"Yeah. It can't be trusted when it comes to you."

I bit back a smile at that. Jules still had feelings for me, whether she said it out loud or not. It was a small victory and I'd take it, but it wasn't enough. Not yet.

"Do you know what my heart says?"

She fidgeted, crossing and uncrossing her legs. "How could I possibly know that?"

Pushing up from the couch, I started pacing back and forth, trying my damnedest to put my feelings into words.

Without thinking, I blurted, "I love you, Jules." Hell, I hadn't planned on telling her like that. At least not yet. "I'm in love with you." Jesus, I couldn't stop myself.

Instead of the smile that I half expected to cover her face, I was met with a scowl. I'd told the girl I loved her, and she was sitting there scowling at me. Could I do nothing right when it came to her?

"Your words. They were always pretty, but your actions were ugly. I don't know how to believe that you mean the things you say to me. And I want to, Cal, I do want to believe you. I just don't know how."

"I know you don't. I can't imagine how I must have made you feel."

"Like a fool. I felt like a fool."

I took a tentative step toward her, her response like a stab to my gut. "Why?" I asked, absolutely hating her answer and that I was the one who made her feel that way.

"Because I felt stupid for believing you. At some point, I figured everything you said must have all been lies. I thought I was smarter than that, that I'd be able to see through someone's bullshit. And when I hadn't seen through yours, I felt like a total idiot."

The knife twisted in my gut. "I meant everything I said to you. There was so much more I stopped myself from telling you because I was scared of what it all meant. You couldn't see through my words because there was nothing to see through."

She swallowed hard, her eyes searching mine for the truth before her expression softened. "I want to believe you."

"And I want you to." The tightness in my chest loosened. "I want to show you something. Would you come for a drive with me?"

Emotions flitted over her face, a mixture of surprise and confusion. "Can you give me a few minutes, and I'll meet you downstairs?"

She was kicking me out. I wanted to argue but knew that I couldn't. I had to pick my battles, and this wasn't one worth fighting about.

"Take all the time you need," I said, hoping like hell she wouldn't leave me out there in the rain all alone.

SECOND CHANCES

Jules

W̲HEN CAL CLOSED the door behind him, I wrapped my arms around myself, trying to keep from falling apart.

Holy hell, he'd just told me he loved me. I'd wanted nothing more than to jump into his arms, but I stayed strong. I had no idea how the hell I'd done it, but I had. Surely, I deserved some kind of award for bravery. Or maybe it was stupidity?

As much as I tried to pretend that I was protecting my heart from being broken again, there was a large part of me that knew my pride was also to blame. It wanted to teach Cal a lesson, to punish him relentlessly because it could. That was almost as immature as his leaving had been.

I grabbed my phone and dialed Tami's number. Apparently, running every romantic decision by my best friend was my new MO these days.

"What's the latest?" she asked.

"He showed up here again."

"Of course he did," she said, as if I was being dense.

In a small voice, I said, "He said he wants to take me somewhere and show me something."

"What the hell could he possibly want to show you?"

"I have no idea."

"Did you ask him why he was here during the middle of the week?"

I slapped my forehead. "No! I keep forgetting. He's distracting."

She laughed. "I bet he's distracting."

"Be helpful. Please."

"I am helpful," she said, her tone so pouty, I could visualize that lower lip sticking out.

"He told me he loved me," I whispered.

"He what?"

"You heard me."

"Ah hell, he doesn't fight fair. What did you say?"

I racked my brain, trying to remember. What the hell had I said when my heart started pounding so loudly, I couldn't hear anything else?

"I told him I didn't believe his words."

Tami laughed again. "Damn. The guy spills his heart on your floor, and you step on it with the heel of your Louboutins."

"I don't own Louboutins."

"Missing the point."

"I know." I groaned. "Am I stupid for wanting to give him another chance?"

"Normally, I'd say yes. But in this case, I'm telling you no. You're not stupid. Look, I like Cal. I don't like what he did to you, and I'll never forget that he did it. But I really do think he's sorry. Seriously, Jules, he's not my boyfriend, and *I* want to take him back."

I chewed on my lip as I agonized over what to do. I didn't want to make a mistake, didn't want to make the wrong decision. But most of all, I didn't want to get hurt again.

"I'm scared," I admitted.

"Of what?"

"That he'll hurt me again."

Tami sighed. "That's always the risk when it comes to love, but we do it anyway. Remember when you told me that you were going to get hurt? You said to remind you that you were going to get hurt when it came to Cal, but that you were going for it anyway. I remember thinking how brave you were, and how I'd never been that brave in love."

"Brave? Really?"

I hadn't considered my actions brave. If anything, I'd thought I was foolish and had beaten myself up for acting so irrationally. But maybe Tami had a point.

"Yes," she said firmly. "Especially coming from you, my little workaholic. You knew the potential was there for things to end badly, but you wanted him more. He was worth the risk."

She was right. I had always known that I could end up brokenhearted, but I hadn't cared then. And I was pretty sure I didn't care now. Cal was here, and I supposed that I owed it to myself to see what he had to show me.

"Thanks, Tam. I gotta go. I'll call you later."

"I'll be dying to hear what he wanted to show you. I hope it's not his penis, because you've already seen that," she called out, laughing hysterically as I ended the call.

My heart racing, I locked the door behind me and gripped my purse as I headed down the stairs.

Cal leaned against a black SUV at the curb, looking ridiculously hot. I hadn't paid attention until now, but he was dressed as if he'd just come from the office. He'd taken it a little more casual after hours, his dark blue dress shirt unbuttoned at the collar and untucked from a pair of black slacks.

When I reached the sidewalk, he jogged over and held his jacket above my head to shield me from the rain.

"Thank you," I said as he opened my car door for me and helped me inside.

Damn his chivalry.

"You're welcome." He shut my door and sprinted over to the driver's side before hopping in. "It might take a little while to get there. I hope that's okay."

I studied Cal for second and realized he seemed nervous, or maybe defeated. I wasn't sure.

"I don't have any plans." I tried to soften my tone, but it still came out somewhat guarded.

When he pulled out of my complex and headed toward Santa Monica, I frowned, a little unnerved that I had no idea where we were going. Trying to be patient, I stared out my window, amazed at how surreal this all seemed.

It seemed so weird to be sitting in a car with him and not have his hand on my thigh. I had almost forgotten how he used to do that, but now that I was sitting next to him, it all came crashing back how natural it always felt to be with him. How easy things between us always were.

When the silence began to drive me crazy, I said, "Can I ask you something?"

He shot me a quick glance. "You can ask me anything."

"How are you here in the middle of the week? You didn't get fired, did you?"

He choked on a laugh. "Fired? No. Why would you think that?"

"To be honest, I'm surprised to see you at all, but I'm even more surprised to see you during the work week. I didn't peg you for the type of guy who took days off to apologize to women."

He grinned. "I'm not."

"So you're not going to tell me?"

My annoyance faded for a second as I stared at Cal's profile. It was sexy. Those stupid lips were still as full and gorgeous as ever. I missed looking at his face, and I hated how much I missed those lips.

He shook his head, and it looked like he was holding back a smile. "Not yet."

"Fine."

"Don't be mad."

"I'm not mad, I'm just—"

"Pouting," he said, speaking for me.

I wanted to stay mad, but I let out a laugh instead. "Yes. I'm pouting."

He reached across the center console and grabbed my hand, squeezing it before he brought it to his lips and pressed a soft kiss to my fingers.

"I do love you, Jules. I know I should stop saying it, but I need you to know I'm serious."

Biting my lip, I pulled my hand away and placed it back in my lap. I wanted so badly to tell him I loved him too, but I couldn't. Not until I knew what he wanted to show me. Not until I knew what the hell was going on.

"I'm starting to believe you," I said. When he grinned at that, I added, "A little."

His grin only widened. "I'll take it."

A while later, he navigated away from the coast and through the winding roads toward Hollywood. I had a feeling he was heading toward Sunset Boulevard, but I still had no idea why.

Was he taking me to a club? Had he set something up with Ron? When we reached Sunset and he made a right, I was still no closer to an answer about where we were headed.

Finally, we pulled into an underground parking lot of one of the most well-known buildings on Sunset. I'd been in this building before, but it had been a long time. It was primarily an office building, filled with everything from entertainment agencies to real estate brokers.

"What are we doing here?" I asked as he parked the car and turned off the ignition.

Cal opened his door and hopped out. "Come on."

He extended his hand to me and helped me from the car, but he didn't let go, twining his fingers with mine. Instead of pulling from his grasp, I gripped his hand tighter.

When he swiped a keycard and the door to the building buzzed open, I was confused.

"How do you—?"

Cal stopped walking and turned to face me. "No questions. Just give me two minutes."

"You're so bossy."

He led me toward a bank of elevators and pressed the call button. When the doors opened and we stepped inside, a flush rushed up my face at the memory of how his body pressed against mine each time we'd taken the elevator in the hotel in Boston.

Wondering if he was thinking the same thing, I slid a sideways glance at his pants and hid my smile. Yep, he was having flashbacks of his own.

The elevator dinged on the seventh floor and we stepped

out, Cal leading the way as if he'd been here a hundred times before. He stopped us in front of a door marked 732 and pulled a key from his pocket. Logically, I knew what this meant, but my brain refused to put the puzzle pieces together. It just didn't make sense.

When we stepped inside the fully furnished one-man office, he waved a hand at the floor-to-ceiling windows that faced Sunset. "Well, what do you think?"

"I don't understand."

"I think you do." He took a step toward me, and I swallowed hard.

"Is this your office?"

He smiled. "That's my girl. Yes."

Overwhelmed, I shook my head, refusing to guess at what all this might mean. If I guessed, I might hope, and if I hoped wrong . . .

My knees were a little wobbly, so I plopped into the leather chair behind the lone desk. Taking a deep breath, I look Cal square in the eye.

"Start talking."

His eyes dancing with mischief, he said, "I talked my bosses into letting me open a branch of the firm out here. It's part-time for now, so I'll be flying back and forth between the coasts for a while. But eventually, my plan is to run this place full time."

When my jaw fell open, I snapped it shut, completely shocked and surprised by this turn of events. "Is this a joke? Are you kidding? Because if you're kidding, it's not funny."

Cal smiled and sat on the edge of the desk. "I'm not kidding. If my bosses had said no, I would have opened my own investment firm here anyway. You were right about how much

California's small business laws suck, and how brutal they are. I wasn't ready to take that on by myself, so I'm glad they said yes."

I nodded, completely understanding where he was coming from. I'd done my own research before making the decision to stay on at my current agency. Going out on my own seemed more hassle than it was worth.

"So you're going to live out here?"

"Part time, yes."

"But how is this happening?" I asked, needing every single detail. "Why did your bosses agree to this?"

"My client list here in LA has exploded."

"Seriously?"

"I think Tabbie and Ron have introduced me to everyone they've ever known."

I laughed as I thought about my old friend Ron. Of course he would have done that for Cal—and for me. I hadn't caught up with Ron in weeks, and before yesterday, I hadn't talked to Cal either.

"That's great. I'm really happy for you."

"It's all because of you."

I shook my head. "No. All I did was introduce you to a couple of people. If you weren't good at your job, none of this would be happening."

"Just take the compliment."

I narrowed my eyes. "Fine. But you take it too."

"Fine. It was both of us. Thanks, teammate."

My cheeks prickled with heat. I remembered feeling that way when things were going well between us. How Cal had been the only guy I'd ever felt that way about.

"Where are you going to live?"

"I'm not sure yet. Know any good real estate agents?"

"No."

He laughed, but I was serious. Kind of. Okay, not really at all.

"You don't? That's a shame."

"I can't believe you're going to be here."

He pushed up from the desk and stepped close to me. Too close, but I couldn't push him away any longer. I didn't want to fight it anymore.

"I wanted to be closer to you," he said softly, "and I figured out a way I could."

"We weren't even talking. How in the world could you make all these plans—"

"I planned on fixing that," he said quickly.

"What if I didn't let you?"

He stepped closer, his lips inches from mine. "That really wasn't an option. But I would have waited for you to forgive me, however long it took. I didn't plan on giving up so easily. I knew I loved you. The second I realized that, it was all over for me. I had to make things right between us. I love you, Jules. I love you so damn much."

I didn't just look into his hazel eyes as he spoke, I dove into them, drowning in that dreamy sea without a floatation device. I didn't want to be saved.

Leaning toward him, I said softly, "I love you too."

His chest rose quickly before his mouth covered mine. It was all he needed. Hell, it was everything we both needed. Forgiveness, acceptance, and a willingness to move past this, all wrapped up in four beautiful words that spilled from my lips like a promise. Words I meant with my entire heart, that fickle organ I no longer hated.

And as we kissed and broke in Cal's new desk, I knew things would be okay. The sense of impending dread that had weighed me down when I first met him flitted away. Now I was filled with something else entirely.

Hope. And I knew we were going to make it.

EPILOGUE

Jules

CAL COMMUTED BETWEEN Boston and LA for the next eleven months. It had to have been hard on him, but he never once complained. He even found an afterschool program here where he could volunteer, which I knew he truly loved.

His bosses were extremely supportive when it came to letting him move out here full time. They knew it made sense to expand their offices to the West Coast, and the fact that Cal brought in a boatload of money made their decision easy. And when his celebrity client roster doubled soon after he opened the office, how could they complain?

By the time Cal moved out here to run things full time, he brought Lucas with him. There were too many clients for him to handle alone, and after Lucas's first trip to visit us, he'd become relentless in his pursuit to move here, badgering Cal every chance he got.

The only problem was that while Cal had quickly become comfortable with dealing with celebrities, Lucas was still a bit starstruck and practically creamed his pants whenever a hot actor came in for a meeting. I kept telling Cal that Lucas would eventually work through his wide-eyed phase, but honestly I wasn't so sure. Sometimes being around celebrities was too much for certain people. I guess we'd see, though, because Lucas was here now, taking over Cal's lease and moving into his apartment.

When Cal told me he needed a place to live here, I urged him to sign a year's lease on a furnished apartment in West Hollywood, wanting to be smart about our relationship. As happy as I'd been that he had come back to me, I wasn't ready for us to move in together. In my opinion, it was way too soon for that. We still needed to get to know each other better.

To my surprise, he hadn't even argued. Instead, he tricked me, staying at my house night after night and slowly moving some of his things in the same way Tami had. Before I realized it, he had nearly a whole rack of work clothes hanging in the guest room closet next to Tami's dresses. And the guest bath's shelves that had once been filled with only Tami's products now held just as many of Cal's.

About a month after Cal and I got back together, the three of us were sharing a pizza one night and Tami had glared at him.

"Don't even think about asking me to move my things out of this room, mister," she'd said with some heat, and he laughed.

"I wouldn't dream of it. I love sharing a closet with you."

"This is still my room. Tell him, Jules, that it's still *my* room!" she'd shouted at me.

"It's still your room, Tami." I rolled my eyes. It wasn't like Cal would be sleeping in there anyway. Unless he was in trouble, of course.

I still kept in touch with Robin, who wanted to fly out and "kiss me on the mouth" when I told her that Cal was moving here. "Best thing you've ever *done,* and I mean that in every way possible," she'd written me in an e-mail. She threatened to come visit all the time, but said that now that Cal was here, she had a real reason. Robin, Tami, and Lucas all in one place might be the death of me. Or the life of me. It was a toss-up.

A month before Cal's lease was up, he convinced me to let him officially move in. To be honest, it didn't take much convincing on his part. I had been dying for us to move in together for months. I'd wanted to play it safe and take things slow at first, but I soon realized that when you were with the right person, slow didn't make anything better. And it definitely didn't always make the most sense.

So today was moving day, the day we moved the rest of Cal's things to my apartment. Admittedly, it didn't take long. He'd already stuffed so much of his belongings into the guest room closet, he didn't have much left at his own apartment.

"Where's my room?" Lucas said as he dropped one of Cal's boxes at my feet. "Tami and Cal have a room. Why don't I have one?"

I shrugged. "I guess you and Tami have to share."

"I heard that!" Tami shouted from the bedroom.

"You know you want a piece of this, sweet cheeks," Lucas yelled back, and I cracked up.

Lucas and Tami had hit it off immediately when they first met, both trolling for guys without a second thought. I overheard Tami threaten Luc once, though. Something about them not fishing in the same pond for guys or she'd stab him in his sleep. Lucas had only laughed and told her that if they both wanted the same guy, then *she* was in the wrong pond, not him. To my surprise, she'd agreed, and then when he complimented her on her forest-green eyes, I'd wanted to punch him in the throat.

"Why is everyone always yelling?" Cal asked as he came into the living room. Not breaking his stride, he walked straight over to me and planted a kiss on my lips.

There's no way I'd ever grow tired of kissing those beauties. They were still just as appealing and dreamy as ever.

Lucas groaned and made a puking face. "Stop being like your brother."

"Never." Cal gave Lucas a smug grin.

"When's their wedding anyway?" Lucas asked, as if he didn't already know the answer. He'd been begging for an invitation to the event since he learned they finally chose a date in February.

"You know when," Cal said, pretending to be annoyed at Lucas before he leaned over to whisper in my ear. "I totally get it now, why Cooper and Katherine were always so annoyingly sweet. It's because they felt like this about each other."

I couldn't agree more. I'd never thought I'd ever be half of a sickeningly sweet couple, but apparently I was.

Three years ago, I would have never pictured my life this way. If you'd have told me that I'd meet someone like Cal and would have a successful relationship *and* a successful career, I would have said you were either dreaming or insane. So convinced I couldn't have both, I'd tried to write one of them off completely.

And as I glanced around our apartment at the people I loved, I'd never been happier to have been so wrong.

The End

Thank you so much for reading! I hope you enjoyed Cal and Jules's story as much as I enjoyed writing it.

Keep reading for a sneak peek of Cooper and Katherine's story, *In Dreams.*

ACKNOWLEDGMENTS

This book was a labor of love. Literally. It hurt me to write it, to share it, to live through Jules's journey with her. Each chapter felt like pulling teeth to get the words out of my guts and onto the computer screen.

It was hard.

The most difficult story I've written to date – if for no reason other than . . . *life is sometimes really challenging and really, really, hurts.*

I hope that you felt something while you read it. I hope it resonated in some deep part of you and helped you feel less alone. You're never alone. To hurt is human. To love is human. To want to heal is also human.

Thank you to my incredible cover designer, Michelle Warren, who continues to blow my mind, cover after cover. She creates so much beauty from a simple image that I find myself constantly impressed by her raw talent. Thank you again for not only being the best in the business, but for being a true friend.

To my editor, Pam Berehulke, who takes my emotional word vomit and makes it decipherable. You would think that I'd be better at this by now, but clearly I'm not. LOL Thanks for always trying to get me to tone down the F-words; one of these days it might stick, but don't hold your breath.

Thank you to the girls who helped me work through this experience (yes, this book was an experience), read an early draft of the story, called to see how I was doing, sent me text messages, checked in on me, or basically made my day by being a part of it: Tray, Becky, CatJacks, Krista Arnold, Brittainy McCane, Jessica McBee, Brina, Jillian Dodd, Tara Sivec, Tarryn Fisher, Claire Contreras, Kyla Linde, Colleen Hoover, and Corinne Michaels.

Thank you to all of the girls in my Perfect Game Changer group for your general awesomeness. I'm always awed by how good you all are to one another—supportive, helpful, encouraging, and most of all, loving. I am so thankful and proud to be a part of you.

Last, but never least, The Boy. Blake always gets a thank-you, not only because he threatens me if I don't (honestly, what's he going to do to me?!), but because he is my most favorite human on this whole entire planet. Thank you, Blake, for not always understanding what I'm doing, but understanding why I do it.

OTHER BOOKS BY J. STERLING

In Dreams

Chance Encounters

10 Years Later – A Second Chance Romance

Heartless

Dear Heart, I Hate You

THE GAME SERIES:

The Perfect Game – Book One

The Game Changer – Book Two

The Sweetest Game – Book Three

The Other Game (Dean Carter) – Book Four

THE CELEBRITY SERIES:

Seeing Stars – Madison & Walker

Breaking Stars – Paige & Tatum

Losing Stars – Quinn & Ryson (Coming Fall 2016)

ABOUT THE AUTHOR

Jenn Sterling is a Southern California native who loves writing stories from the heart. Every story she tells has pieces of her truth in it, as well as her life experience. She has her bachelor's degree in Radio/TV/Film and has worked in the entertainment industry the majority of her life.

Jenn loves hearing from her readers and can be found online at:

Blog & Website: www.j-sterling.com
Twitter: www.twitter.com/RealJSterling
Facebook: www.facebook.com/TheRealJSterling
Instagram: @ RealJSterling

If you enjoyed this book, please consider writing a spoiler-free review on the site from which you purchased it. And thank you so much for helping me spread the word about my books, and for allowing me to continue telling the stories I love to tell. I appreciate you so much. :)

Thank you for purchasing this book.

Please join my mailing list to get updates on new and upcoming releases, deals, bonus content, personal appearances, and other fun news!
http://tinyurl.com/pf6al6u

EXCERPT FROM *IN DREAMS*

CHAPTER ONE

THEY HELD HANDS as they walked down a familiar street. It was the street of her childhood, yet somehow it was different. The houses weren't quite the same and something didn't . . . well, it didn't quite feel right.

Katherine glanced up at the boy whose hand she held. Her mind was keenly aware that she didn't "know" him, but her heart told her otherwise. His hair was short, and the light brown color reminded her of the sand after it had been washed over by a wave. Her gaze traced the shape of his body through the shirt he wore. She could see the muscles in his arms, and the broad shoulders his shirt couldn't hide. His face appeared flawless; it took every ounce of willpower she possessed not to run her hand down his cheek, just to feel the softness of his skin.

Then there were his eyes. Rimmed with thick, dark eyelashes, they sparkled with such blue radiance that every time she looked at them, she wasn't sure she'd ever be able to look away. It was as though he could see right through her, knowing her every thought and desire. She knew she should be uncomfortable with all of this, but for some reason, she was completely at ease with this stranger. He looked down at her and smiled. His perfect teeth and full lips drew her in, making her wonder how those lips would taste.

As they walked, he talked to her. Told her things that didn't make sense at the time. He described where he grew up and how his house wasn't there anymore. He talked about a fire, and horses, and mentioned something about a soldier and war. Katherine listened intently to all the information, but her brain couldn't fully process it. She felt a little lost and confused but stayed silent, content to bask in his attention.

She tried to take in the details he shared and make sense of it, but logic was pushed out of the way. She was too caught up in how she felt. The pure love that consumed her every time she looked at this boy was unlike anything she'd ever known before. If soul mates could be real, this stranger was all the proof she needed. It was as if nothing else existed or mattered in the world around them.

She wasn't aware of the noise at first; she was so caught up in the blue of his eyes. Then she heard it more clearly, the sound of quiet screams that began to fill her ears. Or maybe it was more like muffled wailing. She wasn't sure. But at that moment she felt her stomach drop to the ground beneath her.

"I'll be right back. I have to go in there."

He pressed his lips against her hand and then slowly began to untangle his fingers from hers. "No. Please don't go." She pleaded with him to stay and gripped his hand as tightly as she could.

"Katherine, I have to help." He smiled at her, his blue eyes filled with confidence, and then repeated, "I'll be right back. I promise."

"You promise?" she pleaded.

"I promise," he repeated reassuringly. She let his hand fall from her grasp and watched him slowly disappear through the front door.

Grief immediately washed over her. She fell to her knees and clutched at her queasy stomach, experiencing unease and a sickness she couldn't define. She knew with unfailing certainty that he would never walk back out of that house. The pain and overwhelming sense of loss that thought caused her were so severe, her breathing hitched and nearly ceased completely. And then she heard it, that sound she was expecting, but couldn't have known was coming.

A single gunshot.

"Katherine? Katherine, are you okay? Wake up." A familiar voice startled her awake.

Katherine's eyes shot open to see her roommate, Taylor, standing above her. She focused on the blue eyes staring back at her. Although they had only been roommates a few weeks, they had bonded instantly. Katherine felt like she had known Taylor her whole life.

"My God, Katherine, are you all right? You're crying so hard. I mean, you're like *really* crying. What the hell were you dreaming about?" Taylor's normally pretty face was pinched with concern.

"Dreaming?" Katherine said softly. "I was dreaming? *He* was a dream?"

"He, *who*? Tell me everything!" Taylor's demeanor instantly changed from concern to girlish excitement as she plopped onto Katherine's bed, her blonde hair bouncing against her shoulders.

"I can't . . . talk about it right now, Tay," Katherine

stammered, barely able to get the words out. "I don't even want to move. It felt so real."

"Dreams always feel real when you're in them," Taylor reminded her.

Katherine averted her eyes, looking around at the white walls of the dorm room. She focused on the corkboard across from her bed where Taylor had pinned pictures of the ocean and quotes she liked.

"I know, but this was different." Katherine struggled to put her feelings into words. "Everything was so intense . . . and the guy. I've just never felt like that before."

"What guy? Come on, Kat, you have to tell me. I mean, you were crying! Like *real* tears! And you're acting so weird right now," her roommate begged.

"Taylor, I know this sounds stupid, but right now I'm still processing the fact that everything I just felt and experienced was a dream. It wasn't real. I can't believe he wasn't real." She wiped at her eyes.

"Crying again? Really? What the hell, Kat?" she asked, cocking her head to the side.

"I'll tell you everything, I promise. I just need a minute. Please?" Katherine closed her eyes as she pleaded.

Taylor pouted and stood up to leave.

"I know it's crazy, Taylor. It's just the minute I move, everything's going to fade away. It's all going to disappear."

"What do you mean?"

Katherine took a deep breath. "It's like I can feel him around me. Like my dream is lingering in the air. And I know that once I move, it's going to disappear. I just want to hold on to it for a bit longer. Does that make any sense?" Katherine's brows drew together with frustration as she tried to explain.

"Not really," Taylor admitted. "But I'll give you some space." She sighed and walked into their bathroom, pulling the door shut behind her.

Katherine briefly thought about going back to sleep, but she resisted the urge. She tossed the comforter from her body and slid out slowly from the warmth of her bed. With every move, she could feel the dream and her memory of him fading. She knew it was inevitable, but it hurt. And that confused her.

"Taylor?" she yelled out toward the bathroom.

The bathroom door opened and Taylor's head popped out. "Oh, so you've decided to join the living today, eh?"

"Yeah," she said. "I want to tell you everything. This guy—this dream—it was crazy. I don't even know how to start talking about it because it was more of a feeling than anything else." Katherine sighed before she continued. "Even saying that out loud sounds stupid, I know, but it's true. I mean, not much happened in the dream, aside from him getting shot and killed, which was totally awesome," she added sarcastically.

"What? Who got shot and killed? I'm confused." Taylor stepped back into the room and shook her head. "You have to start from the beginning. And you need to hurry, because we have class in half an hour." She glanced up at the clock on the wall.

Katherine filled Taylor in on every detail she could remember. The house. The fire. The gunshot. The soldier and the war. She did her best to put her feelings into words, although she knew no words could ever do her feelings justice. She described the guy, what he looked like, what it felt like to be around him, her sense of loss when he left her, and her desperation and fear when she heard the gunshot. Taylor wrote it all down, every single word.

"What are you doing?" Katherine asked quietly.

"Taking notes for later," Taylor explained.

She glanced at her roommate, looking like a detective hunched over her pad of paper and pen as she sat on the chair with her legs crossed. "What do you mean, later? You're so weird."

"Really? You have some dream that makes you cry and I'm the weird one?" Taylor teased.

"No, really, what do you mean?"

Taylor paused. "Let's just say for the sake of exploring all our options that your dream guy is real. We need to write down what he looks like and everything else you remember about him so we can find him."

"Real?" The concept of her dream guy existing hadn't even occurred to Katherine.

Taylor's voice rose as her excitement grew. "Yeah! I mean, what if? What if he came to you in your dream and you're going to find him in class or something? What if he goes to our school? You never know. Why else would you dream about this guy and have all these crazy feelings if he wasn't real?"

Taylor's question sparked curiosity and hope in Katherine. She felt her shoulders relax as she pondered the possibilities. "Maybe he is real. Can you imagine?" Katherine smiled for the first time that morning. "I mean, why else would I have had that dream? There has to be a reason, right? There has to be a point to all of this madness."

"That's what I'm saying!" Taylor said excitedly.

"I should probably do something with myself before we leave for class. I mean, what if my dream guy is there?" She hopped up and headed toward the bathroom, smiling.

"You can start by brushing that hair of yours!" Taylor called out to her.

"What would I ever do without you?" Katherine piped back.

Taylor's voice drifted in from the other room. "Clearly, you'd walk around with nappy hair all day."

Katherine brushed her long brown hair as Taylor had instructed her to. "Wouldn't want to disappoint," she mumbled at her reflection in the bathroom mirror. She coated her eyelashes with dark mascara to accent her hazel eyes, and tried to cover up the light dusting of freckles across her nose with some powder foundation.

He could totally be real, she repeated in her head until she found herself saying it out loud by accident.

"That's what I keep telling you," Taylor said as she appeared in the bathroom doorway. "He has to be. Oh, Kat, this is so exciting! We have a mission." Her face lit up with excitement before a cloud settled over it. "It's too bad you didn't get his name or something. Because I could search online for him if you had a name."

"Sorry, Tay, he was too busy getting killed to tell me his name. But if I see him again, I'll ask." Katherine smiled at her roommate, happy that she was slowly starting to feel like herself again.

The two girls headed out of the old brick dormitory and walked through the tree-lined campus toward their class. With fall fast approaching, the leaves were turning magnificent shades of gold and crimson, and some leaves had already fallen, pushed along the sidewalk by a light breeze. Katherine looked around at the stone and brick buildings that surrounded her and smiled. She thought about her home and how no buildings looked the way these did. Southern California was great and she loved it, but had wanted to experience something different for college.

She could have chosen a local college, but knew it would just be more of the same—gorgeous people consumed by celebrity, fame, reality TV, and their future careers. As she sifted through her college choices, she had realized that what she really wanted was a big change.

And what could be more different from the constant sunny days of Los Angeles than the four distinct seasons of the East Coast? When she'd first arrived here, summer was winding down, the days hot and sometimes muggy. Now that fall was near, more often not the days started with a cool bright blue sky that amazed her.

Katherine remembered how she'd felt when the information packet arrived from a school in New Jersey she had only vaguely considered at first. But something about this particular college called to her. She wasn't sure if it was the old ivy-covered buildings or the gorgeous campus liberally dotted with huge, ancient trees, but she knew immediately that she wanted to be there. So when her acceptance letter arrived in the mail, she had been thrilled.

Taylor's voice interrupted her memories. "Is that him? What about that guy?" Taylor scanned the students around them, pointing out boys who fit the description of her dream guy. "Oh, what about him? If he's not your dream guy, I'll take him to be mine. He's nothing but hotness on a stick."

Katherine chuckled. "You're going to make me crazy. How about if I see him, I'll let you know? And really, hotness on a stick? Where do you get this stuff?"

"We could put an ad up on the school's website. Or in the newspaper. We can totally do this." Taylor's eyes twinkled with excitement.

"How about we just go to class first? For all we know, he could be dead. He did die in my dream, after all." The memory of the end of the dream nagged at her from the back of her mind. The possibility of him being dead wasn't something she wanted to accept, so she forced those thoughts aside.

They walked into the large classroom and Taylor motioned toward the last row. "Can we sit in the back? I hate having people sit behind me. It's like I can feel them staring down the back of my neck." Taylor shivered dramatically.

"Wherever's fine. I don't care." Katherine shrugged and followed Taylor's lead.

When they sat down, she noticed Taylor scanning the room and watched with amusement as Taylor quickly jotted things down in her notepad. The sight made her laugh out loud.

The guy seated in front of her turned around in his chair when he heard her laugh. Katherine struggled to breathe as she fixated on the mesmerizing green eyes that focused on hers. His face was handsome, his features so perfectly balanced, that she couldn't help but feel a little inadequate in comparison. Katherine felt herself flush at the unexpected attention, but couldn't bring herself to look away. She knew one of them had to turn away, but he was the one who ultimately broke the connection, not her. When he finally turned back around to face the front of the classroom, Taylor kicked Katherine under the table.

"What . . . was . . . that?" Taylor whispered toward her.

"I don't know, but he's really cute, isn't he? Did you see his eyes? Good Lord." Katherine's cheeks burned.

"Blue?" Taylor whispered back hopefully.

"No, green. But still . . . hello! Is it hot in here?" Katherine laughed softly and fanned her face.

"It's just you. And apparently him," Taylor teased back.

"Ladies, is there a problem?" The professor's voice rose with irritation as he stopped his lecture and looked pointedly in their direction in the back of the classroom.

"No, Professor. Sorry!" they responded in unison.

Katherine punched Taylor under the table. The green-eyed boy looked back for one more glance followed by a quick smile, then settled into his seat. Katherine's breath hitched.

When class ended, Katherine gathered up her things and scanned the room. "Well, that's weird. I mean, where'd he go?"

"Clearly, you scared him so he had to run away," Taylor joked.

She shrugged her shoulders and pulled Taylor toward the door. "Come on, let's go."

They walked outside and into the blinding sunlight. Katherine squinted and quickly reached for her sunglasses. She looked around at the huge green trees and walked toward an unoccupied stone bench.

"Let's sit for a minute," Katherine suggested.

"Okay. I want to ask you some more questions anyway," Taylor said.

Katherine laughed. "What more can you possibly want to know?"

Taylor pulled out her notepad after they sat on the bench. "Why were you crying?"

"I can't explain it. It's the very thought of him. That moment when I heard the gunshot . . ." A gentle breeze tossed strands of Katherine's hair in front of her face. She tucked the pieces behind her ear before pressing her hand against her heart. "It physically brought me pain. It's like I went to bed with a whole heart, but I woke up with it in pieces."

"Kat, that's really intense. We're way too young and too hot to be this crazy over some guy we've never met before," Taylor informed her with a serious look on her face.

"We?"

"Yeah, we. I mean, I'm totally involved in this now too, so . . . we." Taylor folded her arms across her chest.

Katherine stood up from the bench and smiled. "You're crazy. I've got to go to my next class. Chemistry. Exciting."

"I'll see you at home. Did I tell you that Kylie is stopping by to see our place and say hi and stuff?" Taylor reminded her.

"Who is she again?" Katherine asked.

"One of my best friends from high school. Don't worry, you'll love her. I think," Taylor said with a laugh.

"What?" Katherine's eyes widened with worry.

"I'll make sure she's on her best behavior," Taylor reassured her confidently.

"Oh my gosh, seriously? Why? What's her deal?"

"She just . . . I don't know. She can be a real bitch sometimes. She's competitive."

"And she's your best friend? How did that happen?" Katherine asked.

"Eh, it's a long story." Taylor hesitated before quickly saying, "I hated her at first, but then something happened that brought us together. And here we are."

Confused, Katherine shook her head and threw up her

hands in surrender. "Okay. Whatever. See you at home."

"You're not mad, are you?"

"No, you're just weird." Katherine smiled and turned to head toward her class.

"You're the weird one. See ya later, weirdo!" Taylor shouted as she headed in the opposite direction.

TAYLOR WALKED INTO her sun-filled dorm room and tossed everything on the floor except her notebook. She read over her scribbles from Katherine's dream and added new thoughts and questions. When the house phone finally rang, she jumped.

"Hello?"

"Hi. This is the front desk. Your guest has arrived."

"Can you send her up?"

"You need to come down and sign her in first."

"Okay, I'll be right there."

Taylor slammed the phone down and hopped out of her chair. Shutting the door behind her, she hurried downstairs. Once she rounded the corner, she saw her best friend leaning against the front desk, tapping her foot impatiently.

"So, this is what you've ditched me for, huh?" Kylie said with a disapproving frown.

Taylor signed the guest sheet and gave Kylie a tight squeeze. "Don't be a brat. Come on. I'm so excited you're here!"

"So, tell me about your roommate? Do we hate her?" Kylie asked with a tight smile.

Taylor laughed. "No, we don't hate her. We love her."

Kylie scrunched her nose with distaste and Taylor snapped, "Oh, I know that look. Don't be a bitch, Kylie. She's from California and she's really great. I promise."

"Whatever," Kylie said with an eye roll. "I'll try to be nice."

"How lucky for us all."

KATHERINE RETURNED TO the dorm after her Chemistry class, and as she walked through the doorway into her dorm room, the conversation abruptly stopped. Her eyes quickly met Kylie's and she watched as the stunning blonde sized her up with a scowl. She gave her a sincere smile in return, determined that Taylor's best friend would like her.

Taylor jumped up. "Hey, Kat! This is my best friend from home, Kylie. Kylie, this is my roommate, Katherine." Taylor's gaze pinged anxiously back and forth between her two friends.

Kylie stood up and reached for Katherine's hand. "So, you're the famous roommate my best friend loves so much."

Katherine shot Taylor a questioning look. "Uh . . . I guess so. It's nice to meet you, Kylie. I've heard a lot about you."

Unease crawled its way down Katherine's spine as Kylie scrutinized her, the girl's hostility generating an undeniable tension that seemed to fill the room. Something was off with her roomie's best friend, and she wondered if Taylor noticed it as well.

"How long are you staying? Do you want to come out with us tonight?" Katherine pasted a smile on her face, uncomfortable at the thought that this girl could dislike her so intensely so quickly. What in the world did I do to her, she wondered.

"I hadn't thought about it, but what are you guys doing? I mean, if it's some sort of party with really hot guys, you'll need me there," Kylie said as she ran her fingers through her short blonde hair.

"Oh yes, Princess Kylie, for we humble servants cannot meet any guys without your presence. Please accompany us to the party we're crashing later," Taylor quipped back, rolling her eyes.

Kylie eyed Katherine before looking back at Taylor. "I'm just saying you probably *need* me is all. You know that no guy can resist this," she said as she swept her hand in a Vanna White-like gesture across her body.

"Can I talk to you . . . in private?" Taylor snapped and quickly grabbed Kylie by the arm.

Katherine watched as Taylor pulled Kylie roughly into the bathroom. She cringed slightly as Taylor slammed the door shut, and tried not to eavesdrop on the conversation behind the thin bathroom door.

"What the hell is wrong with you?" she heard Taylor whisper harshly.

"Nothing. What's wrong with you?" Kylie snapped back in response.

"Why are you being a bitch?"

Kylie's voice lowered. "I don't trust her."

Taylor laughed. "What do you mean, you don't trust her?"

"I don't know," Kylie whispered. "Call it woman's intuition or whatever. There's just something about her I don't like."

"Seriously, Kylie? If this is how you're going to be, then you should just leave."

There was a pause, before Kylie said softly, "I'm sorry. I'll try to behave. I promise."

Taylor huffed out a long sigh. "Do better than try."

The bathroom door opened slowly and Katherine tried to look busy and uninterested as Taylor walked out first. She mouthed *I'm sorry* in Katherine's direction and Katherine gave her a reassuring smile back.

Kylie emerged and looked briefly at Katherine before averting her eyes. "I'm sorry for being mean."

"It's okay." Not wanting an enemy, Katherine did her best to extend an olive branch. "So, are you going to come with us tonight or what?

Kylie pondered the offer. "Yeah. I'll go."

"And you'll stay the night?" Taylor asked.

"Well, I'm not definitely not driving home at three in the morning."

Taylor smiled. "Good."

"But one of you better let me borrow some clothes because I didn't bring anything party-worthy to wear."

"You can look through my stuff if you want," Katherine offered.

"Thanks," Kylie said curtly, and headed toward the closet.

Taylor breathed a sigh of relief. "Plus, Kylie, you can help us look for Kat's dream guy."

"Seriously, Taylor? I forgot all about him." Katherine tried to sound nonchalant, and hoped she could sell it.

"Liar."

Katherine shot Taylor a look. "It's totally normal that I can't stop thinking about him, right? I'm sure I'm perfectly sane." Katherine rolled her eyes.

Kylie dropped the skirt she was holding and turned around quickly. "What dream guy?"

"Can I tell her?" Taylor looked at Katherine for approval.

Katherine nodded and pretended not to listen as Taylor

filled Kylie in.

"Wow. That's pretty crazy. And you have no idea who he is?" Kylie looked at Katherine with disbelief.

Katherine shook her head. "Never seen him before in my life."

CPSIA information can be obtained at www.ICGtesting.com
Printed in the USA
LVOW08s1724201016

509596LV00004B/725/P